The ountaineers

JONATHAN LOVEJOY

ISBN-10: 0692316612
ISBN-13: 978-0692316610

For every Raven

But as the days of Noah were,

So shall also the coming of the Son of Man be.

Luke 17:26

Part One

_I_'m not just a dyke. I'm an Indian dyke. Or, Native American lesbian, if you prefer. There's something in my heart that's just plain evil, and it doesn't have a damned thing to do with the fact that I like to fuck women. Tattoos (of which I have none) and wife beater T-shirts aside, along with the Mohawk I've felt inside myself for years but I'm too damned pretty to grow. My hair is long past my shoulders and black as midnight rain. The evil that I do might lie in the fact that I don't just like to fuck women. I like to kill them.

The reason why I never got my Mohawk is simple. It's easier for me to operate and move among the people. You bored, dumb soccer moms and busty bodied college moms in waiting. I like to get one of you blonde bitches to trust me so it'll be easier to do what I have to do. And I can't do it alone, so I have two best friends to help me. Two pretty losers like me, whose mommas and daddy's made them understand early that life sucks from a bad bean to a rotten egg, and it's too short to go denying who you are inside. Me? Inside, I'm the Devil, and I'm coming to get one of you shapely suburban bitches.

You won't see me coming, either. Oh, you'll see me on the outside, but who I am inside is invisible. You'll judge my outer appearance; blue jeans, t shirt and cowgirl boots, tanned skin beauty with pretty red lips and almond eyes (Think Roselyn Sanchez. Think hard… yes… you do remember)…the Devil blessed me with a nice package to roll around in. If I were covered head to toe in mud, would you let me in the back seat of your new Camry?

I got a blonde and a brunette helping me do what I do. We live up in the mountains, but it's not a log cabin in the woods, and it's not surrounded by chopped firewood and there's not two German Shepherds chained and barking like monsters at everything that moves. Yeah, the woods aren't too far off, but we live in a brick rancher style home with a big, pretty front yard. There's a big, pretty back yard too, that runs all the way back to those thick woods where wolves and bears live to howl and growl unsuspecting fools. We drive the mountain road into a Triad city every day with our three cars—the hours on our jobs are just too different for carpooling. Chelsea is a bank teller (picture Katherine Heigl, if you can, she's Chelsea's twin). Her blonde hair keeps us safe from cat luck demons that might try to keep us from building our grave yard, across our back lawn to the edge of the Appalachian Woods. We've already buried six women. And Simone, my brunette baby, (my butch bone, my Zeta Jones clone), she told me last night after we saw that stupid assed *Sex in the City* shit, she told me *I can feel the tide rising on number seven*. She said that when we walked outside the movie theater in the evening day, watching all the middle age moms laugh and giggle their horny ways into their SUV's and husbands' flashy new pickup trucks and drive home to their suburban paradises. That's what it is. It's a touch of heaven on earth. But Heaven on Earth is still Hell, and the Devil is always lurking nearby.

We've already got two college girls in our little graveyard out back. The other four are older, all of them had children, though. Two had a husband but no sons. One had children but no husband. One had two daughters and a rich husband. Two young women in our cemetery. Four not so young. When the evil inside me burns the hottest, I need to kill me a soccer mom.

It's so easy for me to get jobs. One look at my face, one reading of my name—Raven Moon—and the cardinals sing and butterflies fly (Google my name and you'll get 13 million hits of God knows what). But two years of college was all I could stand, so I can only go so far. I'm so sick of remembering my job history and writing down my two years of education, so called, just to try and find that perfect job. I'm getting there but it hasn't happened yet. I work a counter at JC Penney right now, but even in this crappy economy, I know they're not going to fire me. They'll cut my hours like a butcher, but they won't fire me. I need to put on these clothes and masquerade. Success breeds ambition, and I am so successfully pretty when I look in the damned mirror that I have to do it. For women like me, life is a daily beauty contest that we always win. Beauty is power. It is the allure of ages past—to my present—and far into whatever future I have left.

The evil that I am builds up inside. Until it overflows. On my break at the mall, I sit in the open, sipping a soda, watching the moms walk with their daughters, enjoying the dynamic between them, the physical age dynamic; the forty-somethings still trying to look twenty years younger, succeeding in looking ten years younger. Lost in the neverland between thirty five and forty five, when they all look like that same, phantom age somewhere in between. Is she thirty seven? Thirty eight? Forty? Forty two? When and where will it be, when it happens to us again? How old will she be, when it happens to us again?

I keep seeing an owl in my dreams. *The owl flies over your resolution,* Simone says. Professor Coronado. Professor Cory. Religious Studies. Women's Studies. *It's a death omen,* she says. It tells me that there is no resolution. No quitting what I am. That things must be what they are, good or bad. I felt this when we choked the judge's wife to death. The three of us are always naked at the end. The women die naked. Chelsea laid beside us and held one of her arms and watched. She whispered over and over *die you fucking bitch. Die you fucking bitch.* She said she saw the moment when the spirit left her body; she felt the woman's arm go limp. The woman fought like a she tiger to live. She jerked upward, over and over again, trying to kick out of the choking I had her in. Her body's steady jerking made Simone cry *God and Holy Jesus* and she bansheed loud enough to wake the dead. It gave me energy. I was on top of the dying woman. Choking her. Climbing my fourth hill in two days. The Missionary of Death. My rubber cock was inside her front. Simone's was up her privileged ass, underneath her. Holding her down. It had been a fight to get our cocks in both sides of her and flip her over. Chelsea made it possible. She always makes it possible. She pulled my hair and clamped her pretty white teeth on my ears to help me. She helped me climb my fourth hill. The woman had a strong spirit, a strong desire to live. To go back to that life we pulled her from. I raped that bitch three times before we finally put her out of her misery. The fourth time was the last. She lived two days in our house before she died. She was the sexiest one we killed. All breasts, hourglass ass and repression. Her nakedness was truly a work of art. She spent a lot of time in a wooden chair in her panties, with her legs closed and tied at the ankles, squeezing, pulling and sucking on her own tits and crying while Chelsea caught it on film. The judge's wife did it with such easy aplomb, like she really understood how hot it is for a woman to suck her own nipples if she can. It is given to but few among us. Chelsea filmed her own hand, gently massaging or twisting the woman's tits hard enough to make her cry from the pain. She tried to block Chelsea's hand. *Put your hands down*, I said to her calmly. *Put your hands down!* Simone had yelled. She obeyed instantly. The middle aged woman was beautiful when she suffered. There's a lot of footage of her coughing and choking on my cock, too. She came by accident when I fucked her the first time. Her mature screams had been deep and hoarse.

Chelsea had been invited to a party at this woman's house. She was invited by one of the loan officers, Connie, at the bank where they work. Chelsea manages to endear herself to everybody—I think it's just because she's blonde and her name is Chelsea. The loan officer invited only her to this party, a whole two hours away from our jobs—three hours from our house. Simone and me followed them all the way to their rich suburban house like a couple of she lions. The house was hidden from the road. We saw many mansions while we drove through. We watched the minivan turn and roll away—up a steep driveway and out of sight. I knew that Simone's Honda was forbidden to make the turn. Chelsea said that going up their driveway was like riding a highway to another world, and seeing a castle rising in the distance, with pine trees and a prairie green lawn lining the road to riches. But the gray wasn't old castle stone and rain clouds, but gray aluminum siding reflected in the sun. I remember that day last summer. The sky was blue.

Chelsea said that when she was introduced to Judge Raynor's wife, she felt a lightning bolt between her legs. The woman's perfectly cut dark brown hair, her pale blue eyes and big smile, forty five years of beauty stuffed in her ivory blouse and gray skirt—all broad hipped, small waisted curves and condescension, chesty and complacent, as sweet and nice and fake as anyone she had ever met—all of it worked together to make Chelsea have to go to an upstairs restroom and stand at the sink taking deep breaths. Premonition had grabbed her insides and squeezed, and she thought she heard the word *Molock* echo in bass around her. She said that all she could think about was me and Simone. She wanted to call us and tell us *I found her*. But we agreed to let nature take its course, which it had done in her body, programmed from birth into her bones and blood, tingling every nerve in her body like an alarm that Barbara Raynor was going to have to die, if it was the last thing she ever did.

At the exact moment in time, the split second when no one at the backyard party was noticing, she convinced Mrs. Raynor, Barbara (why are they always named Barbara?) to leave her guests and come inside the house. *Can we walk the driveway,* she said. *Sure we can, sweetie... you're Connie's friend right, from the bank. Connie said you were pretty. What can I do for you?*

Let's wait until we get on the driveway.

Well...alright Honey, if you say so.

So trusting. So superior. So quick to believe that Chelsea Baxter is worthy of respect and unusual indulgence, because she is so White And So Pretty. Chelsea satisfies the urge passed down from Eve, to have ultimate knowledge and access, to be counted among the elite, to push past the barriers into the forbidden zone of privilege, to cruise the Wealthen Stream like gods, where talent, prettiness and money is beauty, and beauty is worthy to be praised. Chelsea Baxter breathes in the summer air as they step the walkway. Allowing the sorrow of her years to rise the tiding of Number Six, until she is so close to tears as to give pause to the judge's beautiful wife.

Are you alright, baby?

Seeing your house. Your beautiful property. It just reminds me of how I grew up.

Oh, you grew up in a neighborhood like this?

I grew up in a trailer park. I cried myself to sleep at night, imaging myself in a home this beautiful. I only just met you and, seeing you with your daughters, your husband... I really admire what you've accomplished.

Honey, you'll get there. You've already started. That job. That face... just look at how amazingly pretty you are. All you have to do is keep envisioning this for yourself.

But how?

She takes Chelsea's arm. Beside the Great Lawn, they stroll the road to nowhere.

Just keep working. Think positive. Never give up. Never settle for anything less than the best from yourself, and one day, I promise you'll be living in a place that's probably better than this. You should see some of the other houses on this street. Maybe one of those is in your future.

I did. They are beautiful.

I know what you're thinking, I married a rich man, right? Well, he didn't get rich on his own. I slaved to take care of his home and his children while he was out chasing his dreams. And I supported him in those dreams, and was there with him every step of the way. It was a lot of work, but I persevered. The key to success is—

Perserverence?

I know it's a cliché Honey. But it's true. And you just keep telling yourself that while you chase your dream. While you go after the goals you set for yourself.

Perseverance.

And patience. It won't happen for a long time, but it will happen. And that's what separates us from those who don't make it. We understand that it won't happen tomorrow. And we don't give up.

I think I understand. About perseverance I mean. You see, I had a mother... I had a mother who worked very hard. She was always tired. She didn't drink or smoke or do drugs or run around with men. But she was always tired and, I just couldn't seem to do anything right. I was always being punished.

I'm so sorry to hear that.

No you're not—

What?

Chelsea looks around at the lovely, green property, to see that they are all alone out front. She opens her little knife right in front of Mrs. Raynor (No, she didn't pop a switchblade). And she sticks it to this forty five year old woman's throat and says

Shut the fuck up and walk. If you don't I'll cut your goddamned throat right here.

Honey, you don't need to—

I said, shut...up. How do you punish your daughters?

I don't—

I want the truth. She sticks the knife into her back, enough to make her jump.

I... I cut their allowance. I take some of their freedom. I... I—

What else? If you lie to me, I swear to God—

I spank them.

What?

I spank them with my bare hands.

Oh, yeah... Oh, God yes that's what I thought... I know your type. You keep your sex bottled up like a Coca Cola. My momma did the same thing. And one day, she shook it up and pointed it at me when she couldn't take the stress of her life. Do you know what it's like to be tied to a bedpost and beaten with a belt buckle until you can't breathe. Do you?

No... no... honey my daddy spanked me until I was sixteen. I understand. Really I do—

You don't understand nothin'. You and your rich husband and spoiled daughters. And you spout that generic bullshit to me about perseverance. Like you had anything to do with what you've got. You know what you are? You're a fucking prostitute. You whored yourself out to one man for twenty years. You persevered alright, you persevered kissing on his fat face and jerking his little sausage every night until you got what you wanted—

Where are you taking me? I'm going to have to scream—

Chelsea covers the woman's mouth to stifle the scream, and puts the little knife so hard to her lovely throat. Her tears have already started.

When the two of them came walking down the drive way to the empty, tree lined street—that beautiful, sophisticated older woman with the knife at her throat—with that hopeless, defeated, scared expression on her face— I put my hand to my mouth, and I remember Simone saying *Oh Jesus* like somebody had just touched her hot spot, and she jumped out of the car and helped wrestle this short haired, busty and big hipped brunette bitch into the back of our car. Simone pulled her down into the back seat and wrapped her legs and arms around her like ropes. We drove off in smooth silence, down the tree lined street, me watching Chelsea in the rear view mirror turn and walk back up the driveway. We took the three hours with Mrs. Raynor laying down in the back of the car in her tight gray skirt and black heels and soft white blouse. Simone said that her gruff screams vibrated in her hand like a pocket rocket and woke her up down there twice. I remember thinking how she was too stupid to understand that her screaming was exactly what Simone wanted. We didn't choke her or chloroform her on the whole trip.

What's your bra size bitch? Simone asked.

I'm an F cup, Mrs. Raynor answered, defeated, and I took a deep breath while Simone said *Oh my God* and started to squeeze and massage her bra through her blouse. Mrs. Raynor's expression is pure disgust. *I wanna suck 'em now, Raven.*

Not 'til we get home, I say, rather sharply.

Sit up, Simone says, after two hours of laying in the back seat, holding her like a life sized cushion doll. In the last miles of our ride, Simone sits close beside her and studies her shape, how it's possible for a woman so lovely and sophisticated to have such big, miraculous curves without being the least bit overweight. I remember it being the shortest three hour trip of my life. This full grown woman, who had been secure and struggling in the arms of my Simone, who was clearly getting off on every second of it. I had to turn the rear view mirror slightly, so I could see her face—this woman was fine and fancy as they come. *I'm gonna have to wear my cock for this one.* When I said that, she let out such a hopeless wail, such a rare and beautiful sound as a full grown woman's voice in the quiet siren of pleading, the sound that gets men's blood pumping and turns women's blood to fire. It is a call to deviance, a sound brought on by fear and despair, even the fear of pleasure too great to endure, and the despair over its fervent arrival. But this wailing that Simone and I hear, it is the cry of the damned, heard from biblical times, from Eve's cry when they left the garden, to Mary's cry at the foot of the Cross, to the cry of this woman's daughters when their mother never returns home.

We drove until the mountain arose in the distance, looming like a great beast on the horizon. *Your life is over, bitch,* Simone says.

I know, she answered. Sniffing, wiping her eyes. *Dear God in Heaven, I know it. But what about my daughters? Just hold me for ransom and my husband will pay anything you—*

You think this is about money? Simone says. *Those same little college bitches I teach—they come from yall's houses, where you teach 'em nothin' about what it really means to be a good person—not compassion and charity and chastity. No. You teach 'em credit scores, checking accounts and charm, and that money and fame are the best things in life. Not love and loyalty—but lasciviousness. Lust. You... you're the Lust of the Flesh. You're the Lust of the Eyes. You're the Pride of Life. Oh, yeah...I'm gon' enjoy this bitch, Raven. My dick's gettin' hard right now just thinking about what I'm gon do to you—*

Please, I'll do anything—

Simone is so good at this. She lets Mrs. Raynor's plea fall on deaf ears—to coalesce into the air like so much frost, and fade hopelessly into the air. Simone Coronado. My butch baby. A woman with penis envy like nothing I've ever seen. She can cum when I suck her fake cock just right. Sucking and pulling and jerking on it like there's no tomorrow. For this prim and proper lady in our back seat, there is only one more tomorrow, and then she will die.

As we drive, I feel the elevation, the requisite cotton in our ears, the steep sides of the roads where whole towns rest far away below. This is the last part of the miles we take, toward the offences that must come, and where this woman's life is lost, after she must pay in blood the comeuppance overdue in her life. Does she curse the day that Connie Green mentioned Chelsea Baxter to her? Does she regret inviting Connie Green to her summer party—the celebration gathering? Does she wonder how it is that at such a gathering, she managed to be abducted without being seen? What power is the Will of God that operates, that administrates Fate and Destiny? She will cause so much interest—her vanishing.

Rewards offered. Her sister and friends and daughters on the news. They will try to pull Chelsea in on it but she will be no help. What help Chelsea gave was her loyalty to our cause, that we might satisfy our lust and calling.

What about Chelsea? Simone says.

Oh, she'll be along, I say. Looking the judges wife in the eye. Watching the tears roll down her lovely face.

You remind me of my mother, Simone says to her. Then she slaps her hard enough to ring my ears—

My ears ring from the din in this mall. At least I'll miss the five o'clock traffic on the way out, thank God. Soda thrown away, final hour of my day come and gone. I have changed from the business suit, but not in the store. In the ladies stall at the other end of the mall. I don't want them knowing what I feel. I don't want them to see the seventh tide rising. I walk gracefully. Confidently with black, silken hair down the length of my back, to contrast the white t-shirt I wear, tucked inside my blue jeans. I can feel the words *bitch, whore* and *slut* flying through the air at me from the jealous teenage babies and young horny wives, though I am worse than all of their little names for me combined. What is the difference between a whore and a slut? A whore does it for the money. A slut does it for the sex. Every woman ever born is either a whore or a slut at heart. I am a slutting dyke.

The blonde mom I hold the main door open for catches my eye. And my perfect smile. I feel strong. I feel powerful. I am a slutting dyke bitch as I walk. But I am not a whore.

My Camry is my refuge as I drive. Another hour long trip back to the mountains. To the place where graves lie in wait. With all of my heart, I wish that what we do could be done no more. With my soul, I pray to God that it will end, that the tide will not rise to claim a seventh life. I think fondly of the Cross, and in my heart I believe that He died for me. Even for me.

Along the road to Woodland Drive, I see a pretty white SUV on the side of the road. A blonde in faded, ill fitting jeans and a white, sleeveless pullover blouse waves me down. Her breasts are gargantuan under her shirt. (Why would a woman with breasts so big wear a shirt so form fitting?) Her hips are epic, though her waist is small. She has to be a mother.

My daughter took my phone to school, she says. *Today of all days. Can you give me a jump start, Honey?* Her southern, country accent, coming out of that sophisticated, forty year old face is the nitty gritty on my kitty. My soul is laced with pity.

Sure. Let me turn around. I turn my Camry around on this abandoned country road. Amazed at our isolation. Bestowed by the open fields, and the many patches of thick forest groves. She chatters on and on about being named Amanda Hall and how beautiful I am and asking me where I'm from and something about loving Native American culture and her husband being a dentist and her son's graduation six weeks ago and her daughter's dance team until I finally have to say *we better get that battery.*

Oh yeah, she says, with true good natured dumbness—*please tell me you've got jumper cables.*

They're in the trunk. I reach inside the car and unlatch the trunk. So willingly. So helpfully. I hand her the cables and ask *have you put jumper cables on before?*

Too many times, she says. *My daughter's car used to need one every morning it seems, but with things being what they are right now we can't keep using these credit cards. I told her we'd have make do with that old battery until we make another payment…*

I can hardly hear what she is saying over the deep sound of *Molock* in my spirit, and the sound of my own heartbeat in my ears. I look around, seeing no one. Hearing nothing but the call of duty inside, as I pour the liquid into the white rag, still hidden from her behind the open trunk lid. Does she wonder what I am still doing in the trunk. *You can go ahead and attach 'em,* I say. *I'll be right there.* She takes her cheerleader honor society blue ribbon club obligation to its full measure, attaching the cables to her battery, then cheerfully turning to open my hood for me. *It's the least I can do,* she thinks. While her hands are up, I strike like the serpent that I am, using every muscle, every sinew to hold the rag over this country wench's mouth, dragging her struggling to the side of the road, hidden beside her big, white SUV. I drop with her to the ground, holding her until she does not move again. A few seconds more of her full struggle would have overtaken me. She was too strong. But luck has no morality. My killing luck is a cardinal. Her living luck is a blackbird.

While she lays down on the side of the road, I hurry and close both hoods and put the cables in the trunk. Then I drag her one hundred forty pounds of curves across the summer grass, and I place her, ungingerly, inside the trunk and close it. There will be no duck tape. No ropes. No handcuffs. We will let nature take its course. I will await the banging on the trunk. The screaming from inside.

I pull the silver gray car back slowly, slowly away from the dead white suburban vice. Then I glide a U-turn onto the road, ten minutes away from our brick home by the mountain woods.

*C*helsea Baxter counts money. Money that she knows will never belong to her. Money she'll never own. She sits in a cushioned chair in the Money Palace, at the window of drive thru confession. She is the priestess unknown. Unseen by them. Unseen by choice. They see her face, yes. But they don't know her from Eve. Teenagers in their spectrum of life cars, born from one end of it to the other. Twelve year old tin buckets on wheels. Twelve week old luxury hybrids. But who's to say, whether the rust bucket hoopty belongs to them, or their parents in poverty waiting? Who's to say if the luxury SUV hybrid, in stylish ivory mint, was not a gift from well to do kin, in prosperity waiting?

At the window, the beautiful girl tries to let her features be friendly. Knowing so well how they would be perceived if they were not. Pretty enough to make eye contact with every driver. Having to be so careful not to arouse suspicion. Not to cause allure. Or revulsion. The blonde teller counts their money rapidly. Driven forward by the spirits that govern Friday afternoon. They infuse the mind with wit and wisdom. The soul with fun and fantasy, the spirit with expectation and excitement. Acknowledgements of anticipation for the weekend. When leisure calls to freedom. Where work is play. Where diversion is the norm, the purpose for living. She counts the new money from the laughing teenage girls in the hybrid SUV. Comfortable that they admire her place in life. Her station at the money gate. She smiles a big lipped smile for them, mouth closed. Blue eyes twinkling. She slides the money to the driver through the big window drawer. And waits. She waits for the pitiful looking again from the teenage cheerleader, who had thought she was pretty just a moment before. But the beautiful teller smiles a knowing smile so perfect, so reassuring, unable to suppress a wickedly perfect wink from the bluest eye. The pretty cheerleader is disarmed, and cannot hold her own smile inside. She sees the beautiful blonde teller as a visitation. A sign for her to continue her path northward, where the beautiful people go. Where the privileged go to live. And to die.

Chelsea Baxter counts money. All six hundred eighty five dollars of it. How can a poverty mother survive? It is the same amount Chelsea has counted for this woman every two weeks for almost a year, maybe. Six hundred eighty five dollars. That's probably about nine hundred dollars before taxes. Eighteen hundred dollars a month, before taxes. Just over twenty thousand a year. About ten dollars an hour at the plant. The factory. The office. The store. Whatever. Six hundred eighty five dollars. That can barely cover the rent. What about the electric bill. Cable? Car insurance? Gas? For this car, this old gray Civic, there is no car payment, surely, there is no car payment. Is she really a mother? Or is her tired expression from work and financial struggle alone? How does she buy food for herself? Let alone two children? Are there food stamps? Is there Section 8 housing? What does it do to a person, to work like a dog every day, year in and out, and still never make ends meet? To never have enough cash for little extras? To have fun every now and then? To escape the pain of living through the portal that is money? Who are the people in charge, who so easily rip so much from her paycheck every month? What hammer would there be to fall, if the poor became exempt from the high taxes they must pay? From the blood they must draw and give, the blood of finances and need? To say nothing of want, or even the touch of good natured greed. Those who collect vintage cars, some priceless, and those who would wish to collect enough toy cars to make a Christmas morning not be pathetic and puke worthy. Get a better job. Save your money. Don't watch cable. Don't buy your children those expensive clothes and shoes. Why do you have a big screen TV? Why are you driving a new car? Why are you eating out? Why is your grocery cart full of steak and lobster? Why are you watching digital cable? Renting movies? Living in that neighborhood? Why is your boyfriend unemployed? Your husband? You're too stupid to deserve better. You've earned the right to suffer. Your ten dollars an hour should be sufficient to carry you through. Cut up your credit cards. Get a cheaper car. Rent an apartment instead of a house. Learn to do without. To go without. You don't need a car. Take the bus. Get two jobs for five years. Save the money from one job and you'll be free. In five years. Sixteen hours a day. Then go to college. For four years. Working full time. Raising your children. How many children do you have? Three? Four? Six? Eight? You're no better than an animal. Dogs have fewer puppies than that. Use your brain. You're poor. You have no hope. You have no right to children. Your children are a drain on society. You are a drain on society. A cancer. An abomination. A stupid, irrelevant, anachronistic particle of dirt.

The blonde counts the money. She can hardly smile through the nausea she feels. Six hundred eighty five dollars. The woman in the small car takes the money with such joy, such relieved happiness as to be disarming, and the blonde smiles the same good natured relief. Such a big, genuine grin it is. Tempered in beauty. Finished by compassion.

Chelsea Baxter counts money. Hearing the paper plop fifteen times. Hearing the Franklin Flop play a melody of 15 notes. Drawn so casually by the Mustache Man. What blue collar genius is this in this giant Tundra, gray with style? What blue collar paradise gave birth to this, an $87,000 savings account, now over eighty five. Property sold, maybe? A lucky investment? Successful business? Rich wife? Who is the younger man to the side, who the mustache man looks and blows a quiet breath of amazement for the beauty who counts the Franklin Sonata. A melody played where souls drift light as a feather on a summer breeze, where hearts are lifted in awe of their own lifestyles, in the fervent cool of the evening day. Which upper middle class road, which neighborhood streets will they travel? What wife, what mother of his children is there? What kindness, what cruelties hath she inflicted? Fifteen hundred dollars worth. Replaced so effortlessly down the road, when business profits come through. The streets of this town are paved with gold. The walkways are shining marble stone. Brass lamp fixtures cast the golden glow to the bricks and flowers, and perfect green grasses and lawns far below. These are houses bricked by sacrifice. Wood trim painted by struggle. Lawns manicured by perseverance. Flowers landscaped by privilege. The blonde slides the man the envelope, distracted by his manner. Disturbed by means. Disgusted by mammon.

Chelsea Baxter counts money. Five. Six. Seven Franklin notes this time. Notes called forth from the deposit slip, figures too silly or superstitious to name out loud. Read comfortably in secret. Alexander Hamilton fills the phrase—begun on the seven C notes. And now, seven D notes are hidden among the Chords of Resentment. Seven Franklins for the lady. Seven Hamiltons for the Lady. Washington parades in seven to fill the space, the game between joy and sorrow. Joy that there is this ritual, sorrow that there is no peace. Franklin, Hamilton, Washington. Seven times each, these three. Given to the woman who cruises beige Lexus luxury. Reeking of money. Is she forty eight? Forty nine? Yes. Forty nine her license says. That short blonde hair. What color is the deal?

Chelsea Baxter counts money. Twenty one bills. Sliding, flopping noisily to the counter. What is the sadness, the madness wave that floods the Chelsea brain as she counts? The pretty mom face. Those mom eyes. Those big, fluffy mom breasts packed away, smoothly, skillfully revealed through the sky blue blouse hugging them. Tucked into a charcoal skirt. What legs are there hidden from her eyes, Mom? What desire squirms the teller blonde in her seat this Friday afternoon? What murderous rage tickles her fancy? Pulling the hairs on her head in tingling. What is it about the woman in the Lexus? Is it her condescending, superior attitude? Is it the twenty one bills, counted in superstitious, surreptitiously suspicious ritual and lore? What spirit hath whispered to the mom in blue, this career woman, to make her access the $94,000 account? A thousand dollars is a symphony of cash. This, the Symphony No. 94, Chelsea sees when the buttons are clicked. Only 21 bills counted in ritual. Why does the blonde teller take such a deep breath, unseen, as she fills the envelope for the Lexus Queen? Is this the Friday when the address she has memorized will serve? Will she cruise the streets in want, in need, to see where the beautiful middle aged woman calls her home? If so, for what purpose? To see what husband should be a widower, what sons or daughters should be orphaned? This news reporter looking woman—is this her own repertoire, or a collection of works built by another, disguised in her name on this bank account? Who is the Lexus Queen? Is she going to die?

Chelsea Baxter counts money. Slip, sliding it so comfortably, so casually away. The woman takes the envelope, then makes no attempt to endear herself to the blonde teller at the window. She looks the teller in the eye, going only so far as to hide the jealous contempt. She stiffens up, shifting in her seat, almost writhing, pushing her blue blouse bosom out for the young blonde to see. Then she puts her Lexus in gear, and she rolls so comfortably, so calmly, so casually away.

$\mathscr{T}$hump. Thump. Thump. It is the slow, steady rhythm—timed with the beating of my heart, to serve as the counterpoint among her fervent screams coming from inside the trunk. I lean forward in the late mountain afternoon. My cheek against the silver gray trunk lid, feeling the vibration of her pounding, the melody of her voice in my soul. In my spirit, I am nude and running on the plains, a woman among the warrior braves, face painted for the war of the hunt, the hunt of flesh for battle. In my soul, I cry for blood, to grieve the agony of souls, and the lust for the blood of another. In every nerve in my body, I feel the screaming, the demonic crying out for her suffering, and the hunger for her trembling death, and burial in the darkest mountain cold.

This 42 year old soccer mom, mother of a teenage daughter she has belt whipped, and son she has paraded her bouncing bikini breasts for, whose husband will now never again know the taste and feel of her nipples in his mouth, although I most certainly will. I think that Simone may bite one of her nipples off, but I don't know. I feel the pounding of her white fists in the dark underneath me, inside the dark of the trunk. The more she panics, the more I allow the adrenaline to relax me into battle mode, as I lay forward on the trunk, cheek still pressed, t-shirt and breasts flattened against the cold metal. I try to enlist the pounding to my nipples, but I cannot make it happen. I wait for this fine suburban lady to hit the trunk in the right place, to scream the right loudness and octave, with her head at the right angle, or for her to say the right thing for my listening ears— maybe to activate them from my brain. I seek the erogenous pleasure from the sound of her fear. The sound of her despair.

What evil is this that calls out to me, that desires the feel of her naked body? It is a total and complete evil that comes over me, as if she were naked underneath me, cursing God and Christ at me to do terrible things, and in my heart I am the wo(man) she has chosen to Moby *Dick* her into a submission she only thought she understood? But the end result is what the tide rising will bring, the one that the three of us have felt for so many weeks burning inside. It is the awakening of the blue and black fire, the flames of pain and suffering, the heat of perversion too deep to discuss among the normal, ire struck and nurtured through generations, a wrong committed so long ago in our three rivers, in the branches of each of our family trees. In this life, in this world there are victims, and those who victimize. In this life, offences must come. But woe unto them by whom the offence cometh! But the next comeuppance is always overdue, today for this poor woman and her family, for whatever wrongs, whatever sins were passed from her mother who had sex for money without ever calling herself a prostitute, flames that have licked her where she lives, to make her wear such tight shirts over her giant tits—blue flames which dance along the timeline, where it will consume her daughter in the self-same lust and passion. And although she will begin to die tonight, it is written that the sin never dies, and it lives on, to torment future generations, and every warm and cold inhabitant therein.

A cooling breeze opens my eyes in the summer afternoon, pulling me up from the metal, and the dying music of our dead woman's screams. I drift, I walk from the car across the yard to the far edge, nearby the mountain road. I am the omniscient mind, borne by necessity, to travel these roads alone, to see and hear, to feel everything along the road of this life, over the forests and fields, along the entirety of this Carolina mountain range, into the lives of women and men. I know everything by way of mind and spirit, by estimation and speculation, exactly and approximate, and regardless of what is thought or said, it is not independent of me. Their reality is mine, and I am fully unbeknownst to them.

My spirit haunts these roads, until I find the sky blue Chelsea car, formed beyond Jupiter, brought to this earthen plane to serve. I see her cruise the highway in her Saturn, unburdened by the ridiculous $369 dollars a month she must bleed to own it. Unburdened by the newness of the late day, by the sorrow of way she means. It is the way she means to be, to imagine that she hears the chiming of the evening day, and the calling of prices some have had to pay. The bones of six call out to her—the blood in the soil so deep. She can remember being present for each execution. The fumbling quickness of the first, to the artful delay and patient sophistication of the sixth. Today she feels a burden, though she knows not from whence it cometh. The burden to imagine what it might feel like to lay on top of another victim, to suck the milk of hope from them until they are dry—to nurse the milk of life until it is gone. Chelsea burns now, in a lust known to but few, which has her imagine herself naked and bent over, being pounded from behind by me.

But what is the seed, where this desire hath grown? What is the source of this fire? What hath intermingled in her spirit, to produce such a feeling of aggression? These are the roads I travel in my mind—highways extended to the past, the not so far away and distant past for my 28 year old Chelsea, to her eighteenth year in the trailer, where she was raised by her mother alone, likewise as me. By this, her eighteenth year, by this—in the Heart of Memory—gone are the trips to the back room of the trailer, isolated in the country. Gone are the trips to this backroom, where she was once tied to the mother's bedpost with no clothes, and beaten with a belt buckle until she bled. These were as the days before the flood, when violence filled the land the sea, carried to and fro upon the waves of premonition. These were when Chelsea would say merely the wrong thing at the wrong time, to activate the mother's temper, causing her to stand up and get in her blonde daughter's face as though they were the same age—the thirty eight year old woman—confronting the eighteen year old statuesque beauty for epic insignificance, something as minor as unwashed dishes, or trash not taken out, or an answer to a call not given. In the Heart of Memory, eighteen year old Chelsea Lynn Baxter is in the kitchen, confronted by the woman 20 years her senior, pushing her with both hands, trying to provoke a fight because Chelsea had stood at the sink in morose pose and posture defiant, angry at having been called away from her homework to wash a pile of dishes—dishes undone because the mother works too long, too hard at the cleaners to give a damn, when she has a big assed, lazy, good for nothing cheerleading wannabe slut at home to do it. Chelsea stands at the sink hearing *"and you can wipe that frown off your fucking face before I come in there and do it for you."* But it cannot, and will not be done, and the 38 year old Tatum O' Neal woman must claim the wish of their days and ways, to stand up and nearly run into the kitchen area from the adjacent living room area and push her daughter at the sink, as hard as she can on the shoulder. Knocking the teenage woman off balance just enough.

Along this road of memory rides the Chelsea doll, gazing forward over the five and six 'o clock streets of late afternoon summer, feeling the amber call of the sun, which has tinted it pre orange already, for its journey downward to the Western Gate. She remembers this first incident in her senior year, in the cool wind of October, before the tiding of Indian Summer. Chelsea remembers the fear, the betrayal, the electric, bloody stench in her nose from the punching, as though her head had been submerged in swamp water—her mother had began punching and slapping her about the head and shoulders like a slap boxing champion, rocking, knocking Chelsea back and forth between senseless and silly, until all she felt was her mother's hands become fists into her nose and her busted bottom lip. Chelsea remembers the woman screaming *"frown bitch, where's that frown bitch..."* as she kept hitting, then the agony of having her hair pulled with both her mother's hands, bending her over forward, then feeling the stinging, pounding slap of her mother's fists and hands against her back. Then, like the slap boxing prize fighter she was, Alexis Gretchen Baxter, a.k.a. Allie G, upper cut her daughter in the face so skillfully, with such premeditated, predetermined, predestined aplomb as to rock her from silly to senselessness—forgone, making her stumble forward and fall to her knees—*"get up...get your ass up bitch, it's what you want! It's what you want ain't it"* But Chelsea only rests on her hands and knees—trying so hard not to faint. Not to have the sleep of the dead. Breathing through the impending nausea, until it overtakes her and she has to cough and spit to the floor. The spit is pink, she notices—the metallic taste permeates her body—it draws another deep, choking cough, which strengthens to a wretch, to make her thank the Almighty that she had not eaten. She cannot see without a haze, as the dizziness grows, which seems to coalesce in the air nearby, and swing itself hard into her abdomen (i.e. her mother kicked her), making her drop to the floor on her side, fetal position had. In the haze before fainting, in the sickening, hazy dizziness, the dizzy haziness of trauma, she sees the shapely hipped blue jean momma walk from the kitchen, away from her down the hall and slam the bedroom door. In the Heart of Memory, Chelsea lays there. Trying to breathe.

The Chelsea doll drives the road home, crossing the summer threshold into amber. She gazes the golden sun, not quite setting, but hanging so low over the Western Gate. She rolls the streets of Western Carolina, climbing the paved mountain slopes, trying to ignore the side of the highway, where the houses and land sit down and away from the road, where any ill advised, uncareful swipe of the wheel is a trip to the afterlife.

Ignore the side of the road, my Chelsea doll! Stay the course, beneath Sol's journey home, and find your way through sorrow! Use the Light of the World as your guide—stay on the narrow path—cruise the highway in the land of the living, and brave your way home to me! What tears are those, my darling? What is the source of thy quivering vision!

As she drives, she is taken aback somewhat, a little flustered by her own emotions, and how it is so easy for a memory to make her cry. Chelsea wipes her eyes, taking the final major turn in the road, the turn that will bring her home. I stand at the edge of Woodland Road, of Mountain View Road, unamazed that hardly a single car passes the hour, or hardly a moment passes without a sound from Amanda Hall's hoarse, guttural, screaming throat inside the trunk of my car.

Chelsea rounds the rings of Saturn, speeding along the trail of stars, like a comet born in wisdom and light. I stand tall and proud at the edge of the front yard, hardly separated from the screams I hear. The blue chariot rolls along in the distance, seeming to answer the prayer I made, coming home to where I stand in need of my princess Chelsea B, to come home and be with me. What is a partner in crime, truly, as Chelsea is to me? I stand on this end of Creation, alone with this calling too great, awaiting the second in our evil triune. I feel the breeze pick up in warning, blowing the grasses across the field in waves, whishing loudly through every tree, cooling the beads of nervous sweat from my forehead. I am calm by effort alone now, struggling to hold back a shiver. What is the need for nervousness, when you've already lit the fuse? When the pin has already been pulled? As you are vertical in nosedive in your jet plane, to destroy as many lives as you can?

I curse the nerves back to where they came from, taking a deep breath of pure defiance to the God I love, refusing to obey him as I look up to the deepening blue, watching the late afternoon plane shining silver in the sky like a tiny bird—gliding toward the west and dying sun. Of this, Lord, I cannot obey, but I must answer the evil you placed inside me, to do thy bidding as a warrior, to take the souls that you have deemed unworthy to live. Forgive me, O Lord, for what it is that I must do on this eve! Bless me to perform this wickedness in the world! Send my golden haired Angel of Death home to me, that we may do thy bidding, O Lord, to punish the deserving few, and their next comeuppance overdue! God, am I defiant to your voice, or is it your voice that I must obey! The front of my angel's chariot doth speed the straightaway, the straight road to where I am, and I beseech thee O Lord, to forgive me for every sin, for those that I have done, and for those that I must do before thee! Chelsea slows down on the road as she drives close, smiling at me so genuinely, as I return the same smile, but with a knowing stare, one laced with wisdom and tragedy.

Chelsea glides from the Highway of Dreams, born from the trail of stars along the great escape, rolling the car from the asphalt onto the rocks, pulling slowly away from the Road to Nowhere. She gets out of the car in full charcoal gray regalia, the smart blazer pulled so tightly over the matching gray blouse. The fabric is the twin of her gray skirt, so tightly wound about her hips, ending just far enough below the knee for modesty, as it pertains to sensual beauty. She is in monochrome, melancholy, so unafraid to marry the gray purse to the gray shoes underneath, as her own style so dictates. A black purse—black shoes—a white blouse? No. Those she wears were all born from the same storm clouds, where into her reality they rained upon. The site of her raises a lump of fear in my throat, that someday she will wake up and see clearly how wickedly foolish we have been, and will spit in my face as she turns and walks so casually and confidently away.

"It's all wrong, Baby."

"What?"

"Didn't I teach you not to monochrome from head to toe? You look like a storm cloud."

"You want to see the gray nail polish on my middle finger?"

"As a matter of fact, I do."

She holds up her fist, and raises her middle finger up to me with such skill, such violent assurance that it confirms my fears, that within her lies a fierce independence, one that perhaps she has repressed, because she loves me. But does Chelsea need me?

I take hold of her finger roughly, staring her in her beautiful eyes the color of these summer skies. I close my lips around her finger, allowing a strange, oddly serious tone. Chelsea watches me, delighted, intrigued. Apprehensive.

"Money," I say. "You smell like money."

Chelsea watches me suck her finger once more, finally removing it— drying it with my hand.

"That felt good."

I smile, and step against her, hugging her big and southern, squeezing.

"I am so glad you're home."

"Me too," she sighs. Confident that our game has passed. She returns my strange hug, until I feel her purse against my back. "Is something the matter?"

Still hugging her, I open my mouth to answer, flinching deep inside when I hear the weak thump, thump on the trunk. Chelsea hugs me tighter, and I am afraid to see the look in her eyes as she whispers *oh my God... oh my God... oh my God...* I lean back and look her directly in the eye. Waiting for her to tell me to let the woman go and turn ourselves in. The look I see in her eyes is fear.

"I felt it coming today," she says, her voice whispery. "I felt it in my gut all day—I knew it was coming I just didn't know how."

Thump. Thump... *"Is anyone there...is anyone gonna let me out— please let me go home to my kids... don't do it for me, do it for my children...hello...hello... I know you're there please help me..."*

All at once it descends in memory, the childhood she endured in the trailer. I look at my Chelsea's eyes, and I see the depressive spirit take over, and her melancholy lips go to a frown. Lips that I look at, wanting to press mine to them. But I refrain, drawing the energy I need from the bitterness and poison in her spirit, and the vitriolic hatred for womankind that hath descended.

"I'm gonna go get changed," she says. I nod my head, watching her turn and walk in stylish defeat towards our brick mountain home.

*H*aydn strikes a chord in the Cory brainwave, to shudder her from dreams of academia, to longings for the drive into the weekend. Simone looks up from the blue books in her office, carried aloft in Haydn's golden strings, held there by the silver coloring of the horns. The melody swings in minuet played by Adam Fischer's magic hand, in the spirit of the Esterhazy legend, Haydn's Symphony No. 5 in A major. The Gold

Symphony, she would call it, due to extreme beauty of this minuet alone, as it is played by this orchestra, captured for all time. The first movement had droned along in prettiness, unremarkable, as it flowed into the second, certainly no more or less impressive, and then as she neared her threshold of hypnotism for the late afternoon's work, the misplaced Allegro went silent, and then Haydn struck a chord in the Cory mind, and she was suddenly aware of the setting sun behind the Piedmont woods, and the golden glow imbued. She sits enraptured, as this minuet swings into the Golden Trio, where the golden horns have been transformed at their loss of silver light. And as the trio ends, unmercifully, Simone Cory understands that there is a God of Heaven and Earth, and that art is his voice of absolution, to compel and guide the misfortunate and broken hearted to Him.

She closes and puts away the blue books filled with the nonsensical strivings of a pseudo-educated youth culture, and she slides them into her soft leather carrying case. Something for her to do in the weekend, maybe. Trying to understand how little knowledge they have of the Cross, and how little of it there is they desire. Matthew, Mark, Luke and John this semester—but as philosophy and literature, conjecture and literary lecture. This test had been the answer to only one question—*"What part of the Gospel mythology is the most important to you and why?"*She intentionally left out any reference to Christ in the manger, on the Cross, or in the tomb, perhaps out of frustration (she didn't know), or was it curiosity, to see what mind or spirit would guide their erasable ball points and black felts; to stare nosily into the soul of each student as it is revealed on paper, to see who would have fear or reverence, or even mere respect for our Lord and Savior. Perhaps what she was looking for the most was a glimpse into the eyes of the reformed Catholics, such as herself, whose pain and bitter recollection would drip from the pen like excess ink and scatter into every corner of the essay. Naïve little undergraduate brains, too immature to see how bad their answer is, how loathsomely biased against the heart of Redemption, which is that He gave his only begotten Son to be crucified. The Father, the Son, and the Holy Ghost they deride, though without even knowing it inside their minds:

"I think [Christ's] teachings on love are the most obvious way to go—if we love one another, we can all get along and maybe we could finally bring war to an end. But I find it ironic that although he spoke so much about love and turning the other cheek, he never missed an opportunity to insult the Jewish leaders and try to make them look stupid for their beliefs. How could [Christ] have expected them to believe that he was the Messiah? Answer... he couldn't. Yet he spent all or most of his time pushing a dead idea through radical teachings and miracles (which I think the Gospel authors added to make him look more Messianic in nature), doing little more than stirring up strife between the Jews and their religious leaders, and ultimately catching Rome's attention in the end. Except for the Golden Rule, I don't find much of his life either believable or very important for that matter, except for a kind of poetic appeal that is so powerful it has captured and held the world's attention. Too many theories abound that explain away just about every so called miracle and Divine act in his life, so it's just impossible to accept the Crucifixion Myth as fact, although in my heart I wish it really happened the way the gospels try to say it did. The crucifixion is the ultimate irony in [Christ's] life, I believe, because if he had really practiced the love he preached, then he might never have been crucified in the first place…"

Professor Cory had been shocked away from this reformed Catholic, who had no love for the Passion of the Christ, back to the beauty of her reality, which is truth. God is truth, is what sings in the Simone Spirit as she closes her eyes, where the Gold Symphony strikes a chord, to remind her of the Father, the Son, and the Holy Ghost, and that these three are one. *The Voice of God,* she says to herself, segueing into the deepest sigh.

From this sigh, arises the energy to lift her up, and she is suddenly on her one inch heeled feet, turning, strolling toward the window of her office, the dimensions of which she struggles not to know, as they would barely accommodate the floor of a jail cell. Simone, my Zeta-Jones clone, looks out the window. The Friday afternoon campus is the essence of its true self—an empty, ghostly shell of death and despair. She marvels at the difference between this same morning and this sunset, when the summer campus was teaming with living things—walking in loneliness and want—begging for knowledge of the truth, but being unable to find it. Mortgaged, borrowed, paid to the hilt, beyond the line where there is slavery to a cause—a far and distant mirage called the American Dream, where leisure and prestige walk hand in hand, in the aftermath of sacrifice and suffering. Simone Marie Coronado is Professor Cory. Neither sorry nor satisfied with her life, her imprisonment on the road to tenure, so unintentionally longed for, and so unequivocally given.

Simone allows the depressive spirit to come, and claim her body again. Her mind is afloat, adrift on these early summer breezes, to return to a time seven years ago. In her mind's eye, she sees the twenty six year old beauty, which is herself, paying closer attention than normal to the female students, at the request of her young friend and companion. A lovely Indian friend who had dropped out of college, and didn't know what she was going to do. Sitting up in the stacks where she thought no one was looking, crying. The grad student Simone was drawn to, the Indian beauty in the black shirt and dark blue jeans, fascinated by why, by how she could be alone in a library on a Friday night, crying like she had just been beaten. *Two years,* I said, *I just realized I can't spend another day here. I've hardly ever made a grade over a C since I've been here anyway, and I had to fight just to see that happen. I don't know what I'm going to do. I only work part time—the girl I'm crashing with... let's just say things didn't work out and she actually put my stuff in the hallway. Rich white girl—blonde hair, big boobs, big bucks. Thinks the world revolves around her.*

She pulled me in. Made me think I'd found a friend for life. Always talking about how pretty I was—how I was her Indian friend. I know she didn't respect me, but she was nice, I was lonely.

But why are you crying, Honey?

Because my life is over. I didn't want to die. I wanted to live. I wanted to prove my mother wrong. I wanted the last laugh. My mother laughed when I told her I was accepted to school here. She laughed...

Simone does not laugh. She feels like she can never laugh again. Watching me stroll through her memory beside her—a Friday seven summers ago. Knowing that I had found someone rare and special. A woman of beauty and compassion, whose soul had too been forged in blue and black fire, and who had heard the warnings in the lonely breeze. It is written, that the breeze is heard only by those whose loneliness is truly epic, and greater than themselves. In the Heart of Memory, Simone walks the Friday night campus of dreams, beside a loving woman she understood, who had come from the same dark place, a place called the Grieving Land, where there is only sorrow, fear, poverty, and despair.

In her bank of memories, there are no reserves to draw upon, whereas to bring the soul up from the mire of negative recollection. Stored in the professor's spirit are only the solemn days of youth and adulthood, from her mother and father's house in Elizabeth City, to the college campus in

Greensboro, North Carolina. At the window she stands, curiously wishing to undo her white shirt, then spill both breasts forward from her bra and press them against the window for some lucky lookie loo to lay eyes upon. But Simone lowers the blinds instead and closes them, then she walks over to the office door and makes sure it is locked and the navy curtain is drawn over the frosty window with her name on it. Then, she walks over to the mirror on the wall, where the bust of her reflection is the fairest one of all, and she begins to undo her buttons down to the waist of her tight, black skirt. What energy, lust of Vanity, doth move the Queen's hands? What is it that compels my Zeta Jones clone to see herself in the mirror where she earns a smart living, reaching her hand deep inside what I have called her 'boulder holder', her G cup bra, and slide one of her mammoth tits out in the office air, leaving the other one safe inside, glancing at Wonder Woman Barbie on the shelf to her right, seeing none of the whimsy they all associate with her. The Amazon of Paradise Island, the Goddess of Themyscira looks on, her enigmatic stare pleasant, approving, with no judging superior eye. With one breast exposed and hanging free, the professor takes her glasses off and puts them on the shelf beside the doll figure. She then reaches up to her tightly pinned hair and pulls the clamp like a soldier pulls the grenade pin, and she watches the river of silken hair unfurl itself into a waterfall, and spill down and around her shoulders and halfway down her back. With one very large breast exposed, she shakes her head to assist her hair's renewal in full bodied silk, then she reaches both hands back into her brunette mane, which is what it is, and gives one smooth, slow run through with her lovely fingers, even putting it to her nose and taking a deep breath of the soap and honey sent. She tosses her hair to the back, and takes hold of the gargantuan—the DP, the double platinum, the Dolly Parton—getting a good, solid grip on the soft flesh with both hands. With the eyes of Wonder Woman upon her, she lifts her nipple to her mouth, shocked by the appearance of it all in the mirror, and she closes her eyes and sucks her own nipple like a thirsty woman in a hot desert. This is no timid licking, or silly kiss, but a full bodied, vacuum like pulling, trying to lift as much of the flesh into her mouth as she can. Clinging to it for life. For absolution. For recovery. What motivation this is, who can tell? What event, what sight, what sound from her time has burned this wickedly private obsession in her spirit? The feel of her own breasts in her mouth, I've been told, comforts her entire body, like falling free into a cushion of cotton. Since I have known her, Simone's focus has been breast centered, powerfully so, until the sucking of breasts for her is the female fellatio. I have seen her iron clothes and do dishes with her big bosoms completely exposed, as naturally as if they were not there. The abnormal size and swing of them, the unusual heft, the disproportionate hanging is her power, I suppose, her ticket to ride through this life. She pulls, she licks, she sucks herself into a state of relaxation, to a mental place so few have known. Is it a diversion, a perversion, a weirdness, an oddity, her ritual? What business is it of any other living soul, what Simone Cory does to relax herself, to slide herself through the cavern of grief and despair?

She pulls one last, long, loud, sucking pull, looking down at her nipple no longer flattened, tracing the massive areola with her finger, gently touching the bumpy skin bordered inside. Breasts are unique to every woman, she believes, each a special gift of its own right—and most women would agree, the bigger the better. Especially for those women with faces of beauty and bodies besides. These are the goddesses among us, the busty beauties of legend, the focus of every public and private fantasy. The female breast is the universal obsession of mankind, though few would indeed admit to it, dismissing it as vulgar thought, as improper and unripe conversation, a topic fit for lower, less intelligent consideration, or of prurient interest alone. To be the place of sucking for hungry children, or that in private for hungry, lucky men.

Simone lowers her breast from her mouth, leaning her head back with her eyes closed. Feeling the cool office air on the damp nipple. Then Professor Cory lifts it roughly, pushing it, stuffing it back into its rightful place. Blouse still open, bra clearly shown to her Amazon Doll, she strolls back to her semi comfortable office chair, leaning as far back as it will go. *The tiding of number seven* plays loud in her spirit, as I burn bright inside the theater of her mind.

The storms of Elizabeth City often rage the Cory sensibility, planted as the perpetual seed from youth, where they rise and fall in her like waves off the shores of Hatteras. The so-called inner banks brought Simone Maria Coronado into the world, from Sam Coronado, son of a Mexican immigrant. Sam married a young elementary school teacher named Jennifer Cornette, who gladly swapped the pedestrian for the exotic, being Ms. Coronado in school instead of Miss Cornette. Sam Coronado was the typical hard at work bilingual, with a soul of understanding for the merits and morality and money of hard labour, but smart enough to focus and direct it, most likely guided by the Cornette mind. In other words, Jenny Coronado was the smart one, and helped her Latin king to find his gold, repairing heating and air conditioning systems for a living. But nothing as foolish as Coronado Heating, which Sam wanted but his wife knew better. He went to school, got his certification, then to an established heating and plumbing company. Twelve hour days, so many weekends away, working for the man and the money, building time and years, keeping his wife pregnant on and off for twelve years, under the Catholic faith. Simone was 13 years old when Jenny Coronado had her last baby, Simone being the oldest of nine children. It was this year that the storms of Elizabeth City became a part of who she was, when the ritual darkness began, when her parents settled into who they were, Catholic by blood and fear, praying to God for strength of perseverance. But when natural desire is suppressed, it seeks another way out, until that way is found, as the mountain hill that rumbles day and night, rising and steaming dust and smoke, until the molten liquid fire underneath explodes into the evening day.

Simone Coronado was thirteen, when this spirit came unto her. Simone was 13, when the seed and the spirit hath come.

Simone breaks free from the academic prison, the stuffy little book box that dares try to be an office. She walks down the hall, alone with the sound of her one inch heels, carrying faithfully the bluebooks in her leather case, alongside the ambition and drive for tenure—publish or perish, what is that to a Goddess!

She walks the campus of dreams, in the cool of the evening, in the time before twilight and night. Somewhere in the distance, as she looks to the sun's dying light, the spirit of me is mixed in with what she remembers, what she is forced to remember, as she prepares for the long journey to where I am. As to the clouds above, their draperies are caressed in amber, upon the cloth of violet life, and the silver lining that hath turned to gold, in the death of early evening light.

So glad. So happy to be worlds away from the graveyard, the cemetery of her days and years. Not minding this two hour trek from here to there— daily now, while she volunteers to teach the lowlings for a summer session. At least, there are two days free from the drive. Even at this late departure, she'll be home by nine.

Simone—why did you tarry! In your stuffy office of ambition! Now we must wait a little longer, too long on this violent part of our trip, to wait to show the gift we have for thee! Simone! Does your back itch from what thy devastated mother hath done—a mother burdened now by nine children, and a husband crushed under a dream deferred? A husband whose back is broken by labour—unafraid to humiliate himself on some of the Richie Rich lawns and properties—with a leaf blower strapped to his back! What will you do, Jenny Wren, when the ghosts of blue collar failure come to claim you? There will be no business venture! His pay can only go so high! What? His company had to lay off part of its staff? What will you do now, Jenny Wren! Number nine must be the last! Now, what is the outlet for thy perversion? No children? No sex! If you touch your husband, Jenny, you will burn in the fires of Hell!

Simone's back begins to itch, as her body remembers the first time. The day the mother said the words—*you know what? I'm tired of whipping them. From now on if I tell you to watch them for me, I'm going to whip you when they misbehave.* Even now, she can remember the fear that started in her brain, and slowly spread to the rest of her body—as it is written—the types of fear are many, and uniquely distinguished. Among these is the fear of physical pain—the cold terror that comes, to warn of impending torture in blue and black flame. *The lamp got broken because you weren't doing your job, Simone—I told you to keep an eye on them… your grandmother gave me that lamp, it's an antique. Which means it wasn't just valuable to me , it was valuable <u>period</u>—it was worth a lot of money… you think money grows on trees around here— you think the Holy Mother leaves valuable things for me laying around the house to find? You think I've got time to hear you whinin' and complainin' all the time because you're too lazy and stupid to do what I ask you to do—I've asked you literally a thousand times to help me with those kids and you let it go in one ear and out the other, even after I feed you and clothe you and keep a roof over your head you're still as disobedient as Lucifer himself. Now, what is it that you've been disobedient about Simone? Answer me!*

Simone braves the answer as she drives, the truth according to Jennifer Wren. A woman holding claim to a nerd-like prettiness in the face, more suited to glasses than not, but still pretty enough without them, underneath black hair pinned up tightly in the Bun of Legend. Simone remembers that those glasses were off that afternoon, as Jenny had removed them after she stood up, tossing them to the bed where they lay open and upside down. A remarkably, inappropriately attractive woman, replete with skirts and sweaters and one inch heels and no makeup, curves hidden under the ill fitting clothes—sweaters loose enough to disguise the heavy hangers, bound tightly up to prevent the slightest wobble. Pressures built up and suppressed, thoughts and feelings and fantasies resisted for many years, coming at her from inside her own soul in a direct, determined assault bad enough to make her pray for strength, lest she burn in Hell for eternity.

…and you know what, I've had enough… it starts now… and just be glad that I'm doing this without getting your father involved. But this is my problem and I'm gon' solve it right now. I want you to take off every stitch of clothes you have on—every stitch… Simone remembers the little girl she was, the little woman, so incredibly ashamed already of her premature curves, and big, woman's boobs on a young girl's body. Breasts held up so high by time, so undoubtably full and rounded, almost spongy to the touch, uniquely compelling to the destined eye who might see—this preordination given to the Mother Coronado alone. Mother Coronado, unable to stop her own hands from unzipping the gray house skirt, sliding it down from her long slip while she goes to the bedroom door and locks it. She turns around, hardly able to look her beautiful daughter in the eye, who is already in her white underwear and T-shirt! Mother Coronado, behold! Your first born child in thewhite cloth! Her breasts are swollen already, are they not, by the blood of their sinful calling. No! You cannot wet the front of her T-shirt with your spit, while you draw innocence and purity though her nipples with your mouth! Careful, dear Mother, lest you miss the rarest show—as your first born removes her T-shirt and underwear for thee! Young Simone takes off her T-shirt first, covering her breasts with her arm, much to the Catholic Mother's dismal dismay, dug deep and distant down inside. She cannot allow her disappointment at her daughter's

modesty, for it would indicate the presence of lust, which when it hath conceived, bringeth forth discipline (or is it sin!) No, Mother Dear, this is not the sin of lust, you believe, it is the stain of your daughter's sin, which must be cleaned and washed in the blood of the strictest discipline!

… put your hands on your head… behind your head… now turn around… what aches and pains berate the Coronado mind? What fire burns these white feathers to smoke and singe? What plagues the Mother Line Reserves—to open the door, then the lid of this box, to continue Jenny Wren's arms in motion to her sweater, lifting it from over her head to the floor. Then the rapid, steady unbuttoning of the white collar blouse underneath, then the full slip sliding ceremoniously up from the fullest, widest ass this side of the color line, off a waist uncurved but very fit and normal. Ah, the spark that lit the fire in thy father's Latin blood—these unnaturally prominent, predominant body parts to bear. Then, the slip moves upward, does it not, upward over the Playtex Cross Your Heart, the industrial strength cloth holding them bound—then the slip slides up and over the face of Jennifer Coronado, until it lies undeterred at her feet. Bra and big white undies in place—feet as bare as her daughter's white bottom, as bare as if she were on a stroll through a country meadow—she walks over to her dresser and pulls a clean, white handkerchief and two or three panty hoses—then goes, as if pulled along by the unseen, to her daughter's naked body and stuffs the handkerchief in her mouth and ties it secure. The girl Simone looks at her mother with frightened eyes—frightened by her mother's own disrobing—frightened by the sudden silence—frightened by the locked door—frightened by the thought of fire on the skin. *Put your hands between your legs—both of 'em. Now hold your legs closed…*

What humiliation is this, Jenny Wren! For what twisted purpose are her hands pressed between her legs, in anticipation of the first blow? And your heart races, Mother, as your hands reach backward in the flow of Time and History—swinging upward as a pendulum at apex, then rolling smoothly from the farthest secret room in the past, when this country was young and new—your hand glides smoothly down the timeline, gathering speed and momentum, through the line of preacher's wives and teachers you came from, through those secret and selfsame disciplines ever wrought—from the distant far and away, through the near and far, down through the ages to the here and present day, from the sin passed down from the first mother who stripped their daughter to nakedness in the name of Discipline, to the here and present now in burning, and your hand is open, alive with fire as it makes a maximum contact with her buttocks, with the bare white skin of her naked backside in lust and unrighteous indignation. The girl Simone lurches forward, so far as to be knocked off balance by the force— immediately making Jenny grab her daughter with one arm, then bring the pendulum back through time again, letting it fall back through its undulation, until Predestination is found once again. The second hit starts the fire—burning in the same spot hit twice, to warn that continued striking will lead to damage, which will go from one end of the color spectrum to the other, as the damage becomes more severe. Driven, pushed forward by a light inside—a light glowing from red to blue—Jenny pounds and whacks and smacks her daughter's left buttock cheek until it is dark red, hit at least one hundred whacks with her bare hands, understanding now that the bare hand cannot exact the required suffering, and that punishment without proper pain is futile.

I hear your voice, Mrs. Coronado, as you send your weeping daughter walking across the room. Her mouth is gagged with your stocking hose! Her left buttock is a rose cheek! As she returns from your dresser with the

Instrument of Divine Negativity, you know that this is her Heavenly Correction, and that it cannot be given half heartedly. What is the force, Mrs. Coronado? What is the force of energy that moves your body again, to retrieve a second and third stocking hose from the drawer, the first wrapped around your daughter's wrists until they are held together in securest fashion in front of her? She holds the instrument of private pain tightly in her little fist, unable to fathom the whirling of emotions inside, as she feels you tie her ankles together as tight as can be. When the wooden brush slides from her hand to the floor, Mrs. Coronado, it is the fear of revelation that loosened her hand; for please, Mother, have mercy on thy flesh and blood!

Your daughter hears the words *stand still, don't you move, I'll pick it up myself—and that little trick is going to cost you dearly*...Mrs. Coronado—thy name is the Crowning of the Whirlwind! Thine is the face of doom in your daughter's soul—thy voice is the catalyst for her insanity!

Simone pries herself awake on this drive—awake from the daydreaming of Eve, still immersed inside her thoughts like a fading vision—a vision with sights and sounds, smells of stockings and sweat, and the taste of handkerchief cloth in the back of her throat. The sight of how her mother could not resist the devil of desire any longer (having not had sex for two years, as the Spirit hath revealed it to me) and began to fumble with the back of her bra while she walked in front of her daughter. Thirteen year old Simone watches her deeply Catholic, deeply religious mother take off her bra right in front of her, finally sliding the straps off after an eternity of fiddling with the hooks in back, revealing to Simone two great, hanging bells of white flesh—placing the bra on the mirrored dresser nearby, held captive by what she sees in the mirror, holding them both up in her hands with one gigantic, hard and powerful squeeze, pulling the dark nipples forward and releasing them in a biting pull. In the Heart of Memory, the look on the Coronado face is stern—having crossed over severely into intolerance—intolerance for the suppression that has eaten her alive with physical pain, intolerance for the spirit of pretense and behind closed doors hypocrisy, and epic intolerance for her oldest daughter's childhood happiness and peace of mind.

The Lady Simone remembers her mother's renewed spirit—her new command, her spirit's easy flight as her breasts wobble free, hanging long and bulbous, un-flattened and exposed. Simone remembers the twinge of energy in the pit of her stomach, something other than the fear, when her mother's breasts came to light. She remembers the feel of the hard nipple that brushed against her bare back, as the mother took the hair brush in hand to make it ready. She remembers the feeling of wanting her mother to stand pressed against her buttocks and piss hot down her backside and legs—how she had wanted to feel the tickle of her mother's hot urine down her thigh as punishment while her gigantic bosom pressed against her back. She remembers the day the fire ignited, when the wood sent burning embers down through her buttocks; through the skin into her groin, up into her own nipples exposed, to every inch of skin where blood pumped past the stockings, to the gruff feel of her own muffled voice in the back of her throat, and the moist, powerful misting she felt at the top of her inner thighs, and how when she pressed her hand to her groin, it helped soothe the burning of blue and black fire. Simone remembers the loss of breath, the choking hand at her throat at the end of hairbrush fire and blood, then the two handed choking that seemed to lift her up from the floor to her mother's bed, where she remembers the smell of the old brown bed spread with the tassels that dangled just above the floor. She remembers the bedpost, and the dipping of the mattress under her mother's weight as she climbed on top of her. The sudden darkness as her mother let one breast fall full and naked over her nose and gagged mouth—the surprise, the giddy disbelief that begins to course through her veins, as the lungs begin to burn from the poison air inside, and her naked body jerks and twists against her mother's heavy nakedness. Simone remembers the panic, the unbelievable terror she felt, the feeling that she might die from suffocation, from enduring what the scriptures mean, where it admonishes of those things which are a shame to speak, of that which is done of them in secret.

From the heart of this fathom of darkness, from the unfathomable death, Simone claws her way from perverted death into perverted life, where at least there is a breath of fresh air to breathe, amidst the phantom smell of her mother's sweat and perfume.

*D*esire plagues the Coronado mind as she drives, which manifests in the pit of her stomach, to spread outward into ghostly streams—those branch into the parts of her spirit, soul and body, to create a longing for me, and the sensual evils I provide.

Think upon me, Madame Coronado, Professor Cory, thy name is but a shadow of thee. Simone Maria Coronado, who broke the bonds when you were seventeen to your grandmother's house inland, in the Martin County line. Jenny Cornette's own mother, from where the River of Generations flowed, but having dispensed an epic kindness and compassion for thee. From their modest home on Blunt Street, they oversaw your emancipation from Jenny Wren, and your legal name change to Simone Cory. But what truly is in a name, Professor Cory! These scars run so wide and deep, to wounds that bleed still down below, that have often sent lightning into your physical body to make you double over in agony. Phantom lightning in your flesh, born from penetrations you still remember, and have learned and studied and written yourself to death trying to forget. Remember me now, my dear Madame Cory, to try to ease many sufferings inside. But as you will soon see, as you already know, the longing for me cannot soothe the pain you feel, nor the cold, distant craving for relief from the turmoil inside.

I am your Cherokee bride, born and raised in North Carolina, to a Cherokee woman of dirt and straw, who left the mountains with me after my white father died. Think of me, Madame Cory, try to ease the suffering in your soul. But how is this possible, when you see the lonely image of the seven year old girl in the cabin, who was locked in closets and starved for days, and beaten at least once with every passing of the sun? A girl too young to realize that life wasn't supposed to be this way, and that mothers are in essence, our protectors, and are not supposed to make their daughters suffer. Those punishments began when my father was killed at sundown, when he was caught creeping behind back stairs, in time with a mountain girl who was another man's wife. *Thou shalt not covet thy neighbor's wife* is carved in stone, as part of the curse of mankind—to add to his woes when this lust hath conceived—for when *Thou shalt not commit adultery* is seen and surreptitiously broken.

Momma Malina Josephine, *Tsalagi* widow, do not take thy anger out on me! Do not drip the blood from my skin! Stand here, at my dead father's grave, and let the tears soothe the pain you feel! Every mixed emotion that courses through—from his betrayal in life, to his premature departure in death, to leave you alone with what he has done! Stupid Indian bitch! Your husband cheated on you with another woman, and now he lies stinking in the earth because of it! Leaving you alone with a dim witted, doe eyed little bastard out of Carolina! But what whippings she must endure, will not be delivered by a man's hands—but they must come from the mother line—to be rendered in their purest form, from one woman to the next, from a grieving mother to her daughter!

RAVEN

Isolation, physical abuse, sexual abuse

/   \

/   **RAGE**   \

/   \

CHELSEA ---- ---- ---- ---- ---- *SIMONE*

Isolation, physical abuse, sexual abuse   Physical abuse, sexual abuse

Even now, I still nurture a powerful inadequacy inside—a spirit of loserism that courses through my veins—symptomatic of most lives lived, medicated to insignificance in so few. My looks have been the remedy which provides me an escape from my mother's fate—which was to live alone. The evil that burns in my heart—my profound hatred for mothers and their daughters—it does not sour my expression, because so many have eased the suffering inside with smiles and compliments, and no resistance to my initial presence. But on the flipside of this self same blessing is the Curse of God—which causes people to grow tired of me for literally no reason, and they embrace a sudden desire to dislike me—to see every flaw in my otherwise perfect face—to twist it and contort it into something that sickens them, and I'm suddenly an Indian bitch that they can't stand the sight of any more—and I can feel my eyes moving farther apart in their mind and crossing until I'm a cross-eyed sea creature to them—worthy of scourges and neglect and abandonment and death. Simone is unavoidably drawn to the origins of the fish dynamic which is my ultimate curse—to be abandoned unto death—when Malina Moon moved from Pleasant Hill in Cherokee County, trying to escape the spirit of the mountains which had cursed her marriage—dragging me a couple of hundred and 25 miles down east to Martin County, where we settled in Jamesville, so close, and yet so far away from where even my Chelsea Doll and my Wonder Woman could have gone.

Simone—there is no comfort in me! The spirit of me draws you into the rural town, where the Indian woman lives all alone with her daughter! A gigantic breasted woman, the largest bosom we have ever known, narrow of hip and waist, so that the effect is tragicomic at best! Oh, such things as go on behind the closed doors of a home, that no one in the world should see! We are bound together with our Chelsea, you and me—that we are the Lonely; raised by mothers who despised us and beat it into our flesh accordingly—this violence mixed with the buried desire of womanhood— fueled by anger and the frustrations of failure and hopelessness—the three of us, my Simone—think of us as you come home to me! Malina and her daughter Raven, in the three roomed house on Old Mill Road, truly the road to nowhere, as I lived and tried to breathe. A house surrounded by nothingness, seen from the road by the few passers by—nothingness highlighted by a forest of trees and bushes and high grass—a house unkept by hope for the future. Off Old Mill Road is the house of Moon, where an Indian mother lives in isolation with her daughter. A house that had been waiting. Calling out to the lonely and truly dispossessed, who were drawn by preordination. When Malina saw this tiny house—gray with age, broken down by time—the dirt yard and big tree—the tin roof and screen door, the so-called living room and kitchen and two bedrooms, the back screen door and porch, the small back yard and tiny woodshed, the high grasses that bordered the yard at the edge of a thick, dark woods, she knew that she had been called home. A house that no one in their right mind would rent. Waiting for her. A place where she could gladly hide away in, delivering me to the school with enthusiasm every day—dropping me off every morning, rain or shine at the bus stop, then driving off to whatever field or factory she had to labour. How many cold days did I stand there with the other children, ostracized already, neglected, being made to feel different because I was not white or black, rescued from the brink of mistreatment by an older black girl; a light skinned angel who told me I was pretty, and who kept me from descending into tears on so many of those lonely mornings, when I felt that I would implode from pure loneliness and fear. And for the life of me, dear Simone, I cannot remember her name! Only that she was so nice to me, when all the other kids acted as though I stank, and was the ugliest little thing in God's Creation. My eyes were too far apart, they said, and the girls said my hair was greasy, and one of the little girls slapped me on a dare, because I was different from them. My yellow-pretty angel saved me after that. She made them understand that I was to be left alone, or for them, there would be Hell and a solemn ass whipping to pay. Even then, it seems that I was protected outside the house, because I was not meant to retreat from society, having something of epic importance to gain and do. My yellow-pretty angel, five years older than me, who was only seven when she rescued me from exile.

Through that first year in Jamesville, she was there with me at the bus stop, keeping me nearby, ignoring the other small kids, holding my hand as if I were her little sister. I remember holding her hand, and standing so close to her as she chatted with her other friends her age. She was the prettiest among them, I remember. An immature country girl—laughing wildly, running and playing tag with the boys. I always knew that somehow, I was in the back of her mind. That little first grade Indian girl, who had bloody bruises on her body from her shoulders to her ankles. That little Indian girl named Raven, who always looked like she was on the edge of an easy flow of tears. That little Indian girl named Raven, whose voice was as soft as a whisper, and who seemed as delicate as a mountain flower in spring.

The sun sets over the Blue Ridge Mountains, as seen from Blowing Rock and all points west, when the sky darkens from blue to something more profoundly real, and reminiscent of the Truth that lives beyond the light of day. Simone rolls onward, enamored to awe by the disappearance of the last glint of orange sunlight, and the rapid descent of day towards the night. She remembers now why she does not mind the hours and the miles on the road, and why sometimes she stalls for so long into the afternoon before leaving. There is hardly a beauty more profound than the sky after sunset, when the white heat of the sun has died, and there is left but the cool of the evening, when the world begins to reveal the coming night. Simone rolls along, lovely hand on the wheel of Cadillac Luxury, a rolling second home along her blue journey among the stars. She wonders how it is that the rest of these fools on this road speeding to and from nowhere, can look at the unearthliness above them, and perceive nothing of Creation, and the God of Heaven and Earth. Simone looks at the eyes of Venus, at the bright and evening star, knowing it was sent to guide men and women to the Truth, through the wilderness of lies, in the Valley of the Shadow of Death.

The evening day is deep twilight, nearby the edge of night. Shadows recall fair death of light—beyond their feeble sight. Simone breathes in, blinking briefly for too long, then exhaling upon the truth of what she knows—what she feels—that her time with me is divinely wrought, and what we do is a war so sumptuously and sublimely fought. What we do, we *must* do, she understands, as she imagines this same star of the Evening over my mother's lust when I was twelve, and a misery as gargantuan as the bosoms in her special ordered bras. What thoughts plague a person against their will, what feelings torment the body undeterred? She resists the squeeze in her spirit, the desire to reach up as she drives and massage her own breast, while she remembers what she knows, the sight of the evening day over my twelfth summer, and how I am tied to a tree in the back yard. Who can fathom the mother who comes from the evening house, a cute faced Indian woman barely sensual, average sized body in a plain skirt and faded pullover shirt with the three little buttons at the top.

The shirt is a thrift store nothing—faded to a color that does not exist. Her non existent hips are covered in the pleated peasant skirt, her sandals are comfortable and worn like her expression. Those who could have seen, would have seen the woman holding the brown extension cord, and the 1x2 inch piece of stick wood. Simone perceives the phantom itching of old as she drives, as I tell my mother that I will not do it again, though I cannot remember what it is I have done. Something with the dishes, I think, or maybe I ate the last bit of something special she was saving for herself— who's to say? What I do remember, what Simone remembers when she thinks of me, is the woman who has chained me to a tree like a dog. This is the second of three nights and three double beatings I will receive, as my skin is still striped purple and chipped red from the night before. Josephine Moon would appear overwrought to the ignorant, as she often does, except to those who choose to know the truth as it is given. The truth is revealed to me from my Indian mother Josephine, when she lifts her pullover shirt up just enough for me to see the two heaviest hanging and flopping breasts under the sun on a woman of her normal pounds can create, and she grabs me and proceeds to whip me with the extension cord hard enough to stripe tiny bits of blood under my dress. Her breasts swing and wobble like two great swinging bottles of milk while she whips me, and in my young mind, she exposes her breasts simply because she needs freedom to move better. To me, it has nothing to do with epic domination, the ironic twisting of motherhood from comfort to discomfort, from coziness to discord, the systematic unraveling of me from a whole person to pieces, the infinite confusion while she draws pleasure from the infliction of pain and suffering. She pulls and yanks and jerks me around like a rag doll, growing irritated by my high pitched screams and squealing. She ties the extension chord around my wrists until they are bound so very tightly, and then she takes her shirt off completely in the evening day, and I know that I am going to feel the stick wood across my arms, my shoulders, my back, my buttocks, my thighs, my shins and my feet.

The windshield is the theatre of the mind, as Simone watches the vision while she drives, of the great busted Indian woman as she beats the little girl's squeaks and squeals down to mature guttural screaming, cracking the board across her buttocks and then breaking it across her back, then moving ghoulishly calm as if possessed, putting the two pieces together as one and concentrating hard on the little girl's buttocks, on my buttocks, until the bruises whiten to injury, then begin to darken to the edge of death and blood. Fifteen minutes passes, I suppose, over the rise and fall of this impossibility, of the woman on Old Mill Road, who whips and beats her daughter in the evening. As the vision fades, Simone feels the burden of it lifting just enough to lift her up, and push her forward through time to seven summers ago, when she was researching her dissertation *The Second Coming of Christ,* which I know for a fact she had to fight for.

What did we know of Fate, Destiny and God before then? Of how people are drawn together according to his purpose, whether it be good or evil? What judgment for the unworthy hath He wrought through our hands, through the hands of the mountaineers, to exact death and destruction to such a deserving few? To bring a hammer down on the foot of complacency, on the fingers of hypocrisy, across the skull of civility, until it lies bleeding and dead? Simone and I left the stacks that late afternoon, strolling the campus of dreams, in the splendor of renewed hope. I sensed something in this beautiful woman—a quiet and powerful understanding—that she knew the meaning of the word pain, and had felt the spirit of the word suffering.

The Mountaineers

I want you to come home with me. It's a two and a half hour drive, but at least you'll have somewhere to stay tonight.

So, the professor and I are adrift. Two souls in mourning for what once was, and for the tiding of what will be. I remember the old champagne colored Taurus she drove, how it seemed to me a paragon of virtue, a gift of luxury bestowed from God, rolling righteousness on four wheels. I had met another angel, I believed, I *felt,* that would take me away from this life into one of peace and tranquility, to protect me from the woes of sin, and the corruption of salvation lost. I drove West with Professor Simone Cory that summer twilight, knowing in my spirit that Destiny had called me, but wondering how it would end, because so many of us are called, and so few of us are chosen. What is the calling, that the beautiful, intelligent woman took pity on me, to invite me unbeknownst into her home? I could hardly breathe, I was so filled with anticipation and uncertainty, like a feral cat pulled from the streets and put in a strange car, and was taken to a warm and cozy dwelling I had never seen before.

It's pretty isolated. I'm sorry about that. But don't worry, this isn't Alfred Hitchcock Presents, I'm not going to kill you and bury you in the woods... and I laughed a genuine nervousness, one that she sensed because after nearly two hours of hearing me tell of what Malina Moon hath done, she finally reached over and took my hand and said... *we can make it,* which infused me with such a sense of belonging, such a sense of home that I had to look away and take deep breaths through my nose, because I most certainly did not want to appear as though I were manipulating her through tears, nor did I want her to know that I was crying inside.

The miles continue to flow past us—above, below and all around us, until the evening fades to night, and I see the sign post up ahead, *Welcome to Black Mountain.* It seems that we have driven out of reality into another world, where the stars are brighter, and the shadow of earth is darker than the night. *This feels so familiar,* I say. *I haven't been here since I was a child—the mountains, I mean. What made you come here—so far away from your job?*

For some reason, I love the drive. It feels like you're going on a long trip every day. I get to see the sights, which I never get tired of.

I look around at the shadowy landscape of fences and open fields, and the black forest silhouettes beneath the disk of the silver Summer Moon. *This reminds me so much of where I grew up. It's really strange, but you're a college professor, about to get her PhD, which means that you're something of a people person, yet you chose to live out here—*

In the middle of nowhere?

Yeah.

Half of me is a people person. The other half of me can't stand the sight of 'em. Their smell, the sound of their lying voices. People are so filled with lies—with deceit. Have you ever...

What?

Nothing.

Please say it.

Have you ever just wanted to reach down into yourself—and unleash the pain you felt, and make everybody else in the world suffer? Like a volcano that spews enough black ash into the sky to dwarf itself, and block out the sun for days?

Oh, God! What questions stir apprehension into the soul? What answers raise the Spirit of Fear!

That half of me, she says, *wishes I had never been born.*

When a door is opened, the Door of Opportunity, one does not stand there in dumbness, dumbfounded, wondering what to do. These words spoken, so genuinely and casually spoken into reality, a formal declaration of truth—this Amazon Goddess, speaking the words of my foolish life—telling me that half of who she is…is the whole of who I am. It is the Door of Opportunity opened, and I so casually, so genuinely step forward into it as we drive—this door to another dimension—a dimension of friendship and love, where blood ties do not exist to corrupt the bond of matrimony—the marriage of two kindred souls to bear. I take this opportunity as we drive, and I take her hand into mine as though it is mine to have, not even daring to look at her. Then I lift the beautiful hand to my lips and kiss it gently, then I rub the lovely white hand firmly against my cheek.

And as this vision too fades into Simone's memory, there is no lightness in her spirit besides, as her mind traverses the dark miles still left, to where I stand waiting, underneath the Stars of Heaven.

"*I'm dying of thirst*"…thump…thump… "*I'm dying of thirst… I can't breathe*"—

'Shut up' is the other side of the duet I hear, with Chelsea slamming her hands hard on top of the trunk.

"*I can't help it, please help me—I'm dying of thirs—*"

"You've only been in there for four hours you dumb bitch so shut the *fuck* up!"

"I'm dying of thirst…"

"You're gonna be dyin' of something else if I hear one…more… WORD!"

I can hear the stress and impatience growing in Chelsea's voice, like a hungry hyena nearing a carcass at night, whose laughing voice grows more high pitched and sinister with his determination the nearer he gets to feeding, as even the lions must become wary when the laughing jackals are in need.

Our victim's pounding from in her tomb never ceases, having no knowledge of the dangers if the lid of her metal coffin is open.

"When are we gonna kill this bitch? We should just go ahead and do it and get it over with and show Simone the body when she gets here. We don't know when she's coming."

"She'll be here. I know it. And she'll be here sooner than you think."

"How do you know? You wouldn't even let me call her."

"We never talk on the phone to each other when this happens."

"I know. I just need to fuck this bitch and kill her with my bare hands. I feel like I'm gonna die if I don't."

"Me too. But we have to wait. We can't even unlock the trunk until she—"

"What?"

I mouth words to her, but there is no sound. She watches me only slightly bewildered, more frustrated than curious, as I take the same steps toward the road that I had taken this afternoon. This night is a crystal clear summer's evening, with every star visible above the tree lines, and the open field of grass across the road. I can feel the rise of impending doom for this poor blonde woman in our trunk, a force approaching like a wave, as the third part of our trinity rides the last mile.

We are all prisoners of our Destiny. Free to roam about at random, as chosen and administrated by Fate—like animals in a moving cage, like passengers on a moving train, condemned to rail against the confines of the un-breathable space to none effect, with no power to prevent oneself from going where it is that train is bound.

As the Eyes of Light glide eerily past the curve down the road, no longer hidden by the trees, I know that she does so by preordination, even down to the time of this arrival, and that she could not have left for home a minute sooner if she had tried. All of our lives, we have fought against the same dark destiny, the paths which were divided into three, but which have since merged into the same road of blood which flows us along like a river, to carry us to the darkness of this night, where we are called and chosen by Him.

I take Chelsea's hand, and we turn away from the road towards the house, where the Camry coffin is parked oddly in the grass towards the woods. With an apprehension that approaches that of a soldier nearing the battlefield, we stand in front of our brick home in the Black Mountain Night, watching our companion glide hidden behind her Eyes of Light, turning slowly, noisily onto the gravel rocks, rolling to a slow and smooth stop beside the rings of Saturn.

The light soon pops on inside her car, to reveal the face and hair of the Goddess of the Hunt, brow wrinkled in something like profound confusion at why my car is parked so far into the yard and why Chelsea and me are standing like two mountain ghosts in the light of the Milky Way.

She is a tallish, very heavy breasted brunette with a small waist and big hips—a strong legged silhouette of a woman in beauty more extreme than what we see in the mirror. She switches those tight skirted hips in the dark, so unafraid of us, her silhouette lit up by the white blouse in the pale moonlight.

I should have called, I'm sorry," she says. "Please don't be mad. I brought dinner, see? You love KFC, don't you?"

"Chelsea, go put her things in the house." She obliges, taking the burgundy cardigan sweater, big leather carrying bag and the red and white dinner bag, moving with such diligence, such determined obedience that Simone is taken aback again, this time allowing civility to fade.

I suspect that fear, the extreme side of it, has silenced our Lady inside the tomb.

"You two are acting like you're going to jump me or something. How about somebody telling me what's going on?"

The trees whisper loudly in the mountain night, as they try to answer, by a breeze strong enough to blow my hair and cool enough to forecast a warning. Chelsea comes back out of the house and walks boldly up to our bewildered partner, getting close behind her and hugging her tightly around the waist. Simone touches Chelsea's hand.

"Did somebody die? Did something happen to somebody in my family?"

"Somebody's going to die," Chelsea whispers.

I see a sudden boldness come over Simone's face, to hide the sudden terror that washed through. She doesn't know if she is going to wake up, or die in demonic betrayal inside a dream. She locks eyes with me in the dark, ready to fight me and Chelsea to the death if she has to in love, fear and cutting. I step close to her and touch her face.

"I brought you a gift. God sent her to us. Another white, corrupted sheep to be sacrificed. Another wicked, sinful woman with too much time and money on her filthy, disgusting hands. A middle aged, middle class mother—whose life is so filled with wickedness that it led her right to me—"

"We've got her in the trunk," Chelsea says, breathing the words. "In Raven's car."

Revelation descends upon our Simone in full, to transform her expression to wide eyed amazement, with her drawing in a loud breath, and putting her hand to her mouth. I turn and walk towards the car, while Chelsea escorts our Lovely behind me.

"Hey, *Bitch,*" I say, banging hard once on the trunk. "You ready to go home?"

"Yes, oh yes please.... please..."

"Let me hear you beg for it you fucking whore!" Chelsea yells. "Say *please*, over and over!"

The sound of her squeaky, fear laden, high pitched pleading twinges every nerve under Simone's skin, and it is suddenly winter chill in her body. Then the cold flashes to a sudden heat, pressing down in her groin to her bladder, all encompassed under the deep, booming sound *Molock* in her ears. She tears away from Chelsea's grip and runs through the yard into the street, as if trying to find a space in the world with enough oxygen for her to breathe. She goes (lumbers in one inch heels) across the street into the grass and lifts her skirt, pulling her black underwear down and off, and I can hear even from this far the sound of her pissing in the grass. And mixed with that sound is the loud, gruff voice of release, as though it is her calling to announce in bellowing the sound of Death and Hell in her soul.

"Go help her Chesea," is the quiet chirp from pretty Indian lips in the dark, as the blonde obliges with wisdom and willingness, crossing the street hurriedly as the obedient lady in waiting. Somewhere in the dark, I

see silhouettes in a moonlit night, moving mysteriously nearby the mountain road. The Spirit of What Needs To Be Done is not through with our Queen, causing her to cough until it grabs hold of her and she cannot see but how to focus on the dark ground at her feet, lovely mouth open in coughing that rises to gagging, and now a loud and sickening dry wretch or two. Chelsea helps her to her knees for the long series of dry heaves that jerk her body and take her breath, so that she has to wonder how she will ever again breathe free. I see the beautiful women in the moonlight, one standing bent over, attending the other on her hands and knees in nausea and revelation, as her body accepts and incorporates the spirit of the deepest perversion. Chelsea helps her to her feet, her bare feet, and in my mind I hear her say the words *you ready?* And I see the Queen of Babylon nod her head amidst the deep breath and dry mouth.

Simone! There is no vomiting of the evil thou must perform—the Angel of Death has a calling for thee! Thy breath will be sweet in the mountain night, in the aftermath of dry heaves!

"I heard you throw up".

"I almost did," she says. "But it wouldn't happen. I need some water." Chelsea hurries inside for the glass of cool and clear life. Simone walks in her bare feet to her car and pulls the Big Red from the glove compartment, unwrapping the red stick of cinnamon gum, chewing it, breathing a deep sigh, tilting her head back, chewing until she is satisfied. When the chewing ends, I know the gum has been swallowed in renewed hunger. Chelsea returns water for the Queen, who drinks it all in a thirst unknown, a drink from the well of living water. She nods her head when the last swallow is gone. We watch our blonde maiden take the glass back inside— to give Simone and me one last moment, where nothing is hindered between us and agreement—and when I look at her, she closes her eyes and nods accordingly.

The blonde returns one last time, slowly, her spirit girded for battle. In the glow of the house light, under the light of the Summer Mountain Moon, I open the door of the rolling tomb and pop open the lid of the trunk—

I hurry back around, in time to see the white fingers claw through the opening (oh, how I need to break those lovely fingers!), and a white arm pushes suddenly through, pushing the trunk lid up higher, lighting the dim insides of the rolling coffin—

A middle aged white woman—in a sleeveless white button down blouse and blonde hair climbs out in hurried clumsiness, panting, falling like a sack to the ground behind the car. The sight of the unfamiliar house, the beautiful blonde, and the brunette stranger mix rapidly with me in her mind, her helpful Indian friend from the road a while back—and we all begin to spin a turbine in her brain, and we flash electricity to every cell and instinct in her body. Without hesitation, she gets up in the dark and runs away from us toward the road, but I quickly run past her, between her and the street, my expression as calm and dark as the forest silhouette. She jumps and yelps, startled, confused, turning again, running past the gravel driveway to her left, stupidly toward the back of the house like a confused deer—but there are no helpful and safe neighbors to hear her. Only the three of us listen with the solemn grass and trees, hearing her scream *"Help! Help!"* so loud and deep, as to cause one to incorrectly say 'at the top of her lungs," which is the phrase I hear. Yes, she screams at the top of her lungs to be helped, to be saved, to be rescued, to be redeemed from the nightmare that is abduction, and the curse of God which is death and burial.

When she is in the middle of the back yard, there is nothing for her to see but moonlit blackness, the shapes of Paradise Lost, a forest too black and menacing to approach, and three figures who have left dignity in the night wind, and have descended to animals in human form. Yet, we are not vampires or werewolves, as some would call the daughters of Eve. We are women, suffused with a divine and demonic gift for blood. But when it is the fight for life, the survival instinct says flight! Even to a forest at the edge of Hell itself! She tries to run into the woods down and away from the house, not knowing how close she is to where she will be buried. Chelsea blocks her way into the atramental forest—and she turns again, confused, out of breath, expending the last of her old cheerleader energy, suburban work mom energy, middle class might and perseverance, running again to the mirage that is hope, towards the lights of the only house within five miles of where she will die.

We run beside her, keeping up with our scared prey, the middle class mouse running in the dark. She makes it to the back door, in time to see a strong, shapely brunette step between her and abscondence, her retreat from judgment and reward. What evils were done by her ancestry, who oversaw what atrocity in the mother line, deep in the past, in the branches of her family tree, to have caused this to be visited on her flesh, and the souls and spirit of her grieving children?

Like the dumb, stupid sheep she has always been, she runs again to the middle of the big back yard, finally into the arms of exhaustion and half hearted surrender.

"I swear to God…I won't tell anybody….*please* let me go…"

In total silence, we all look at her. Stunned. Speechless. Exhilarated. Awestruck. Disbelieving. Like hunters who have cornered a trophy buck against a hillside in the woods too steep to jump or climb, watching him slam repeatedly against the dirt and leaves, falling clumsily down over and over again. Or three gangster girls, less appropriately, who have cornered the bitchiest cheerleader in an abandoned locker room after school.

Giddy with instinct, I step to the side, to open the gap between her and freedom. In the vast mountain dark, in the great open space of night, she bursts from the grip of our sight and tries to run around the other side of the house *"to get to the car"* her spirit whispers to her, to punish her with one last flash of false hope. She runs, all hips and ass in her jeans, running without confusion this time, as if her mind has presumed to give her a plan. She watches the house get closer, seeing it approach as slowly as it can, soon passing her, and she is unsafely on the other side, noticing the bricks and two windows, the thick woods on the other side, and the unseen grass beneath her feet.

'My shoes are so fast' tries to smile in her brain, when suddenly her legs do not move anymore, and she falls forward like a tower of Lego blocks to the ground. Chelsea lies on the ground with her, arms wrapped around her legs in a tackle tight enough to have stopped a man. The woman screams, then she screams again when I fall on her hard enough to make her grunt from the impact. We turn the woman over, lit up by the feel of her body writhing underneath us, and the sound of her breathless, panicked screams. She lies on her back now, with Chelsea and me pressed on top of her with both her arms pinned, and her legs pressed against the ground. While I watch her tilt her head up and back, screaming for the stars to hear, I can feel the epic loss of compassion in Chelsea beside me, and

the epic loss of dignity in the woman underneath me. She struggles and screams, face dirty and puffy from dust and stress, makeup smeared to a mess of discoordination, revealing her natural and sensual cuteness as a mother. Simone gets on her hands and knees close to us, so that she can look down at the face of the woman.

We all rest here. Feeling the lights turn on in our bodies, the rising of a fervent heat, then the burning of blue and black fire.

*O*ur walk inside is perfectly casual, as the muses are so inclined, that even the condemned are treated with respect on their last mile before they die. The stroll into our humble home is a surreality of middle class décor, provided by our three incomes, and our blonde guest to endear herself with the requisite *"you have a lovely home."* The sound of her pathetic pleading sickens every inch of me, and I have to resist the urge to call her on her epic bullshit and tell her to shut the fuck up. But my own frustration is reflected through the Chelsea Doll, who pushes our white shirted guest hard in the back, enough to make her stumble forward and nearly fall in the middle of our living room floor.

Chelsea grabs her by the hair, which seems to prevent her from completing her long fall, and pulls her upright while we stand in a small circle around her. The expression on Simone's face is sheer delight disguised as calm civility, as though the woman were an honored guest to be admired. Chelsea's expression betrays the purest contempt I have ever seen on her lovely features, like a pit bull held in check by its master, while the lust for blood runs and courses through its body. I think at this moment, she carries a vampiric lust for the woman's blood, to easily hold her down and bite one of her shoulders until she is able to taste and swallow the blood. Will she be held down at some point, and bitten to a screaming frenzy? This I do not know. When I look at her, I am sickened by the sight and smell of her blonde self righteousness and old perfume, by the air of entitlement she wears around herself even now, as though she has a divine right to be successful here, and walk free from inside the Gates of Hell. We are good cop, indifferent cop and bad cop, standing around some fool we have captured, hoping to wheedle and needle our way to a confession.

"Ring around the rosie Bitch," Chelsea says, trying so hard not to smile and laugh over her hatred. Her hand flies by us all at lightning speed, and we hear the loud smack of a gigantic slap that makes the woman yell and stumble towards Simone. Simone grabs her gently and shushes her calmly, quietly, reassuring her that all is well, and that Chelsea will not hit her again. "Right Chelsea?" she says, which brings only a response of strong hairpulling, which Simone allows, so she can enjoy the look of pain and fear on the poor woman's dirty, pretty face. Tears do stream the dirt, along with the beads of sweat and a runny nose, as if she were working in the fields all day from sunup, and just told that her daughter was found dead in the river. The fear and exhaustion on her face is part of the pain she feels, and it feeds us as fuel for this fire. Chelsea punches her suddenly and without warning in the pit of her stomach, and the sudden, sickening yelp tells us all that she is a stranger to real pain and suffering. After the punch in her stomach, Chelsea holds her up by the hair and watches her hopeless expression, keeping her from absorbing the blow. "Chelsea," Simone says, shaking her head no. Chelsea turns, frustrated, and walks away from us into the kitchen. The woman turns to the only warmth and compassion there is nearby, and she hugs Simone and cries to her for mercy. Simone moves on the wings of compassion, escorting the suburban mother weeping to the back bedroom down the hall, the bedroom whose window overlooks the dark'ned grass where the four of us had lain. Chelsea watches with disbelief and jealous fascination at the weeping mother in Simone's caring arms, being escorted so gingerly down the hall.

"Hey," she says. "Hey Simone—" Quickly I reach out, stopping her from following them down the hall.

"But she's taking her—"

"I know, just let her do what she wants—"

"What's she gonna do, give her a bath? Should we fix her a plate?"

"Just relax Honey. Let it grow. Let it happen the way it's meant to happen."

"And what am I supposed to do until then? I want to kill that fucking bitch, Raven. I want to beat the fuck out of her and then kill her with my bare hands."

"You think I don't want her gagged and hogtied right here on the floor? Babe, you've got to learn to be patient—don't disturb the natural order— the supernatural flow of what we have to do."

"I want to do it *now* Raven. I want to do it now—"

"I know you do, and so do I. But I have a feeling there's something else that has to be done first. Something we're not meant to see."

Chelsea looks me in my almond eyes—alive with spiritual power—the energy of dark renewal.

"I want to run down the hall like an idiot and slam on the door," she says. "I want to do it so bad."

The sound of whimpering drifts through the door to where we stand unaware of how, or when she will suffer again.

"You want to eat? She brought your favorite."

"I can't eat now."

I would like to taste the chicken, sweetened with the herbs and spices some claim to know but have no clue, but I take the red and white bucket to the stove, imagining a happier time for us, where we would all be sitting at our little dining table eating, laughing, talking of where we will go on vacation at the end of the summer. I suddenly see us in our hotel overlooking the Hawaiian surf, amazed at the endless expanse of blue sky and water. From behind me, in my vision I hear a whimper that pulls me backward to this present, past the blackened forest silhouette and bright stars, into the brick rancher house on Mountain View Road.

This whimper falls from the heart of fear and hopeless longing, sitting on the edge of the bed behind a closed door, woven in Privacy's warm embrace. The woman of knowledge stands up, still in her white blouse tucked in her tight skirt appropriately black—keeping a watchful eye on every movement, every breath, every hidden and unhidden inflexion of this forty two year old dead woman.

"How old are you?"

"I'm forty two."

"Really?"

"Yes."

"How many children do you have?"

"I have a seventeen year old daughter and a nineteen year old son in college. They're names are Aiden and Alison."

The voice of this lamb chokes on the syllable of motherhood, as she remembers the sight, sound and smell of her daughter—her best friend and secret girlfriend.

"Does your daughter look like you?"

"I don't know... I guess."

"Does your daughter look like you..."

"...she ... uh...her body is smaller than mine. But she's got my... my bosom... she's real pretty in the face but she gets that mostly from her father."

"I think you have a very pretty face. Pretty blue eyes."

"Thank you. People always say she looks just like me but I know it's because we've got the same hair."

"Dark blonde."

"Yes. And we've got the same personality too. People always mistake us for—"

"Sisters?"

"How did you know?"

A pause…

"Is your daughter a virgin?"

"I… I hope so. I think she might be. She tells me everything."

"And your daughter's a cheerleader. Like you."

"Yes."

"You allow your daughter to dress in a costume designed to inspire lust in women and men?"

"I don't know what you mean."

The sound of the woman's lie penetrates Simone's skin like a ghostly butterfly, fluttering through to the pit of her stomach and into her spine.

"Tell me… who really has the biggest breasts? You or your daughter?"

"I don't—I don't…"

"Answer the question."

"Mine are bigger."

"Oh? And how do you know that?"

"Well… she's my daughter, I see her all the time."

"How do you know yours are bigger? You said she had breasts like yours."

"Because I've seen her."

"You've seen her what?"

Mother! What memories burn thy suburban blood! What images have plagued your mind tonight, of you and your daughter laughing together topless in front of the mirror?

"I've seen her around the house."

"Did you see your daughter's naked breasts?"

"No… I"

"Did you see your daughter's naked breasts?"

The woman's mind cannot keep from flashing to the lengthy and private sessions of bra fittings behind a locked door, or the shared bathroom time in front of the mirror, when the daughter brushes her teeth with the two perfect globes sitting strong and straight, nipples outright, breasts jiggling and shaking in such pretense as her arm moves back and forth in the teeth brushing—the daughter in her skin tight black jeans and no bra yet, while her mother applies her own makeup in her bathrobe, because *Doug is in my bathroom fogging it up and the one in the bedroom doesn't have the right light,* or the long yoga sessions beginning fully clothed and ending with only bikini underwear and no bra or anything else.

"Were you ever… intrigued by your daughter's body?"

"Well… she has a beautiful body. It's like looking at a real life Barbie Doll. Her breasts are so high and firm. She hardly even needs to wear a bra."

"What else do you like to do with your daughter?"

"We like to dress up and go dancing. We like to compete and see who can get the most phone numbers."

"Is this in a nightclub?"

"Yeah. My best friend got her a fake ID."

"Did you ask your best friend to do this?"

"Yes."

"You got your daughter a fake ID?"

"Well… I guess I did."

"You like to compete in nightclubs, and see who can get the most phone numbers."

"We used to. But we stopped because for some reason I always won. Those young guys really seem to like older women. Even my son Aiden was—"

"I don't give a god *damn* about your son. Do you understand?"

"Yes."

In my mind's eye, I see the frustration—I feel it grow from the Simone orthodoxy, from the Cory sensibility, the core of reprehensibility grown. She turns and goes to the fancy mirrored dresser, with its carved wood designs and shelves up either side of the mirror—where a few porcelain figurines rest in uneasy tranquility.

"Do you enjoy watching your daughter wear that cheerleading costume?"

"I—"

"Watching her bounce up and down and side to side—shaking those pom poms for the mothers—and men. Jumping high up into the air—spreading her legs wide open to every upskirt fantasy. Whose thighs are lean and clean up to the crotch? Whose thighs have more wiggle and jiggle in between? Which one of them is a slut? Which one of them is a virgin? Which one of them is a fucking whore? Which one is a fucking prude? Which one had their auntie's finger down there when they were a little girl—who was split wide open by their daddy's cock when they were twelve? Which one of them has old scars on her back, and old bruises around the wrists and ankles—which one knows what the tip of a curling iron feels like in the middle of her back? Which one knows the sound of their mother's laughter after they've been whipped so long the blood comes through their white t-shirt? Which one of them knows how to deep throat like a sword swallower because that's how their mother taught them how to do it on their father's cock—which *ONE!*"

Through the wall of hearing, I see the insanity come to claim the Cory mind, as she is bent over at the mirrored dresser—resisting the loss of breath control.

"Come here."

Amanda Hall gets up obediently, her expression as demure and pitiful as it can be. Simone guides her into place, standing behind her in front of the mirror. *I want to kill that fucking bitch!* rings loud and distant through the walls of our house, an alarm sounded in Chelsea's voice, and the epic slamming of a door.

"You're not going to let them hurt me are you, hmm? Because we understand each other don't we? Because we have an understanding..."

Simone begins to remove the pins from the woman's hair. "Don't worry about them. It's just me and you."

The woman's dark blonde hair falls about her shoulders. "A woman's hair is who she is. To lose your hair, is to lose yourself."

Simone begins to unbutton Amanda's blouse. The woman's cleavage is big in her bra. Her fascination shows on her face, the quiet shock, so complete that she feels like she's in a dream. Then she watches her reflection have a woman's hand reach inside the partially unbuttoned shirt, inside the white bra, and slide the soft globe of white flesh out slowly, exposing the nipple, amongst the strange feeling that this too, apart from her reflection, is happening to her as well. The brunette beauty in the mirror reaches inside again, into the other side of Paradise, and slides the other breast out slowly and completely, until the blonde reflection stands there with hair unkempt, wearing a grass stained white shirt partially buttoned, with her two Double D heavy hangers exposed for them to see. The woman is overcome suddenly with despair, and she shakes with a whimper unheard, her lovely face contorted by grief.

"Your ass is grass, Bitch! Do you hear me, your fucking ass is GRASS!" These are the sounds of her impending life, of what is left of it, amidst a

hard slam and thump against the door. Simone feels her flinch and stiffen, as her exposed nipples harden on their own, stimulated by fear alone.

"Please let me have a piece of ice. Just one little piece of ice."

"No water. What you need is the Truth. You need to listen to those sounds you hear. They require your confession—so you can be forgiven."

Then she sees the brunette reflection lean down, and feels the wet pulling of her nipple into the brunette's mouth. The sucking is so deep, so rhythmic that Amanda has to close her eyes from the sensation, as each pulling draws energy up from her groin, to ignite the flame she has felt and desired toward her own daughter, the burning of blue and black fire. The brunette releases it after some time, clamping the same perfect, moist sucking to the other, igniting the pilot flame from her groin to her breasts, and every involuntary twitch in between. What good or bad luck is this, what blessing or curse, to feel such a rich perfection of expertise upon her nipple, a nursing such as few women have ever known as perversion, that can bring nothing but arousal to the body? After another time, the other nipple is released in the selfsame wet and noisy pull, causing a visible shudder to the woman, whose body is already addicted to sensual pleasures unknown.

"Are you gon' kill me?" she whimpers in sweet southern discomfort.

"I'm not going to kill you. I'm going to save you."

"You gon' save me from them?"

"I'm going to save you from yourself. When you confess to me—you confess to God—and he'll forgive you for your sins."

"And then what's gon' happen?"

A pause. To eternity.

"Life. And freedom."

Amanda draws a loud, long breath of protracted shock, when she sees white fingers lock onto the nipples in her reflection. The shock is a jolt—to increase to fear and cold in her body.

"Did you ever spank your daughter?"

"No…"

Then the pressure upon her nipples clamps down suddenly in a sharp bite, making her yelp and squirm. *"Put your hands down"* is what she hears amidst her own squeaking and squealing voice. It is repeated without pain, until she puts her hands down at last. Chelsea rushes out of her room again, moaning *oh yeah baby, oh yeah…* with the longing of a she-wolf witnessing a slow kill in the Appalachian forest snow.

"I want the truth," she says into Amanda's ear.

"I told you the truth—I swear to God and Jesus I told you the truth."

Simone squeezes again and this time, the woman screams as if her nipples are clamped to a hot wire.

"I didn't," she says… "I didn't…"

"Do you want more?"

"Six months…"

"What's that?"

"I spanked her when she was six months old because she wouldn't stop crying. I was mad at her father and I took it out on her because she wouldn't stop crying. I slammed her in the crib and I had to take her to the emergency room for a broken arm. I told them she fell out of the crib and they believed me."

Simone closes her eyes and hardly hears the *oh, yes* come out of her mouth.

"You never spanked your teenage daughter?"

"No. I swear to God no. I never did."

"Have you ever hit her at all?"

"I slapped her one time. I slapped her because she told me to shut the 'f' up when I said her boyfriend was a f-ing loser. She said *'you shut the fuck up, you don't know what you're talking about—'* and then I slapped her as hard as I could. I called her an *ungrateful, smart mouthed little bitch don't you ever talk to me that way again.* Then I walked out and never apologized for slapping her."

"Did she apologize to you?"

"Yes. Then she hugged me and started crying."

"At that moment… did you want to kiss her?"

"I did kiss her, but not a lover's kiss. Just a regular kiss."

"Did you want to fuck your daughter?"

The woman squeaks something unintelligible, then she feels lightning grab her at the nipples like white fire.

"Yesss!!" she screams. A deep, loud scream that reverberates the mountain night, through the Chelsea Doll and her Indian Bride, through the walls of our brick home and beyond. I bite my thumbnail, fearful for mankind, watching Chelsea lean against the door, pressed in meditation as though trying to phase through it to the scene.

"You want your own daughter—"

"I wanted to punish her by fucking her up the *ass!*"God help me I did. I *do!* I fantasize about fucking my own daughter up the ass. I want to strap on a cock and…"

The woman melts into despondency, at the release of this truth from her spirit.

"What about your son?"

"I thought about it once when he was taking a nap on the couch. He was laying there asleep in his gray sweats and no shirt."

"What did you want to do?"

"I wanted to undo his sweat pants and put his penis in my mouth."

"Put his what in your mouth?"

"His pen—his cock. My son's cock."

"You're pretty comfortable with the word 'cock' aren't you?"

"Yes. Yes I am."

"You may as well be. Saying 'penis' doesn't change the 'cock' in your mind. You think God doesn't already know what's in your heart? What you feel? You really believe you're not going to Hell because of what you *think?*"

The woman screams again from the twisting, in sorrow for the pain outside and in. "You think that just because you never actually fucked your daughter, that you have no sin to be forgiven?" The twisting activates the screams again, this time into my own spirit, and I have to walk over to Chelsea and take her by the hand for my own sake. "Don't resist the pain," I hear her say. "Breathe and flow with it—that's it…" The woman cries a river of sorrow, this for several minutes past a quarter of an hour, while Simone exacts confession from her through fiery bruises, done by pinching and hard breast spanking, and nipple twisting that makes her call the name of God and Christ. Simone exacts this confession from her, everything from how she threw black women's job applications in the trash when she managed a Hallmark store, to how she used to sunbathe in the nude to make her neighbor jealous and she used to wear her bra sometimes in front of her son hoping he would notice her double D tits and how she refused to do her husband more than once a month out of pure spite though she made it a practice to give herself an orgasm at least once every other day by straddling a rolled up towel on top of a stack of pillows on the corner of their bed, while watching Days of Our Lives or All My Children, or with one of her husband's secret Danube Women's Wrestling tapes in the VCR sometimes for a half hour, and how she and her 44 year old best friend have been fuck buddies for five years and how they love to go to strip clubs and hotels in the middle of the day in towns a hundred miles away and do missionary tribadism (crotch grinding), fully dressed in business suits with underwear on until the first orgasm has come and gone.

"My God," Simone says. "A closet dyke. You really have been a bad girl, haven't you? I want you to know that I understand. I understand the fire that burns. The heat that gives you a pornographic mind, that makes you crave your own son and daughter and makes your husband disgusting, and makes you and your best friend have to go to a hotel and grind each other to death. I know that feeling—that craving that makes it impossible to be a Holy woman, to have to wear a mask in public, to pretend you hate sex and pornography so people won't judge you and ridicule you. I know how the burning gets too hot, and it flares into a sun inside your groin, and it radiates this lust into every cell in your body."

By now, the torture of breasts has ceased to be, transformed into a rough, determined squeezing. Simone's eyes are closed and teary, while she leans firmly onto Amanda's back. Simone takes one of Amanda's breasts in hand, and pushes it up to Amanda's mouth. "Put your mouth on it," she says. "That's it, suck it like you mean it. Suck it like the rich, suburban dyke you are. This is the upper middle class, white suburban secret, that half of you bitches are closet dykes, burning for each other like a coven of backwoods witches. Suck your own breast, woman. Yes. Feel the power of your witchcraft. You are a modern, secret witch, using sex to contaminate the world—the vulgar, pornographic way you live your lives—what churns beneath your cultured civility—the way you dress—the way you walk—the way you parade your daughters in public, teaching them how to conquer each other by cattiness, by being the skinniest, the prettiest, the cutest or the hottest. To teach them this same witchcraft over all women and men. You don't know whether you want your tits and ass flat like a little girl or round like a mountain momma, you sheep listen to whatever the magazines and the men tell you, so you binge and purge and starve and nip and tuck yourselves to death, then you spend thousands of dollars to shove bags of silicone into your tits and mutilate yourselves into skeletal freaks with two rock hard tits that make all real mean sick to their stomachs at the thought, but make you dumb, stupid women proud and jealous of each other. And you go around shoving those deformed, stretched bags of silicone skin into your daughter's faces, to teach them that fakeness is the new reality, and that the lust for tits burned you so hot you had to go out and buy some. Oh, but you my suburban momma, my *W*hite *A*nd *S*o *P*retty, my soccer mom, the Mother I'd Like to Fuck, your tits are so big, so soft, and so real."

Simone lowers the woman's breast, and they stare at one another in the mirror—both in tears, both anguished to the end of endurance.

"Have you been raped?" are the words breathed into the air, to reactivate the beginning of sobs and pleading. "Thou shalt not suffer a witch to live," Simone says, "but that is for God to decide. But now, I must do what it is He has called me to do. And I know that as sure as He is my Redeemer, as surely as He is risen… I'm going to have to fuck you."

Desire pulls Simone from behind her immolation, sending her adrift to her closet. This, she does as if unaware, on a treadmill of sorts, moving from one point of origin to the other. *Take off your clothes* she says to our number seven, watching her give in to what life she has left, and undo the rest of the buttons on her open blouse. Simone turns to her own affairs, turning away from the blonde. She finally, after so many hours of waiting, unbuttons her blouse and pulls it away from the black skirt, hanging it up inside the big closet. Then she unzips the top of her skirt and slides it off from her big hips, to reveal a mountainous waist curve ratio into strong, muscular thighs; a natural, feminine muscularity bestowed from a Mexican grandmother she never knew. She reaches up to the back of her big black bra (yes, a *black* bra), unhooking the strap quickly, then sliding the shoulder straps unceremoniously away. Amanda Hall cannot help but stare, to see what nature hath wrought to the front of this Amazon whose hips and buttocks can only conjure the word "ass," with the combined bubble and spread of so few. *An ass is an ass and that's all there is to an ass* plays in Amanda Hall's mind, as she watches the tallish woman slide the black French cuts off to the floor.

Simone's hips are big by proportion, though perfectly shaped and impossible to ignore (picture Beyonce Knowle's wide hips on a white woman and you've got it). Amanda Hall is somewhat intrigued by the knowledge that the hips don't lie, and that her captor sports a figure that out classes even her own—something she had never really seen before on a white woman, not even her own mother. How is it that even in captivity, the jealous wave cannot be denied access? It flows through Amanda Hall like invisible water, where it coalesces to green crystals in the heart and lungs, then is pumped and breathed quietly away. Then Simone turns to lean down into another part of the long closet, and what Amanda sees returns the green ice quickly to her lungs. The biggest, wobbliest breasts she has ever seen outside of pornography and pin up photography flash in her vision—knowing that if she was a DD, then Simone must surely be playing the key of F or G Major. Simone leans over, her expression sullen, huge breasts hanging down like two great skin bottles of milk. The word Amanda is searching for is *Amazon*, though she will never find it. Amanda stands nude now, arm crossed over her own bosom, the other arm in front of her stomach with the hand covering her private. Like a lovely statue in alabaster she stands nude, modest, frozen in this moment 'til the end of time.

Simone stands up, upon a toss of her brunette hair, with the bundle of straps in her hand. These straps are soon sliding up her legs into place and she carefully inserts the short, black protrusion on the straps into her vagina—closing her eyes and savoring the entry. Then she lifts the harness up into place, the protrusion deep inside her, the main instrument hanging free—the fullest extension of who she is—hanging down in realistic member form. *"This is your absolution,"* she says. *"Your reason for being. To accept all of what it has to give—what pleasure—what pain."*

The Queen tells the Maiden to lower her arms, which she does reluctantly, wishing not to engage the spirit of Sappho tonight, but to go back to Boone where she came from, and curse the day she ever laid eyes on the sign to Black Mountain (Why did she have to visit her mother today of all days?) Simone walks over to her in new confidence, masculine energy burning inside. She stands tall in front of Amanda, who looks her in the eye in pleading for compassion. But Simone cannot be comforted by righteousness. The comfort she seeks strides the power of carnality—it rides the wave of forbidden sensuality. Her lust is fueled by memory, the memory of childhood atrocities—the infusion of demonic rage—anger that fuels the blue and black flame, and the need to express herself through the forbidden. In this power, she is Queen—to draw such sensual, moaning kisses from Amanda Hall as she never thought possible—heads leaning side to side, eyes closed, tongues probing in rage and fear. In the fierce, instinctual spark of Hope, Amanda is driven to lift both of Simone's great, heavy breasts to her mouth and go back and forth upon them like a woman possessed, prompting the loud grunting from Simone—announcing to us that this has begun. The two of us stand outside the door—listening with hardly a breath to breathe. Nervous as soldiers on the Battlefields of Dawn, waiting for the first signs of battle in the new day.

The heart of Simone is perversion. We are three, joined with her as one. Simone hearkens her spirit to Sapphic images she has known, and words crafted in Lust, Beauty and Sin. They carry the spirit of her evil, the possession she endures—these words spoken from the Fantasy Chamber— the chamber of Lasciviousness and Death:

> *"In the beginning of time, the world was split in two—day and night, male and female. Between them was an undying essence , the desire for reunion, to merge back together, the urge to create the future. This is the engine of life. All creatures—from the smallest insect to the largest fish in the ocean—are driven by this power...*
>
> *The essence has many names—Aphrodite, Castrati, Venus, Isis—and we beg to be filled with this. We are all a flame waiting*

to become an inferno. We are all a breeze waiting to become a storm. We are all still water, waiting for the crash of the wave. We're naked. We're open. We're waiting.

In the Fantasy Chamber, there is no gender. No male, or female. Only that which lies between us. The giver of life."

These words ring out, echoing their counterfeit truth, stripping us of our feminine dignities, to bury our desire for chaste womanhood and delusions of morality. We listen to the squeaking of the bedsprings, craving to see the blonde bouncing up and down, grinding the member she straddles— giving herself and her body for dear life—this, in Truth, believing that she can literally whore herself into forgiveness and harlot herself into a pardon.

I stand behind my Chelsea Doll at the door, my hands inside her black, unbuttoned capris', pressing firmly against the bulge of soft flesh I feel through the silken cloth down below. Then the bouncing on the bed ceases rhythm, like music in transition, as the blonde is ordered to her knees, and the big brunette is on her knees behind her. The next sound I hear corresponds with what plays the Theatre of My Mind, as the woman must put her head down and scream to God and Christ, having never been entered anally by such a large member—lubricated by spit and time, as every inch of it is shoved into her backside. The woman must cry real tears of pain, no longer a virgin of this kind, by that which was done by those in the twin cities in the Valley of Siddim, before the judgment of fire and brimstone. Simone pins the woman's arms, letting the member rest deep inside her—sliding it out slowly and back in again, shocked by the smoother flow and the appearance of lubrication by blood... *"please it hurts please take it out"* is the melody of this phrase, as Simone is only driven to drive it deeper inside—to hear the woman's loud and pitiful yell once again.

What is the energy of sadism, what wine of light does it provide! What is the electric trembling that this sends to Simone's innermost region, to make her shake her own head in unrelieved, brief disbelief and grieving? She pushes the bloody member in deep again, as deep as is possible, putting her head back in a quiet, violent grimace that betrays the painful level of desire she feels. She grabs a handful of the woman's blonde hair and pulls her head back far enough to create another source of pain for her, and another source of pleasure for herself. She gives herself over to the Spirit of Perversion—calling it in, saying *"Spirits of Death and Darkness, I call to thee—"*and then I hear the rhythm of the moment change again, as the blood soaked member now slides into the back of her, into her vagina from behind, strangely the giver of Life, and the giver of Death as well. The place of birth and purity, now transformed to death and immorality— as we hear the slapping and popping noise of flesh against flesh—rhythmic and slow, switched to fast, then slow again, beneath the flow of a new melody from the voice of Amanda, a voice of pleading to God for endurance against the wave of unwanted energy building up in her body. *Let it flow*—Simone says—*let me hear it in your voice, let the sin gather itself inside you, let your daughter's cock save you from your sins, yes, fuck your daughter's cock Bitch, now get off, get off Bitch, yes, that's it—come on your daughter's cock!* And I suddenly hear Amanda's voice change from a hopeless whimper to a hard, animalistic yell just below a scream— then I hear Simone say *Oh, my God no... Lord Jesus help me...* and upon this syllable rises the Cry of the Banshee, a high pitched sound that climbs far above a scream to become a siren, a noise that penetrates every particle of wood and fleck shard of glass around us, a sound that seems to command that all be silent, from where we breathe quietly, to even the frightened night creatures of the Appalachian Wood.

$\mathscr{C}$helsea keeps watch as I dream, roaming the property like a mockingbird—patrolling the grounds of our fervent dysfunction. I lay curled on the couch as if I had fallen asleep watching TV, remembering the night's events in my dreams as such. Away from our waking reality, my mind cannot process the night's events as real, dismissing it all as a projection of non reality, until I see Chelsea burst through the front door with a terrified look on her face—running over to me and grabbing me by the shoulders, shaking the daylights out of me and saying *Its coming!* *Raven its coming and the world is going to burn! Burn, Raven! Burn her up in fire!"*

I wake up suddenly, in time to see Chelsea walk in the front door.

"Did you say something about fire?"

She turns me no answer, only a bewildered stare and shaking of the head.

"You want me to watch now?" I hear myself say in half sleep.

"I'm too wired", she says. "Go back to sleep."

This, I do by no choice whatsoever, as if a spirit has descended to pull me away from my waking reality. I close my eyes in troubled sleep, to end the pain of my exhaustion. But the tired soreness in my body follows me into the gray world this time, where it is enhanced into pain.

The skies of my youth have descended once again, as I find myself awake at the tree I am chained to. Pain has risen from the Earth I know—moving in front of the lovely stars I see. These clouds have gathered over my last evening here at the tree, as the scrapes, welts and bruises mingle with the cuts to tell the tale, of a girl punished in mountain backwoods style. I hear the booming rumble from above as the clouds quickly come to life, and in the next instant, I feel the cold drops of rain. There is no shelter from this raining, only my soaking wet body and hair, in a rain so blessedly warm in the summer evening.

I hear my voice crying in the wilderness—*Momma! Momma!* Hoping that she will have compassion and that God will have mercy—but there is no rest for the weary on this side of the grave. And for those of us who are in pain, there is shared a common gift—that one day the suffering will cease, and the pain will be taken away. It is the light that guides us through the midst of prolonged suffering—the focal point of *this too shall pass*, though at the time we don't realize that's what we have done. I did not realize this as the calm descended over me, as something told me inside *"it's just rain"* to ease my nerves into comfort. The dusty smell is so strong in this rain—as it splashes the dry earth to awakening, washing the old dust into the air around me, where it will soon all fall back to earth as mud. I go to the tree trunk and accept my Fate. I am a mud dauber, a common dust wasp, about to be soaked to the limits of her calling.

I lean against the tree in the dark'ned rain, unafraid of what wolves and bears may do, carried into the deepest sleep imaginable, where it is a bright and sunny day, and I am at the bottom of a grand waterfall in the mist, soaked to the skin, in awe of the rainbow that has suddenly appeared. At the bottom of this waterfall, I think I feel someone come up to me and put a coat around me—then I am suddenly removed from this dream back into the night at the tree, with my mother's old raincoat draped over me in the storm.

I am pulled awake from this dream within a dream, feeling the drops of phantom rain on my face, still with the musky old scent of my mother's raincoat around me. This raincoat is a blanket I find, draped over me some time ago by my blonde Lady.

The digital clock shines 4:04am from the satellite box under the old school RCA, a 36-inch dinosaur of a picture tube square head type TV with a picture that cannot be beat. I see my early morning silhouette clearly in the big screen, sitting up from the couch, feeling anxious in my soul that what we have to do, we must do it quickly.

Stopping to where I can see down the hall, I notice Chelsea sitting on the floor, leaning against the door of Simone's room, her eyes closed in something vaguely resembling half sleep. Whether or not she can sense me, I choose not to know, hearing the call of a strong breeze outside, and a fervent, powerful warning whispered in anguish from the trees. When I open the door, I can sense the whishing and waving of the entire forest, bearing down on our little scene. I step quietly outside, hoping not to wake Chelsea, my hair blowing wildly in the dark morning wind.

This is the start of what was forecast by Heaven and Earth, by the so-called weathermen, and the spirits at work and play in my dreams. The stars are a memory already, hidden by clouds moving rapidly underneath them. It is the sadness that gathers this brief storm, to coalesce into tears of mourning. This warm wind blows up from the southwest, to be transformed quickly into the clouds I see moving in the dark. A sign that He sees all, that He knows exactly what it is we have done. What beauty there is of our mountain paradise is now cloaked in shadow and suspicion, suspended over the edge of a grievous canyon divide.

Crossed arms over a bosom in D minor, aching with desire, I step into the grass to take the requisite early morning stroll, unable to ignore the rising wind, and the silhouettes of every tree line moving for my attention. My evil step sends a wave of energy far into the earth, where the roots of the tree lines reside, sparking a message through the network of this entire region of mountain woods—there she is! An evil destroyer of mankind! A witch more wicked than her mother Eve, who plunged the world into darkness and despair! Behold, a scourge, a blight on Creation, how can she escape outer darkness, where there will be weeping, and gnashing of teeth!

I shudder a chill, strolling the grass by the dark morning woods, breathing in the dusty scent of approaching rain. Dreading the digging of the seventh grave.

"I think she loves her," is the voice I hear. Drifting up behind me. I turn in time to see Chelsea rounding the corner to where I am, though not as leisurely.

"I didn't mean to wake you."

"You should see them in that room. They're both asleep under the sheet. It's like a god-damned honeymoon in there."

"The honeymoon's over for that bitch. She's gonna wish she'd never been born."

"I want to do it now, Raven. I don't want to wait. I don't even want to hump her, I just want to kill her and get it over with. It's what I feel. I feel like I *have* to do that."

"This one's special, Chelsea. It has to be done right. It has to be done in a certain way. She was given to us. Her fate was sealed by God. I have to acknowledge that. This woman is the last sacrifice."

"You having second thoughts?"

"Of course not. But I want to do what we talked about on this one—"

"Look, Raven. I'm not feeling any ritual on this bitch but a good choking to death. I want to do it myself. I *need* to do it myself."

The tone of her voice guides me to revelation, as does the look in her eyes—the feel of strength in her hands as she takes me by both arms. I see the inspiration flowing through, powerful enough to affect her presence as a warrior, bound and determined to a course of action.

It's on.

"She's all yours, Baby."

The house resounds from within and out, as our knocking mixes with the voice of thunder from the clouds. Inside, they both awake with a quick start as though they might have, but are unsure of, whether or not they heard the Trump of God.

"Simone," I say loudly. "We need you to kiss her goodbye."

From inside, I hear a whimper and a deeper, falsely reassuring voice. I slam on the door again. Thunderously. The whimpering increases, until a quiet crescendo of words appears. *"I didn't mean to be, Simone. Please help me... you said you wouldn't... you said you wouldn't Simone, you said you wouldn't—please forgive me—please forgive me Simone—"*

The door swings open to her demise, and to her surprise we stand there waiting, as flopping naked as she. I reach in and yank her out, and Chelsea quickly puts the brown extension chord around her neck, secured by the strength of a madwoman with no clothes on, wearing black leather gloves, fittingly winter gloves, to protect her hands from the iciness of her deed. I help secure the struggling, choking woman in place, with hardly enough room in the hallway to move without us hitting the walls. *"How 'bout it now Mom, Huh? How 'bout it now..."* she says—face twisted in an angry, animalistic frowning grimace that robs nothing from her beauty. By contrast, the suburban woman kicks and pushes and pulls and chokes in the ugliness of damnation, and a near epic loss of what dignity she has left. Every part of her body flops and jiggles while Chelsea drags her choking to the open living room, the woman's eyes wide open in shock, face bloated and bright red tinted blue already, spit foaming at the mouth as what she knows of breathing ceases to be. Chelsea falls backward to the floor on purpose, wrapping her legs around the woman, still pulling the brown extension chord around the woman's neck. The woman kicks strong—strong enough to threaten freedom, so I have to take hold of her legs, much to Chelsea's fervent displeasure. *"Let me kill her myself!!"* she screams. And I let her legs go. Chelsea holds on while the woman kicks, legs flailing open, thighs and buttocks stained with her own blood, as are her mouth and lips now from where she has bitten her tongue.

Thunder claps loud enough to wake the dead, but making none of us jump, as we feel it an extension of the power we have over nature. I watch with breath held tight, unable to breathe just yet, watching the strong, blonde mother lose her strength in the kicking, while Chelsea pulls as tightly as she can from underneath her. *"Oh yeah,"* she says. *"There you go, Momma. There you go. Now die bitch. Just shut the fuck up and die."*

And now I find myself breathing, breath trembling in and out, as I watch Chelsea Baxter continue to pull and choke a woman who will certainly never breathe again. Simone stands by, but not in idleness, her white sheet draped around her in mourning, fully engaged in the power and the glory of what we have done.

$\mathcal{W}$e are gravediggers in the rain, the blonde girl and me, preparing a place for our seventh to be laid to rest. *Buried* is more appropriate, I think, as when one kills an old dog and dumps the carcass in a hole in the ground. And even though it better captures the essence of what we have to do this morning, part of me still believes that this seventh lady was a divine gift bestowed, and should at least be paid the minimum respect. So, unlike it was with every other victim, who were all buried without thought or feeling, who were all dumped in a hole naked and forgotten, Amanda Hall is wrapped in the whitest top sheet we own, laid ceremoniously on her back, her hands crossed over her chest in repose.

The motorcycle I plan to get roars and rumbles inside my head. It only adds to the headache I feel, the sickness rising in my body—as I swing the pickaxe into the wet earth, dreaming of sunny days with Chelsea on my black Honda with me, with the wind at our backs, crossing a railroad track or two into nowhere. Chelsea stands with me, at the edge of these mountain woods, her head cloaked like the reaper himself in her black raincoat. We had tried to be troopers in this storm, but gave in quickly to the human need for protection from the rain. "Hand me the shovel," I say, giving her the pickaxe in exchange, refusing to let her strike the first shovelful of earth. After all, I was responsible for bringing her here, right? So it stands to reason that I dig the first hole in her grave.

The mountain soil is hard to manage, even in a hard summer rain shower such as this, pouring and blowing like a hurricane all around us, though it is only a noisy shower of doom. Carrying a warning with it too late to heed, and a prophecy too devastating to believe. It is the manifestation of our deed, the rage of our lives sparking and rumbling from the sky. The Shadow of Fears untold, coming down in tears all around us.

Chelsea removes her hood, and I see the still angry, depressed look on her features; her big, pink lips being the most prominent mirage in the morning dark. Somewhere behind these clouds, the sun rises on her final hatred, in mourning to burn our scene in the Light of Day. The demonic energy takes over her once again, and she tires of my clumsy chopping around in the wet dirt, taking the shovel from me and digging twice as fast as I was. As she digs like a wet girl recruit in the training field, I know full well the source of this final rage she has bought and delivered.

I met Chelsea among the racks of JC Penney, at the Four Seasons Mall in Winston Salem. Only six weeks had come and gone since I met the goddess in the stacks, and now, I see another one in the racks. What stacks and racks are there among the gifted, those blessed with curves too magnificent to ignore? Five feet ten inches of pure, yellow blonded perfection, with big blue eyes and thickish pink lips, but with a serious expression besides, colored by both melancholy and an extraordinary touch of humility. Her Levi's are a perfect fit over Barbie Doll hips, the envy of every woman alive, legs long and set naturally apart, so that the space between them is perfect and permanent, beneath wide set buttocks the shape of a heart turned upside down. *The best ass I have ever seen* rises up to my mind from somewhere within, as I observe a woman who is truly more model material than I. But the thing that amazes me the most, even more than the perfectly small waist and DD cup bosom in the blue T- shirt tucked in—is the fact that she clearly has no idea of how beautiful she is, and that she could have already been a very wealthy young woman.

"There's not a single dress here you wouldn't look good in," I say. Noticing the strong attention she paid to the compliment before she broke her frown—a smile of such genuine sweetness and beauty as to have power, and is heartbreaking to behold.

The Mountaineers

My sales lady instincts kick in, such as they are—so confident in my own prettiness, my own ability to flash a kick ass smile and a twinkle in my bright eyes. Before long, her arm is draped by two pretty dresses priced so far below their lost potential, which is why JC Penney is the best anyway, the Walmart of ladies casual if you ask me. While her arm is draped in dresses, her spirit is draped in me, as I am now part owner of this princess, with sole access to her personal space. A space replete with loneliness. This same loneliness that has plagued me since I was first a child in the Blue Ridge Mountains, and then the wooded farmlands of eastern North Carolina. This space of dreary despair that surrounds her—it is mine for the taking—mine to possess, for I have the power to do so if I wish—and there are none brave enough to stand in the privileged space I'm in. Yes, she is literally too pretty to talk to, carrying a sullen, no nonsense look that might would be unfriendly, were it not for the flashes of humility. Yes, this is the girl I own now. The girl whose life and space I am in.

Seven summers ago, I meet this young woman when she is twenty three and I am twenty four. We stand at the rack still talking, drawn by each other's manner and appearance, doing the dance of greeting so smoothly as to be without effort, with not a false smile or phony laugh to get in the way. "I majored in psychology," she says. "It was the only thing I could stand. Learning about how screwed up people are... (we both laugh a little...) how *fucked up* they are..."

And for some reason, we are gripped with a spirit of giggles and laughter from here, flooded with a sense of relief and assurance—as though a ticket has been bought and paid for, and finally redeemed at the grand event. These tickets are bought and paid for by the lives we were given, by the blood of the lash, taken and torn by the spirits of who we are.

We have been divinely ordered to embrace the moment, to go to where there is common ground, so that we may till the rich and fertile plain as one.

We are as one already, when the fortyish woman brushes past me without so much as a gesture of manners, as though she is too good to acknowledge 'those young bitches,' who she finds inferior to herself in every way. What beauty there is of her is aged to perfection, curves grown soft and rich with time, twenty years an expert of what makeup to wear and how to wear it, when to wear earrings and when not to, what power there is in a good credit score, how to set up an engorgement meal to keep from getting fat, and how to give herself the best possible orgasm when she is alone. The truest signature of a woman is her orgasm. How mild, how intense, how soft, how loud. In the orgasm, a woman is the truth. God is truth. And these are the privacies, the secrets that He knows, and has placed conditions of morality upon, that when we are overcome by this truth, we are overcome by Him, and must call out to his name for mercy. This truth is universal, bringing pleasures to all that are indescribable, rising to another level in some, to where the approach is as agony, and must be endured. But for these, after this agony is done, the pleasure is a drug to their minds and bodies that enslaves them, so that the rest of their lives revolves around this essence. This truth.

Our spell is broken by a witch more powerful. Humiliated, we slink through the store under a burden of memories, soul and subconscious recall, bad enough to have grabbed the fabric woven between us and ripped it in two, until Chelsea says—

"What the fuck was her problem?"

"Some rich bitch. Thinks she's better than everybody—they come in here all the time. They'll buy five hundred dollars worth of stuff and lie to their rich ass friends about where they got it."

"I know," she says. "I heard a girl say that's what her mom does."

"Really?"

"I would listen to 'em talk in class. One of 'em said '*my mom shops at places like JC Penney and tells 'em she ordered it from Macy's.*'

"No bullshit?"

"I swear to God, some slut named Donna DaVetta said it. So you're right—that's exactly what these bitches do."

"How do you know she was a slut?"

"When a girl you don't even know says in your ear one day *'have you ever fucked another girl'* and then laughs about it, then I guess she's a slut."

"She said that?"

"Yep. Back in my junior year, one of my psychology classes. Donna DaVetta. You know, it's about the only thing I remember that whole year. The whole five years, really. Yeah, it took me five and a half years to finish. I had to work all the time."

"At least you finished. I know somebody who just got their PhD in Religion. She's only 28 years old."

We share one last collected, melancholy gaze back at the older woman. A look burdened by heavy contempt.

"Have you ever wanted to just—"

"What?"

"I don't know," she says, "just… beat the Hell out of one of those women?"

When she turns to look at me, the look of shock and surprise on my face cracks her into a thousand pieces, which all fall to the carpet as tiny diamond jewels.

"I'm sorry," she says, hand on her double D-cupped chest, red faced with embarrassment. "I'm really sorry. I didn't mean to say that—"

"No. Its just—my God. I thought I was the only one."

"The only one what?"

"What you said."

"No, I didn't—"

"No. I heard you. You meant it. How often does that come to your mind?"

"Every day."

We are briefly lost in one of the rarest moments in human history, when two people feel themselves leave their bodies and connect in space, then return rapidly to the physical body as lightning to the groin and spine.

"How long have you felt this way?"

"A couple years, I think. My Mom and me didn't get along too—"

Suddenly, A pile of blouses and skirts falls on the counter between us.

"Could you please watch this for me—I've got some more shopping to do."

The polite request was a thinly veiled order, one that I heard clear in the clap-clapping of phantom hands when she slammed those underpriced skirts and blouses down—and the irritated, superior tone of her request for me to *'please watch this for her.'* What I heard in my mind was *'could you please—you're supposed to be helping me, not talking to some blonde slut—now get your little Indian ass in line or I'll have you reprimanded.'*

I move about $300 worth of clothes to the side, from where they had buried Chelsea's two for $50 special dresses, which I can sense she can hardly afford. She pays me in cash, then takes the bag from me. Remarkably, we both speak at the same time, a desperate plea lost in confusion and laughter. Before we can recover—Miss Money Britches switches stocking hosed hips back to where we are, four dresses firmly in hand. I feign politeness for the older woman the best I can, pointing the stupid laser and folding the clothes loosely as I move them over, watching her total rise up until it hits five hundred and beyond. I glance at my new blonde friend, noticing her staring at the suburban mother, arms folded, face devoid of the humility I saw before. On her face now is only boldness and contempt, mixed with scorn and disdain, finished and polished by disgust.

The older woman breathes a deep breath of impatience, pulling her cell phone—and calling someone that must be her daughter. After what seems an eternity, her clothes and credit cards are all beeped and clicked and swiped, and five hundred and eleven dollars is signed away in rapid signature. Then she takes the bags and looks at my blonde friend like she is lower than dirt, wrinkling her mouth and shaking her head several times as she walks away. The look on Chelsea's face is extraordinary—her cheeks are as red as if she had been slapped, and her eyes are as cold as a serpent's.

I call a lesser peon than I (a skinny, half unattractive black girl with a sweet voice and no hope for the future) over to my register, saying "I've got a bad family emergency I have to take care of—if anybody asks just tell 'em I had to rush off for that—but if they don't ask, don't say anything. Don't ask—'*don't tell*'," we whisper together. She takes her meager, underpaid little teenaged position at the register for me (she is more underprivileged and cursed by birth than she realizes), and I walk past the shapely, athletic blonde with only a tilt of the head, my charcoal skirt halfway up my skinny, black stocking thighs, just below where mankind cannot see, the lace elastic tops of these self-same stockings and black thong underwear. Fate was kind to my little ass, rounding it out just enough so that it can be called a cute little booty, instead of just a plain no-assed Indian dyke. Who the fuck do I think I am?

"Who the fuck does she think she is? Lets follow her to her car, okay?"

My blonde friend only looks at me—slightly unnerved, slightly bewildered, and totally exhilarated. The mall is teaming with lost souls, as usual, drifting from one light station to the next. We follow this burgundy bloused, brown haired blue eyed beauty through Hell's Lobby, so inconspicuous ourselves as part of the desirable landscape of broad and wide loops downward—a road that spirals outward so far that the turns are not noticeable, with so many detours to that straight and narrow path, signs of the Cross, and an arrow pointing to the way.

We follow this middle aged sophisticate down the wide and crooked path, through the noise of pride and anger, lust and envy, greed and gluttony and sloth, watching her exit the doors without assistance, walking through the busy summer afternoon traffic, halfway down the full and flowing traffic lot to her appropriately black luxury something or another (who gives a fuck?) and Chelsea hurries ahead of me by pure instinct, in time to meet her when she opens the back door of the black chariot with gray leather interior (I can smell the leather right now). She turns around suddenly, too proud to be shocked, that even in her heels she's not the tallest hen in the coop this time, as the blonde stands a full five-ten and a half in her own sandal strapped clog heels.

In the early summer sun, her capris jeans are divine.

"Can I help you?" the woman says, in smug, sarcastic bitterness.

"You know what," the blonde says, reaching into her black pocket, pulling out a small knife, "as a matter of fact, you can…"

At the feel of the knife point in her gut, the woman's expression does an unbelievable one eighty turn and descent.

"…you can get your fat ass in the back seat and sit down."

"I will not," the woman says. Wide eyed with shock and the arrogance of fear and shame. But then she yips a suppressed *yipe*, and I know that she will soon bleed where she was pricked with steel.

"Get in," the blonde says. They exchange a look of epic rage and fear, as the woman leaves dignity to disperse in the summer breeze. From what I see and hear inside the black luxury vehicle, I am piqued and unsettled enough to be astounded, putting the big bags on the back of the car to cut visibility inside, which is the blonde raising her fists up and bringing it down over and over to the woman's face, in a chorus of muffled, quick and surprised yelps and grunts. *"Who the fuck do you think you are looking at me like that? Huh? How do you like it now? Where's your smart mouth now, bitch?"* This, amidst the chorus of smacks and punches to her face, with the woman's grunts threatening to rise into cries and screams at any moment.

When I suddenly hear nothing—I look inside and I see the blonde's knee in the woman's stomach, holding her hair down to the seat with one hand and covering her mouth with the other. *"Say something,"* the blonde hisses, the back seat packed to overflowing with their bodies *"I said…say…something…"* each word marking the hammer of another punch to the woman's face, her voice now descended to the pathetic whimper of a woman being gently raped in private. Something in me moves my body to grab each bag and throw it in the front seat. I get inside the driver's side—nervous but empowered now, finding the keys in the bitch's purse, remembering the bloody glimpse of a mess her face is now while I start her fine car. Something compels me to pull a smooth, slow back and right turn down the full parking lot, suddenly in a haze of motion as inside a dream, obeying every traffic courtesy while the blonde girl holds the older woman down in the back seat, holding her hand over her mouth. At the traffic light—two people behind us are hardly curious at what the beautiful blonde is doing leaning over in the back seat, seeming to struggle with something unseen. Is it a dog, a wayward child? A stack of papers—shopping bags? Then, the blonde goes down out of sight and the light changes to green, and I turn to where the next several lights will lead to interstate forty west, and to the digging of the second grave.

"What's your name?" The blonde says. "What's your *name!*" No response, then a sudden struggling and a deep scream.

"Diaaa...Vaaagh"

"What?"

"Diane Vaughn..."

"How old are you?"

No answer.

"How *OLD* are you!"

"Forty eight..."

"What?

"Forty eight!"

"Oh, *yeah*, Mama. You got any kids? Any daughters you want to fuck?"

"Three dau..."

"What?"

"Three daughters you bitch... *HELP ME!*"

Even in the traffic, in the broad light of day, I see the blonde beauty raise and lower her fist in punching, in hammering to the woman's face in blood. Then the woman's screams begin to fade, until I only hear the noise of the punching, which begins to sound like digging and chopping, until I can no longer see the daylight and the blonde is a figure in the rainy mountain night, swinging a pickaxe hard into the rocky mountain clay.

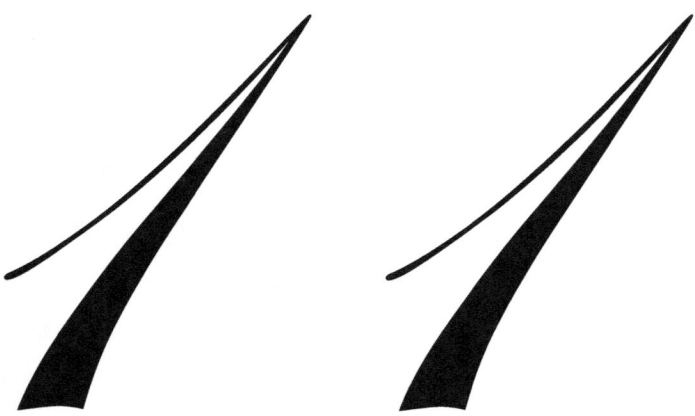

*Y*es. From where this rage comes that we bury in the clay, I know from whence—as it was seven years and a day, when Diane Vaughn was abducted and murdered on the highway, rolling many miles down business 40, where there are trees to hide when the Devil does his bidding.

I know from whence this rage hath come, that chops through the nighttime mountain soil, when we drove 10 miles outside of the city to the

Piedmont Woods, and we took turns beating the woman with our bare hands until she closed her eyes in sleep, yes, the sleep of the dead—but not just yet was she dead. We stripped her naked in the daytime Piedmont woods, then with the crowbar and jack from the trunk of her luxury car, we broke her skull open to blood. In the daytime darkened Piedmont Woods, we broke her dead face and skull—and brains we laid open to blood. Chelsea watches her body in the woods, while I drive back to the area of the mall, parking in an isolated space near the Forsyth County Hospital. Then I walk so calmly, so fashionably in my miniskirt and heels through the many parked cars that day, crossing the busy highway in JC Penney casual, so beautiful in Indian hair, making my way to the mall parking lot in the afternoon, thinking suddenly of my lady Simone at school, then of the blonde whose name I never knew, wondering did I conjure her in a dream, or are my hands really cut and aching sore with blood?

In the Four Seasons Mall lot, I find the older Camry which is mine, still not obsolete in forest green couture, to match the very blouse I killed the woman in that day. I care nothing for that stupid job at this moment, as I slide back into my car, so glad I have my keys in my leather bag with shoulder sling—a bag my instincts told me to pick up when we first followed Diane Vaughn to her luxury car.

I drive in nervous leisure back to our wooded scene just 10 miles from civilization, driving the car so much farther in the woods than the black luxury car had been. Yes—I know from whence the rage hath come, that powered the blonde's muscles to pound a hammer drive, until Diane Vaughn was no longer herself, but merely a dead naked body with a bloody mess of teeth and bones for a face. *"Cover that bitch's ugly face,"* I say—and the speed and diligence of the blonde's obedience sends lightning deep into me. I know from whence this rage hath come—as it wraps the woman's head covered and out of sight—as it drags the body to my open trunk, and as it helps me place it so carefully inside. Though she is dead, her breasts are of magnificent design, full in the key of C major, smaller than ours, but so high and so perfectly formed.

"That's some rack," the blonde says. I reach inside to the body and fully squeeze the firm, rounded flesh, feeling the nipple besides, wishing badly to nurse her posthumously.

"Feel it."

"I ain't touchin' her dead titty."

"Go on."

"Why should I?"

I walk forward into her, through the veil of rage—and I hug her. "Do it for me. Do it because I told you to. Do it for me."

Suddenly, the rage I knew hath dissolved, rising above the trees of life, and she looks at me with such humility, such childlike wonder that my heart is broken. Yes, I know from whence this rage hath come, in the Woman of the Carolina Wood, who squeezes so full and lovingly the spongy and firm breasts of a dead woman. With each passing squeeze, I hear again a digging noise among thunder, and the woods around me is black again, and my hair is soaked with a nighttime mountain rain.

Yes, I know at last the source of this summer storm, built up from a year ago, when July flowers blossomed under the Prairie Moon, and our sixth victim was dead and buried. The rage that Chelsea poured into this, our Number Seven, the fire she had shown last night, when she choked her in front of Simone and me, it was reborn one year ago, in the days of the Prairie Moon. Believing that we had buried our last victim, she drove the highways north to Chesapeake, Virginia—to where her mother had tried to abscond, to hide from the pain and agony of her calling. Having met a man in full Cinderella style, who was brave enough to follow her home from her restaurant job to her trailer in a silver gray Navigator, and literally ask her to dinner that very night, marry her in a private ceremony a month later and take her to an exclusive gated community to bear his blonde, beautiful blue eyed children in upper middle class style—a man she never loved but tore her legs open for willingly because he stank of some sweet music and money.

Two years into this dream, Chelsea's mother was no longer Gretchen Baxter, But hiding as Mrs. Donna Turner now. Lovely landscaped garden community, my Chelsea drives her Saturn through. Looking for absolution, and relief from the pain inside. *It was something right out of An Officer and a Gentleman,* her co-workers at the Town and Country restaurant had said, when he carried her out of the restaurant in his arms laughing and joking, with Chelsea's pretty mother smiling ear to ear. *Chesapeake, Virginia* they said. A place called *Camille Harbour,* they said.

Yes. I know the rage by which we bury Number Seven, at Camille Harbour Estates, and the mansion on Harbour Wood Road.

A sky blue Saturn parked. A pristine, dark concrete walkway. A blonde beauty steps free of capitalist craving, her high heels onto asphalt luxury. No fountain, no statues. Just a massive, perfectly cut and kept lawn colored golf course green, from the front walkway, steps and white door of the brick home all the way to the residential street beyond. In tight black pants and frilly white, pink flowered top hanging loosely, innocently below the waist at the hip. The decorated doll steps from the asphalt to the brick walkway. Taking each step in fear and memory.

"What the Hell are... how the Hell did you find me?"

The woman's shock, Donna Turner's shock, clouds her reason, to disperse the hatred the tiniest bit, where Chelsea can step forward and give her an anguished, awkward hug.

"Hey, Ma. I just thought I'd come and say *Hey*. I get to missin' you a lot. I needed to hear your voice. Can you believe I went to that old trailer? A black and white couple live there now.

"I know. I sold it to 'em."

"Like I said I... I just needed to hear your voice."

"You can hear me just fine over the phone."

"I know. I did try to call. Remember?"

"I don't have time to talk to you about nothing. I've got a husband. Kids to take care of—an ex wife to worry about... a restaurant to run... as a matter of fact I should have been gone already—"

"Can I come in, Mom. Just for one second. I've... I've got some real problems I need to talk to you about."

"Well, tell me something I don't know. You've had nothing *but* problems since the day you were born. You looked like a roll of pan sausage when you were born. You were so underweight they almost kept you in the hospital. Problems? I've spent the last 10 years of my life recovering from what you did to me."

"I know," she says, nodding her head. When she closes her eyes, a tear falls. But she wipes her eyes through a smile. Sniffing. Trying too hard not to look pathetic.

"Look at you. Still grinnin.' " (Gretchen's word for *crying*). You came into my life and fucked it up. Yet you're the one who's always sniffin' and grinnin' about it."

"I know. I think that's what I need to talk to you about."

"Like I said, Chelsea, I don't have time. If it's money you want you can just…"

"I just want to *talk*, Mom. I just want to talk to my mother."

Gretchen (Donna) folds her arms. Bewilderedly. "Okay. Then, *talk*."

Chelsea smiles—wiping her eyes again. "This is a beautiful house. It's like a dream."

"I cain't help it my man's rich. And he ain't stingy with it, neither. What's his is mine—that was part of the deal. Otherwise I'd still be waitin' tables and pressin' suits in Martin County. Now I'm waitin' tables in my own restaurant—and A Cleaner World is pressin' my suits. And those three little witches he calls daughters, runnin' back and forth between here and Norfolk to his poor assed ex wife—I got somebody who comes in every day and watches the two little ones for me so I can do whatever I want. And she watches *my* baby too. My daughter."

"You had a baby?"

"Yeah, I had his baby. Prob'ly gon' have another one too… I cain't keep 'im off me. Tell you the truth I don't mind it too much. He ain't good lookin' but he ain't ugly neither. Typical nice guy, spends too much time workin'. Bald, slightly out of shape but he's really nice. I actually felt sorry for him when he asked me to marry him. Fuckin' slut of an ex-wife didn't know how good she had it. She ran around on him like she had a fire in her pants. Wasn't never satisfied 'til he had to dump her for it. Caught the bitch in bed with the contractor."

"Is he good to you?"

"Look around. What do you think?"

Two little urchins, with faces like ten and twelve year old girls appear at her side. "Hi," they say. "Donna, who's that?"

"Nobody sweetie. Go back inside. Watch your little sister for me."

"They are so pretty. Your stepdaughters?"

No answer.

"What's the baby's name?"

No answer.

"That's… that's good, Mom. I'm really glad for you. I just wanted to say—to let you know how sorry I am for the way things were between us."

"That's all you've ever been is sorry. The morning I brought you home, there was a blackbird on the roof of the trailer. Like something right out of a bad horror movie. There it was—screamin' and barking its head off while I got closer to the trailer. I was so poor I had to take a cab home from the hospital… I didn't even have a car. I had to get rides to work and the grocery store…"

A pause.

"He was a good lookin' man. Your daddy. And I think that was his problem. He loved me but he didn't need me. Girls and grown women clawed him with their eyes everywhere we went. They wouldn't even let me enjoy my own husband. In the store I'd hear things like—*damn, how'd SHE get lucky?* Group of young, ugly ass black girls once said—*what's he doin' with that trashy bitch.* Bunch of yard sluts calling *me* trashy."

"They were just jealous, Mom. I swear that's what it was because you're beautiful—"

"Your father was so handsome that he made me look ugly. I ain't no prize but I know I ain't ugly trash neither."

"No. You're not."

"I been hit on too many times by too many different men. Women too. One look at you and I can see you as salty as a bowl of peanuts."

"Salty?"

"You can't hide it in that blouse, Baby. You swing the other way don't you? You're a dyke."

"What?"

"God only knows where you been and what you been doin'. Its written all over your face. And I'm gon' have to admit it... you look like a goddamn movie star. 'Bout the prettiest thing I..."

A pause...

"When I look at you, I see your daddy. You look more like John Baxter than you do me."

"Mom, you're beautiful yourself. You really are..."

"I don't need you to condescend to me, Miss USA. Standing there in your frilly Mall shirt and tight cut off pants. Look at you. The fact that you ain't married to a rich man yourself by now is just what I'm talkin' about. You're bad luck, Chelsea Lynn. Your luck is as black as a crow's tail. You came in the world on a moonless night. It's prob'ly how you gon' die."

"Mom, how can you talk to me like this?"

"Because I raised you bitch. And I got split open to bring your little ass into this world."

She laughs. Cruelly.

"The doctor said you looked like a little blow pop, your head was so big. I can talk to you any way I please. The sight of you. The smell of you is making me sick.

"Please tell me why you hate me..."

"I hate you because I didn't want you. You understand that you dumb bitch? You ruined my life. I had to suffer eighteen years of Hell because of you. Because I got pregnant with you *before* we got married. Do you know how hard it is to take care of a whining, clingy, needy little bitch with no man and no money? A stinkin' little piss ant I never asked for?"

"Mom I'm sorry."

Gretchen, *Donna* rushes from the doorway, shoving Chelsea backward in the chest and slapping her hard, making Chelsea scream once in despair. Then she pulls Chelsea upright by the hair and neck.

"You shut the *fuck* up. He left me because of *you*! Did you hear me? I had a dream man and he left me because of you!"

In the fog, the haze of her vision, Chelsea can see the little girls and a young woman in the doorway.

"I loved him! I loved him with every cell in my body. And when I got back from the hospital, all he left me was an empty trailer to live in and a goodbye note I still can't throw away. And you ask me why I hate you? I hate your fucking *guts!*

She shakes her daughter's head, her daughter's big, pretty head on the last syllable, genuinely sickened by her wet, teary face and nose.

"I never want to see you. I never want to smell you again for the rest of my life. You fucking *cunt.* If I do, I swear to God and Jesus I'll take my husband's bat and beat you to death."

"Please forgive me… please forgive me… please give me one more chance…"

"As the Devil you came from is my witness—if I see you again… I'm gon' kill you."

Her mother tries to walk away, but Chelsea grabs her by the arm, and Gretchen begins to beat her daughter on the head and in the face by memory. By this same memory, Chelsea has to let go and cover herself, while the nanny comes out and interferes, pulling the angry leopard off the deer she is forbidden to eat, pulling her into the house and screaming "Just go! Just Go!" To the blonde stranger on the lawn. But the stranger can only follow her mother to the door until it slams in her face—knocking repeatedly and ringing the doorbell in tears for a full minute, as the screams are muffled down to nothing inside the house.

The air around her cools in the summer gray, as the sun is now hidden by the passing clouds and thunder. Chelsea turns in a fog of confusion, walking through the rising summer wind, jaw muscles strained from holding her mouth open. Even before she gets inside her blue Saturn, the wind blows its voice violently, spitting spots of cold water in her face—admonishing her to run for her life—to flee the wrath to come. She does not hurry, savoring the big, cold drops of water on her back, finally sliding in the car, as a bolt of lightning sparks in the darkening clouds.

"Crack that whip," says the car stereo. *"Give the past the slip. Step on a crack. Break your momma's back."*

I'm going to shit in her grave, the blonde says to me, in the aftermath of fervent rain, where surely my own ancestors too were compelled to have pissed and shat. These sins are through the motherline— the Cherokee blood that screams inside. With full understanding, I hear my Chelsea Doll, understanding her in the morning twilight, in the hour before dawn's early light. She pushes the woman in the wet sheet up and over the mound of dirt, and she falls unceremoniously into the pit, where her body will return to the dust from whence it came.

In the breeze of early morning renewal, in the passing of the storm, the Chelsea Doll climbs down into the wet grave—her black soft shoes anchored in the mud. *What are you doing* comes to the tip of my tongue, but I hold it prisoner, swallowing it into oblivion. She undoes her black stretch pants in classic form, sliding them down and all the way off and throwing them up to me. I fold them with hardly a thought, as she slides her tiny black underwear down to her ankles—leaving them in place—with her black shoes still on, and her legs anchored on either side of the body. Beyond even my expectation, she folds her black shirt up until her breasts are exposed under the black cloth resting on top of them. Her white skin glows in the morning mountain dark, as the coolest summer wind chills me to the bone and blows solace in aching disbelief through the trees, while the blonde woman squats over the dead body in the sheet, her face anguised in despair. I look closely, to see her features twist in ways I have only seen at the precipice, when she nears a release of energy into her body.

What devastation, this desecration, this energy of defecation in ruin, defiance of every natural law of man and spirit, this consecration of such sublime denunciation! The ultimate, most intimate and impudent imputation, this impartation of divine subjugation, of the body in the grave of eternal desperation!

Her face twists in the pain of a calling too terrible to speak, and she lets her voice out into the early morning breeze, as the most vile part of who she is defiles the body underneath her. I am amazed at what I see, shaking my head in awe, as she desecrates the white sheet in completion. A quiet, determined *Oh, God*—then another straining, to crescendo into a final, triumphant bellowing like an animal. *Yeah, take that you fucking bitch* I hear from the grave, watching her clean herself on the sheet like a cat in the grass. Then she pulls her shirt down and her underwear up, and climbs out of the grave almost on her own, until I grab her hand and pull her away from the stench in the pit.

The clouds begin to depart in the morning twilight, nearby the edge of night. Like a madwoman possessed, like the man hating dyke I am, I drive into the damp earth with a speed and fever unprecedented, to bury this last tragedy of what we've done. I stop only when the half hour of hard labor is behind me, to stand up as the gravedigger, every muscle in my body sore, every nerve on edge of pain and suffering. But I breathe deeply the cool mountain air, athletic from breast to bone, able to endure what brief recompense is due.

When I look at the sky at predawn, I know that not every omen is confined to the earth, as I see the bright and morning star shining so brilliantly in the heavens above. It is the light that I need, that guides me into the Truth of all things. This is the truth that brings fear or solace to the soul—depending on which road is traveled. Those that walk the straight and narrow path, as it moves through the Valley of the Shadow of Death, as they endure the roar of every lion, and the screaming voice of every crow, the Light appears to them in the morning or the evening day, when the wind of renewal blows a break in the clouds, and their soul is filled with passion, the power and love for our Lord and Savior Jesus Christ; his death, his burial, and his resurrection from the tomb. But for many, this Star appears above the wide and crooked path, a path landscaped by roses and lawns of forest green, and every detour of pleasure and perversion known to man; every blessing of love and finance, of beauty and admiration, of talent and achievement—and every answered prayer known and loved, every earthly glory fought and won, even of wars fought in the name of freedom and justice, and all manner of works for the cause of righteousness and wisdom of man—even above all of these the Star will appear, to those who travel the wide and crooked path of hypocrisy, complacency, lack of compassion, false charity, love of riches and glory, hedonism, atheism and vice. When the Star appears in the evening day, above their wide and crooked path, they understand the meaning of the word *fear*, and the terrible knowledge of the truth, that will set its feet upon the Mount of Olives, and split the sacred ground in two, as the Star gives their souls premonition and the dread of death, beyond which is outer darkness for them, where there shall be weeping and gnashing of teeth. And some hear the calling from the wide and crooked path, seeing for a brief time the exit sign to Redemption, but having not the courage or the strength to go the way.

As I smooth out the dirt—I look away from the light, thinking only of my Simone Baby and my Chelsea Doll, and whence forth came the evil and rage for what was done. Yes, Chelsea. I see you at school in your eleventh grade year. So eaten alive with craving already, to be free of your mother's sting! So joyously desirous—to dress in the cheerleader cloth, and feel thy womanhood grow. To feel the expansion of thyself in leaping, jumping, bouncing high and wide—to be the best cheerleader they have ever seen. To focus and direct the pain from your home life. The black fire from your trailer, tinted blue, to burn in the cheerleader's lust. To explore your sexuality in carnal cleanliness like they have rarely seen, all covered except your legs and the fat of your young thighs, clean and smooth when you jump and spread your legs—your shapely, wiggly bottom pulled tight in the royal blue underwear, the center of yourself on fire as you are held up by the other girls—the cooling, orgasmic release when they drop you down into their arms, from whatever pyramid or other form they desire. To cheer and be cheered, to see and be seen, to be adored and worshipped by them, for every ounce and inch of the beauty and body that God gave you. To have fun. To enjoy life from wholesome worldliness, from worldly wholesomeness, and thighs baked half naked in the sun.

This, you desire for thee! To have yourself a high old time, though the gate to this freedom is already closed and locked. You ask Gretchen as far back as the summer can you try out for cheerleading, and Gretchen says *Who's gonna pay for it?* And Gretchen says *No.* But the desire comes, at the beginning of your eleventh grade year, when the other girls are alive with this energy, the other pretty, blue ribbon club babies... when the want and need of it decides that your resistance is futile. It decides then and there, when you see the sign for open cheerleader tryouts, you decide to stay after school, even though it might require a beating from Gretchen if she knew. But what lies are this you tell, Dear Chelsea, when you know what prevarication must be, that your friend *"begged you to go with her to a key club meeting,"* to try and persuade you to join! So you go to the gym, all aware that quiet and beautiful Chelsea Lynn Baxter is going to try out for cheerleader this year, and that it is a spot already held in the future and gone.

The Mountaineers

For a week you lie to your mother about this club and that club and this committee and that committee and this girl you're tutoring and that girl you're tutoring (*You?* Gretchen says. *Tutoring what? How to look like a whore?*) until it is understood that the Junior year Chelsea may not always be home when the mother is. And after the week of tryouts is done and the names are posted on the gym wall, there are no last names that start with A, so that your name is above every other name, and Chelsea Baxter is on the cheerleading squad. Which one of the lucky boys will take you, my Chelsea, or which one of the busty girls in secret. You do not know. But you're a cheerleader, aren't you? So surely you are a slut for the boys, right? What else could be so wrong as their formula to judge your sex, for where they see that sugar is sweet, there is none that you require, for you are as salty as tomatoes on a country picnic under a chestnut tree.

In the twilight of morning, as I gaze the fading stars that twinkle, I share the same vision as they, as they remember Chelsea Baxter ten years ago, as though it were but a turning of the day. To every star in Heaven, a day is as a thousand years, and this thousand years is as a day. Our lives are a whimper, a whisper, a gust of wind that blows to and fro upon the face of the earth, until it is lost in quick and fervent time.

I smooth the unholy mound of dirt, packing it to the grave, to make the bed for the seventh rose bush in bloom. This, a white rose, to symbolize our last gift from Him. I press the bed for these roses, my Chelsea, in the aftermath of a summer rain, breathing such a cool and determined wind from above. In the Heart of Memory, I see the horror on your face, dear Chelsea, when you come home from practice today, when you see the strange car in the dirt space by the trailer. Already, you know who it must be inside, because you have seen its owner get inside of it before and drive away from the school…

You get out of your friend's car, head pounding from the sound of the words *What's Miss Gorham doing here?* Meredith Gorham. Cheerleader coach extraordinaire. A human deer—doe eyed in perpetual youth, in permanent slick back ponytail and narrow hips, a sweat shirt and matching pants for every occasion. Meredith Gorham. Wife of Dr. Gorham—young teaching physician two hours away at Chapel Hill.

Meredith Gorham. So driven. So dedicated to the cause of perfect cheer. So bound and gagged by the rules. Haunted by the rules of protocol. Unable to keep her mousy promise to her prettiest new member, to not yet say anything to her mother about being on the squad. *Just let me handle it,* Chelsea says, *I'll tell her when I can.* Let me have this one chance to be free, Ms. Gorham. Let me be a cheerleader. *I'll invite her to our first game, and then she'll see and she'll understand.* She'll be so shocked, so impressed by me that she'll have to be proud of me. *It might be the beginning, Ms. Gorham, of something between me and my mother that I've always wanted.* Something I've never had before. A connection—the ability to look in my mother's eyes and see something else besides hatred. *Help me, Ms. Gorham.* Please let me do this in secret. Don't call Gretchen Baxter. In the name of the most High—in the name of God, don't call Gretchen Baxter. *Help me do this my way,* Ms. Gorham. Help me win my mother's heart. Help me to breathe free.

I see you, Chelsea Doll, when you walk into the house. A look colored by fear and epic disbelief.

"Hey, there she is," Gretchen says. "Miss Gorham told me about your little stunt. So, you made the squad. That's pretty... it's pretty impressive." She laughs a giddy, nervous laughter with Ms. Gorham. "Boy, she can get it done when she puts her mind to it, cain't she?"

Meredith and Gretchen so heartily agree on your condemned, broken behalf. Unmercifully, Ms. Gorham stands up to leave, confident that the only trust broken is the one that doesn't matter. But in the grand scheme of things… her ass is covered. It is written, *The bureaucratic mentality is the only constant in the universe.* As such a thing ought to be, perhaps, to preserve order in the midst of chaos, in the teeming masses of illogical motivations that is humanity.

"I want you to come to one of our practices as soon as you can Ms. Baxter", followed by a fake hug and tap on the back—then a "I'll see you at practice tomorrow Sweetie… and see, I told you I'd take care of it didn't I", she says with a knowing look and confident whirling out the door.

Amidst the sounds of daytime darkness, and the ghostly echo of Ms. Gorham's voice in memory, you watch your mother at the trailer window beside the ugly flower made sofa in perpetual thrift upholstery. The sound of her car signals you to step forward, to ease your mother's impending wrath and disappointment. But no sooner than the car sound fades away, than the lioness stands up and whirls around, and you see a lightning bolt and feel one side of your face burn in blue and black fire; your eyes are closed from the sting of such a powerful slap, and you touch your face in the agony of revelation, and the pain of what is real. Then the requisite tightening of your throat while your ears ring from the slap, and a pulling in your hair that burns your scalp to acid. Choking you with one hand, pulling your hair with the other, she ushers you over to the flower made couch and sits you down hard and straddles you, pulling your hair and holding your throat until the tears stream down your 17 year old face, already more blonde and beautiful than she.

Why does she straddle you, dear Chelsea? To subjugate your soul to grieving? Why does she press so hard against you, dear Chelsea, to acquaint you with every curve of her anger?

"What did I tell you?"

"You told me not to—"

"What did I tell you?"

"I don't know."

The next sound heard in every non-existent ear, is the sound of your deep yelling, the rise of your deep, young woman's voice into a legitimate scream for no one to hear. What pains are there, dear Chelsea? What are the varieties and severities of pain? Is this chiming of the lovely ear as such to wring a dizziness to your brain? Why does she twist your ear, dear Chelsea, and press herself so hard and heavy against you?

"What did I tell you?"

"You said don't do it—"

And after you answer comes the sound of your screaming again, but this time from the chiming of both lovely ears, as she twists your ears back like a German Shepherd dog. Here, in the wake of a mountain's passing night, my shovel still in hand, I see you dear Chelsea, and the pain and suffering you grieve to bear. Now, I see her lay you down on the flower made couch of thrift—*you gon' quit tomorrow,* she says. But though you would like to agree, the words *I can't* slip from your crying mouth, followed by the screams again with your head held back, and your mother laid flat on top of you on the sofa.

I'm gon' strip you, she says—*and I'm gon' beat you black and blue. Get up. Get up!* she says in noisy intention, watching you strip down to your Barbie Doll breasts and hips, then she punches you in the face, still fully clothed herself in jeans, t-shirt and mother's button down blue collar. She slaps and punches you again and again, pulling your hair and hitting you in your stomach and your crotch, telling you *I'll bet that's your problem, shaving your pussy already like a fucking whore*, and she hits it again square on with her fist, then she hits you in the nose while you're unprepared, causing the blood to run free down to your mouth. Another punch quickly to your face as you cover it, then so many to your sides and your back while you bend over crying loudly, hitting you in the back hard enough to make you think of coughing—and dream of when you can breathe free.

Chelsea! Young Woman of Straw! What is the sound you make when she wrestles you to your own bed on your stomach and holds your hair down, punching you hard in the cheek, saying—*How 'bout it now bitch, why don't you fight me now*—bashing you hard enough to rattle your brain, then getting up suddenly and leaving the room briefly, returning with a silver instrument; not the knife that she held at your throat in the kitchen after you disrobed, telling you that if you ever disobeyed her again she would kill you. No—this is the silver shape of so many private fears and fantasies, that vibrates in buzzing when lust hath conceived, bringing forth sin. *Put your hands underneath you, between your legs*, she says, but when you move too slowly, my Chelsea Doll, she beats you in your sore back and ribs hard enough to make you cry again, so you do it quicker, naked face down, with your hands underneath your groin.

You wanna disobey me? she says, her shirt up to expose her nipples. On her knees, her pants unzipped and low on her hips, the sullen and sour look of an addict preparing a fix, she turns the device on to a light buzzing, and affixes the tip of it to your anus, dear Chelsea, where she spits in satisfaction. *Relax your ass… relax your ass or I'll put a knife in it* she says, then she pushes the device into your bottom without mercy, in disbelief of what your screams at this moment do to her mind and body. She slides her underwear down, affixing herself against the back of the buzzing silver device, so that it buzzes against her groin—then she lays down on your back, pushing the device further in you with her own slow pelvic squeeze against your buttocks.

Chelsea, do not cry for thee! Do not cry for thyself, for the life she hath taken from thee! The gruffness, the hoarseness, the hopelessness of your voice feeds her hunger, as she squeezes herself to thee! As she pushes the silver blade deep inside you, the buzzing dagger, to cut and burn the life from thee! What is the trembling you feel from her, my Chelsea, as she grunts *Oh, God* in your ear in such low pitch bellowing as you have never heard, mixed with a brief howling as a heifer, and the convulsing of her body in full, as she whispers over and over in your ear *I'm gon' kill you bitch, I'm gon' kill you bitch, I'm gon' kill you bitch*—for you know where this breathless trembling, this Heavenly Correction hath come, dear Chelsea, to infuse your soul with blue and black fire.

*I*n the cool of the evening, upon the turning of the day, the three of us gauge the view of our mountain paradise, upon the rising of the Summer Moon. Above the tree line across the road and beyond the field rests the dark Appalachian woods, highlighted in the evening day by the light of a full moon rising low above it, looking as big as life and as golden as dreams of a blessed fade to night. The golden yellow moon looks down on our deed, in the aftermath of the storm sent to cover our wickedness, at the edge of starry skies that we will see, that will carry our sin from Earth to Heaven. A view of us unfettered, uncluttered for every star, and every grieving angel at the Throne of God.

"The eyes of the Lord. Staring right at us. Reminding us that we're going to Hell for what we've done."

"Says you," Simone says. "I know he died for me—just as sure as he died for all seven of those bitches in our back yard."

"I hated every one of 'em," says Chelsea. "I'm glad they're dead."

"Why? Just because you hated them?"

"Because they were sinners." Simone says, protecting her Chelsea. "She passed judgment on them. Gave them what she determined they deserved."

"And what do we deserve? What have we got coming to us for what we've done?"

"Well... I've got a pizza and a movie coming to me. Damn this guilt trip you're on," Chelsea says, turning and walking into the house.

"You can eat pizza 'til you're as fat as a pig, Chelsea. It won't go away."

"You're just projecting, Raven. You're so guilty it's ridiculous."

"How am I supposed to feel? Happy? Satisfied? Maybe that's how it is in books and in the movies, but this is real life, Simone. God, you and Chelsea... you guys don't feel anything. Chelsea is a pure -T sociopath."

"And what are you?" Simone says, snapping a little. "A sociopath with a conscience? That makes you better than us, huh? You think that because you feel guilty, that makes it alright? You're not fooling anybody, Raven. You're just scared because you think a demon's gonna come out of these woods tonight and get you for what you did last night."

"I didn't do anything."

"You what?"

"I said, I didn't do anything. I didn't kill her. I didn't even rape her."

"Well, I don't know what the Hell *that* means, but I do know you're not sorry, Honey. You're scared. Because if remorse was what you felt, you'd be on the phone with the cops right now. You gonna turn yourself in?"

"No."

"How 'bout us?" she says. "You gonna tell on us, and wait to see if we rat you out?"

"Why are you attacking me?"

"I'm not attacking you. I just don't like the idea of you trying to drag us down into your guilty party for something you pulled us both into."

"I know. But for some reason, I feel guilty as Hell this time. I keep thinking about her poor, dumb ass on the road. No cell phone. No hope. All she talked about was her family."

"Well, now it's the other way around. Now, all they're ever gonna talk about is her. All Alison's ever gonna talk about is how much she loved her poor, missing Momma. Poor little Alison, with the ass just like her mother, I'll bet. When I think about that woman we just buried, you know what comes to my mind? You found her, I fucked her, and Chelsea Lynn fucking killed her. That's all I feel and that's all I *want* to feel. And I don't like the idea of being made to feel guilty about it. Least of all from you."

"Least of all from me—what does that mean?"

"It means you're turning into a fucking hypocrite of the worst kind, Raven. Which makes you ten times more disgusting than any of those bitches fertilizing our back yard. If you're going to do what you do, Honey, at least have the courage to own it."

"Who the *fuck* wants to own this, Simone? I know how screwed up this is, I am at least partially aware of what we've done. Are you? Don't you have any conscience left at all? Don't you feel any remorse?"

"My momma burned my conscience away when I was sixteen years old—and you know what she did? Yeah, I'm talking about the curling iron incident baby, that's right, where my father had his dick up my ass, holding my hands behind me while my Momma burned a fucking ditch into my back—you wanna talk to me about conscience? *Conscience seared with a hot iron…* you goddamn right. I can't even believe you mentioned the word remorse."

"Look, I know what we went through when we were young. But when's enough gonna be enough? It's no excuse for us to spend the rest of our lives taking women and girls from their families."

"What?"

"You heard me."

"My God," she says. "You actually think you can talk back time. You think you can click your heels three times and make this go away. You just buried a woman five feet underground covered in shit and blood. And now you're gonna stand here crying about it in front of me and expect me not to get sick to my stomach? I still cringe at least once every day when I think about what my mother did to me. And if I have to kill a hundred women to make that go away then I will. And you're the one who turned me into this in the first place. Remember? Remember that night in the parking lot? Huh? And now you're gonna stand here and try to make me feel guilty for it? As if that can undo anything that Chelsea, me and you have done in the last seven years."

"Ouch. Must have touched a nerve."

A pause. A hurt, bewildered look.

"Well, you can just go to Hell Raven Moon."

As she turns and walks toward the house, I feel words forming at the tip of my tongue, causing my mouth to move independently of my will.

"So, I guess I'll see you there, then?"

The shapely brunette acknowledges me with an extra bouncy step onto the porch and a middle finger turned up toward me. What sights dispatch a fervent heat into a woman—this, the heat of rage? I follow her into the house on wheels of frustration, with something that can be called ire poisoning my bloodstream.

"Hey... show me that finger again. Hey..." And on that 'Hey' goes a strong, humiliating push in her back that stumbles her forward, making Chelsea look up from her movie at us with a serious, worried (wounded) expression.

"Raven... keep your hands to yourself," Simone says.

"You told me to go to Hell. Now, why don't you send me there?"

"What are you doing?" Chelsea asks, walking towards us with a cautious, anguished (wounded) look. "Raven, what's the matter?"

"Ask her."

"Simone?"

Chelsea's voice douses the heat just enough—enough for Simone to remember herself as too mature for my reckless nonsense, always prepared to die to protect my glass emotions. She turns and walks down the hall in heavy steps, steps burdened like few others in the history of womankind. Her bedroom door closes on a cushion of restraint.

"Raven what happened?"

"I..."

I can only shake my head and walk calmly to my bedroom for my keys. With Chelsea still watching me pitifully in confusion, saying *I was gonna order us a pizza*, I take the requisite walk past her, out the door, into the evening day.

Who the fuck does she think she is? Telling me to go to Hell and to go fuck myself? I almost hit her in her fat-breasted, big assed, broke down Catherine Zeta-Jones wannabe looking mouth. Telling me to go fuck myself? I'll go fuck myself bitch, with your teeth marks on the back of my right hand, and a clump of your ratty hair in my left.

Amazon bitch.

I drive on in the mountain twilight, not really knowing where I'm going, suddenly remembering that Chelsea said something about pizza. I'll drive to Marios. It's a half hour away but I need to clear my head. Besides, Chelsea thinks Pizza Hut makes good pizza and I keep telling her it tastes like crap. If I eat pizza tonight its gonna be Marios. I'm going to get this pizza because it's what *I* want. Who cares what they want. To Hell with both of them.

To Hell with what I know their doing right now. Chelsea on the bed near tears, her arm around a brooding Simone—aching from stress and guilt I caused her to have. Religious guilt she swore she'd die before she would allow herself to feel again. To Hell with Chelsea saying *"Let's go take a bath... we both need it,"* and Simone's coy, embarrassed look as she gets up in agreement that a whore's wash off was certainly not enough in the aftermath of a rape and murder.

To Hell with Chelsea's blonde, giggling fun and jiggling removal of all Simone's clothes even before they get to the bathroom, and the good natured slap and wobble of Simone's giant tits, followed by Simone's girlish, sly giggle—tongue firmly in cheek. To Hell with how much of it is playful perversion, as opposed to perverted play, when Simone puts her hands above her head in mock pinup fashion, while her blonde lady takes hold of both of them and mashes and wobbles them like two giant sagging water balloons, to Hell with the slapping sound I can hear even from the miles—the sound of those two great bags of flesh being slapped together until Simone has to stop laughing and pretending it's not her devastation. To Hell with Chelsea's good natured and hard pulling of just one of those great nipples into her mouth as hard as she can and have it still be comical, releasing it in a loud smacking noise that is the call to their clownish carnality.

To Hell with them. To Hell with Chelsea and her perfect assed Barbie Doll body, naked as a jaybird now, running their bathwater in the huge Jacuzzi bath. To Hell with their naked splashing and suds foaming on the water as they forget all about me, Chelsea sitting on the edge of the big blue marble tub with Simone resting back between her legs. To Hell with Chelsea's patient and vigorous rubbing and washing those bloated floating bags of fun and freedom, now lifting one of them up and leaning over

Simone's shoulder, pulling the big nipple into her mouth like an overgrown suckling, moaning, giggling during the moan in non-committal, Simone staring at the sight in rapt amazement, that a woman such as herself could be so lucky. To Hell with her as she closes her eyes, and allows the energy of the suckling to pass from her gigantic breast to her heart, lungs and into her arms, and inevitably into the pit of her stomach, down to her legs and the trembling tips of her toes.

To Hell with them.

$\mathcal{T}$he Pizza Girl was all of sixteen, which had set my mind and body to racing when she took my order, of what I might have done to her perfect little breasts with my lips and tongue. Don't act so shocked and innocent; you don't know how many of us, including *you* maybe, have thought the same thing. Especially when we go into a restaurant and get "serviced" by a pretty young thing, all decked out in their little paper hats—young, tight curves all smooth and bound up tight in their little servant's uniforms, all smiles and happy, bouncy ponytails to go with that happy little personality. Some of you horny bitches know exactly what I'm talking about, especially you suburban mothers with daughters their same age, whose lusts are an unspoken, unfathomable hurricane of contradictions, whirling from your mind to your groin and back again—even if it's only to have suddenly, the entire restaurant emptied, so that the only two people in the world are you and that little underage girl, so that she can spend the next few minutes at your smiling, beckon call—you white women especially, when one of the servant girls is a pretty, black haired Latina with dark eyes and an exotic smile. If her ass is big enough, you picture it over your knee, don't you? Getting taught a painful lesson in mother-daughter humility. But some of you are more cruel than that—and would like to see them standing stark naked, with their hands behind their back at first, while you torture their young sensitive nipples with your teeth, lips and tongue until she is crying from the pain. *Hands in front, little girl*, you'll say, and then you spank her little fat ass until the palms of your hands are raw, and your heart is up in your throat. Oh, don't act so shocked and innocent, Mom. You know what I'm talking about. Especially you corporate types and teachers and boss bitches, who are one hundred percent comfortable around people, and think it nothing to relax in the presence of sexy young women. Avert your eyes, Mom, from their pretty face and young, tight and wiggly little bodies as they make your sub, fill your fast food bag of goodies, funnel your French fries or stuff your taco, or spread the ripe, red tomato sauce on the pizza you just ordered. Yes, I do the best I can to call her with my eyes, this little Pizza Girl, who must have thought it strange when I asked her how old she was and when I told her she was pretty.

Coming from me, I think, with my Latina looks that people don't know is really white and American Indian, coming from me I think she found the compliment worthwhile.

I am amazed at the size of the pizza box she eventually brings to my counter, which dwarfs a so-called medium Pizza Hut box. I hand her my twenty, telling her to keep a five dollar tip, knowing full well I have just gotten more for my money here than I have for a long time buying anything else under the sun. Oversized pizza box in hand, I flash one more smile at the young girl, bothered and a little fascinated by my body's involuntary need to flash images to my brain, of me on top of this 16 year old girl in my bedroom, with her arms pinned to her sides, taking what is left of her white suburban virginity with my strap on penis.

My car is now a pizza delivery service, its driver grieving to partake, not realizing that she has not eaten a full meal in two days. Curiosity gets the best of me and I open the box, greeted by and treated to the white, tangy Mozzarella cheese and pepperoni pizza. I actually say *"Oh, God"* aloud, then close the box, so I don't spend the next 10 minutes in the parking lot worshipping the sauce and cheese and thin crust masterpiece. Some of the cheese near the crust sits so delicately at the edge of browning as to be miraculous, while in the center, some of the rich red sauce can be clearly seen through the white. A thin crusted pizza pie, it is, that surely cannot taste as good as it smells. I close the box, shaking my head while I crank the car, heading back toward our brick house mountain Paradise.

The miles roll along—each hungry minute building one onto the other. The minutes and miles stretch into a millennium, until I know the spell is meant to be broken. After 10 painful minutes, I fly open the pizza box with my right hand, understanding that this is a job for two hands. I pull over to the side of the road, comfortable in the dark, in the shadow of the approaching night. Like one dedicated to a cause, I break one of the cut slices, made hungrier by the melted cheese, swallowing from just the sight of it. I raise the slice of Heaven to my mouth, biting down and pulling the melted cheese away. After one bite and chew, the taste rings my ears and I have to close my eyes, saying "Oh…GOD," with the emphasis and respect on Him that he deserves. With my mouth still full, I bite again like I am starving, breaking the melted cheese again, leaning back and closing my eyes, breathing deep through my nose as I chew. This is not mozzarella cheese alone; a blend perfected over time, combined with a sauce that compels one to bite deeply, to seek out the cure for what ails you. *Pure Italian*, my mind says. Food for the gods, pizza for the angels. Even as I drink those first two bites, my mouth opens for a third, then I put the slice down at last, finding a napkin in the glove compartment for my soiled hands and face. In my thirty one years, it is truly the best meal I have ever tasted. "Mario's Italian Pizzeria," I say aloud, putting the slice on a napkin, positioning it to die a slow, delicious death in one hand while I drive.

Back on the highway, inevitably this incredible meal on the go activates the Theater of my Mind, as I remember the night when my two Beloveds first met:

"We're going out tonight."

"I don't know, Honey," says Simone. "It's my day off—you know I can't move on my days off."

"I'm in the mood for a sit down dinner, just the two of us. Just put on your gray skirt and that navy shirt I bought you. I'll drive."

Three hours away from our new cemetery, we sit in the Pizza Hut restaurant in Winston Salem, North Carolina on the busy Four Seasons Mall boulevard. Our mountain graveyard is fresh enough to be macabre, with the bodies of our first and second victims rotting away, safely apart from the tiding of number three.

"You don't even like Pizza Hut, Raven. What are you doing?"

"I like the setting. I just wanted to do something different for a change, Professor. Maybe you like laying around that house all the time but I like to get out every once in a while."

"And being on the road 5 hours a day isn't enough for you?" The beautiful brunette looks at me with tired suspicion, sipping her coke again.

"Here comes our waitress."

"It's about time," she says. "I'm starving to death."

I lock eyes with the beautiful, tallish blonde— irresistible in her servant girl braid and uniform. She asks to take our order, smiling at me and looking over at Simone like she was the Queen of France. She takes our mundane, corporate cliché of a cheese lover's whatever order and whirls away.

"Do you know her?"

"What makes you say that?"

"I don't know. You seem awful chummy. You've got chemistry like… wait… now I get it. You like this big bird, don't you? This little, yellow chirp of a waitress, and you brought me all the way back here so I could watch you fall flat on your face. Raven I don't feel like—"

"Shhh. There's something about number two I never told you."

"Number two? You've got to take a dump now? Then go ahead."

"You're not listening. I said *Number Two*."

Genuine bewilderment crosses her expression, until her mind flashes the image of the 2nd grave. Her lovely features all react accordingly, relaxing into renewed interest and revelation."

"You mean D.V?"

"Yes."

"What about her? Is that waitress her daughter or something?"

"No. When D.V. (for Diane Vaughn) left the store, I wasn't the only one who followed her. As a matter of fact, there was somebody else in the back seat with her while I drove. Somebody who held her down good, Simone. She made that woman cry and I almost pissed myself when I heard it."

The somber, awestruck look on her face is a masterpiece of non verbal communication. Simone turns her head slowly, scanning the restaurant until she finds the other woman of straw. Watching her walk around the restaurant like any ordinary college grad making a quick buck while she waits for her real life to come along. Taking the customers' orders like any ordinary pretty girl, begging to be liked for a tip and a fake pat on the back. Simone looks at the tallish, well shaped blonde. Then she looks at me, and for the briefest moment, her soul ices cold in fear.

After the requisite eternity, our dinner appears in Italian form, and the waitress breaks protocol by permission from her manager, and she sits down at our table.

"She said I could take my break now," she says, flashing a big, toothy smile and pink lips. Her face is all features; big eyes, arched eyebrows and thick lips. Like a princess in disguise.

"It's so nice to finally meet you," she says, shaking Simone's hand across the table. "I'm Chelsea. I met Raven about a month ago."

She glances nervously at me.

"Go ahead and tell 'er," I say.

"Miss Cory… I know you don't know me, and I don't blame you for thinking how weird I am. And if Raven told you the whole story then I know what you think of me. I begged her not to do this but I couldn't stop her. Raven wants me to tell you that the managers here… '*don't know it yet, but this is my last night.*' That I'm gonna be moving to Black Mountain."

In the Heart of Memory, I see Simone's look soften, phasing through from suspicion to unresisting compassion, as she gazes into the eyes of a killer. But these are the Eyes of Mine—those of a child born in hatred, nurtured in discord, and raised in blood and fear. From this, the two of us have blossomed into the women that Simone Cory sees, women in the pain of a Divine Calling—to live and perish by the sword.

When the miles have come and gone, in the wake of another vision faded, I return to the house on Mountain View Road. Divine dinner in hand, I open the unlocked front door and go inside, an hour forward and back again, hearing the words *Oh thank God* from Chelsea's voice. She takes the pizza from me as if I were the life of the party, and throws her arms fully around me.

But when I see the burden of Simone's lovely face in the hall, the tears in her eyes, what well of sorrow there is overflows in me, and I hug the beautiful brunette woman, sobbing every regret among the river of tears I cry.

"The sun is too good to be true—
I must be seeing things today
Cause everything keeps happening
In the most peculiar way"

"It may be unbelievable
But it happened just that way
You came into my life—
And now I want you to stay"

The brightest rays of sunshine permeate our Sunday morning vista, above our Garden of Lost Hope, where we tend the planting of the Seventh Rose. This seventh rosebush is a sapling now, to be cared for by the sun and the rain, until there are white roses in bloom, to mark the purity of our final calling. Though we have not yet fully discussed it, I think we all can feel the finality of what has happened to us this weekend, though we never had any plans for it to be so. I was the first who brought this horrible thing into being, this destroyer of lives, be they innocent or deserving. But it is written that *"Deserve's got nothin' to do with it,"* as to what comeuppance is overdue, and we truly all have it coming, when we will have our great and terrible day in the sun.

Chelsea and Simone look so adorable, so cute helping me tend my garden, both on their knees—Simone in a pair of jeans and college T Shirt hugging her magnificent bosom, a sight to cause wonder in any human being, for whatever reason plagues their sorry, sinful soul of curiosity. Whenever she stands up from the weeding of the garden, I am sure not to miss it, but then I have to look away in favor of preserving her dignity.

Though she claims no ill effects from it, i.e. back pain or shyness, I know that the years of stares and comments and rude, heartless snickering and laughter has taken its toll, adding to the heavy resentment I know she already feels toward other people. How she can stand her chosen profession baffles me to no end, though she has been drawn away from lecturing by choice, with research and publication her focus. *"The Road to Tenure,"* she says, *"is paved with published work, but eventually that road always ends, and there is suddenly a river gorge between where you are and where you want to be. And then you have to build a bridge to the other side, and this bridge is your academic masterpiece. Your greatest work."* But why Tenure at a university, Simone, when I know that sometimes the sight and smell of their phoniness, fear and hypocrisy makes you sick to your stomach? This resentment she has, this began when she was only 14, when her mother saw that what was happening to her body hearkened from the farms and fields of Mexico, bypassing her own curves even at such a tender young age. Simone was a prodigy, so to speak; that she was already a triple D at 14 years old, with a bullseye painted on them, where Mama Coronado threw darts every chance she got. By the time Simone was out of that house and living with her grandmother, she was convinced that her gargantuan breasts were "bloated bags of sin," and that her curvy body was painfully botched and misshapen.

But this, she overcame, having gotten away from Jenny Coronado's poison, in time to learn that her body and her demure personality worked together like magic to cast a spell on everybody in her new school and beyond. A year of worship from her peers and teachers did the proverbial trick, until the beginning of the confident, self-assured woman began to emerge like a flower under a full moon. From a childhood the grandmother never knew, merged with the breast worshipping stares and smiles and comments, Simone Coronado fell in love with her own bosom, until she herself had a fetish for them; her own, and other women's as well. I know that nothing lights her body up as to have another woman's breasts in her mouth, especially one extremely younger than she, or a woman old enough to be the mother of a twenty one year old girl. This, from the way her own mother deflowered her nipples when she was only twelve, and the way she was made to suckle her own mother's bosom long enough to bring her mother to full orgasm in the evening day. Of this particular mother-daughter perversion, only Chelsea does not know, but Simone and I are of lengthy and powerful acquaintance.

But Simone's shapeliness is complete, truly Amazonian in nature, born to near completion when she was only 16, a year before she had to leave her home after the brutal fight with her mother. Jenny Coronado's pleasure had been to make Simone understand that sometimes there were private needs that had to be met, private and pensive punishments that had to be undertaken, where she would stand behind her daughter in front of the mirror, with her aroused groin pressed against Simone's very wide young hips, those hips from the Latin motherline, that Mexican grandmother she never knew. A sight that used to keep Jenny occupied many a night, as she dreamed up weeks in advanced how to have her overdeveloped daughter naked in front of her and weeping. When this nakedness was achieved every so often, she would be behind her daughter in front of the mirror after sunset, when the other children were at mass or a movie, when the husband was working overtime into the night, she would be pressed hard against the middle of her daughter's big, young ass, watching her daughter lift and suck her own nipples, telling her to *suck 'em like you mean it*...until Jenny could do nothing but begin to slam herself in full flesh clapping sound against her daughter's backside, watching her daughter nurse herself in the mirror, slamming against her until the movements were no longer voluntary and she had to cry out once, and steady herself against the violent trembling that would not cease in her body. This, Simone endured for at least a year before other cruelties took their toll, and their fight was brutal enough to have her removed from her mother's home forever.

"I didn't even know I had dyke blood until I started lecturing," her professor friend Ms. Baker says to her. Her short curly do is fried, her legs are spindly in her short blue gray skirt. " I can tell you cause I know you know what I'm talking about. I'm married with a teenage son and two grown daughters, and I'm telling you sometimes I can't keep my eyes off my own daughter's friends. And these girls that come in here with these tight jeans and tight shirts. Sometimes my husband thinks I'm horny for him when really I'm fantasizing about these girls, Simone. What the Hell is that, Simone, I'm not even gay. I've never even been with a woman."

"What about your own daughter," Simone says. "You ever wanted to... you know."

"You mean, sex with my own—well, I don't really think of my own daughters like that. Maybe they're not my type, I don't know. But I tell you I have spent many a morning in a long, hot bathtub thinking about this one girl I saw with my oldest daughter. She had long dark hair and smoldering eyes. And when she turned around her ass just went on forever. I could NOT stop thinking about it. Everybody's always talking about cougars and young men but I'm telling you I would take one of these young girls over my knee and burn the skin off her little fat ass if I had the chance."

"If you had the opportunity, I mean...if one of these girls were to hit on you, say for a grade or something, would you do it?"

"The Professor's Peach. A kiss for a grade. Every one of us would take a bite of that one, Honey. If it looked sweet enough. I know somebody who teaches in another school, who is a member of something called a 'Mother Daughter Exchange Club.' It is high class and highly classified. So much so that they'd probably pass a lie detector if you asked 'em about it.

"A mother-daugh—"

"That's right. They get together with other Moms in these exclusive, really high end neighborhoods, you know. Those golf club looking neighborhoods with the brick castles a half mile apart from one another. The goal is to meet other mothers and daughters for a weekend of "fun." And sometimes the Moms will go off alone with each other's daughter. Usually a trip somewhere or cooking or golf or sight seeing or shopping or spa or whatever. And this friend told me she was invited to meet someone's daughter, and if she had fun she could bring her own daughter next time. Just something to kind of broaden their horizons, so to speak. Help them bond with other mothers and daughters, gain some experiences, maybe learn something about themselves. Well, I'm breaking a solemn oath by acknowledging this out loud, Simone, but she told me her and that girl exchanged a lot more than phone numbers that weekend. She said the girl was only 17, and that young girl was on her nipples like a vacuum cleaner. She said the orgasm it gave her… ruined her life forever."

I watch Simone's demurity in black ponytail braid, wondering how it is that she is not aware of being so extremely beautiful. *A face and a body to match*, I'll say to her sometimes, usually when I catch her unguarded; cooking or cleaning our house on Mountain View Road, or even doing the laundry of her two demonic companions. I remember her being shocked to tears that night seven years ago, when I told her what I had done.

It was only twenty four hours after I met Simone that it happened. That the spirit came unto me in the evening day.

"Josie, you've been stabbing me in the back since I got here. You asked me to come here, remember?"

"Wait a minute, I asked you to come? You practically invited yourself— what was I supposed to do? I felt sorry for you. 'Josie I can't afford housing this semester. I don't have anywhere to staaaay.' Meowing at me like a fucking ally cat. Thank God you're finally getting the fuck out of here."

"You asked me to come live with you, Josie," I say, a tear already forming. My vision is hazy from it but I know I can't blink in front of this girl.

"Yeah, I asked you. After you told me that sob story. 'Oh, Josie, my momma didn't have enough money to help me get here. The dorms were full and I don't have money to rent a place, I guess I'll have to sleep in my caaar.' I lent you money for your books too, didn't I? You still haven't paid me back either."

"Josie, how can you stand here and say that? You know you said don't worry about it, I've got this."

"Yeah, and how's that not a loan? Just because I said don't worry about it, I meant don't worry about it that day. I need my fucking 500 dollars back."

"I—I'll have it as soon as I can."

"Yeah, right. I'll believe that when I see it. They said this was gonna happen."

"Who said it?"

"My friend warned me about you, that's who said it. They told me to watch out for your sneaky Pocahontas looking Indian ass—they told me, 'Josie she's gonna suck you dry if you let her in and then she's gonna put a knife in your back.'"

Josie, whence forth cometh such bitter lies as this? Is it because your friends talked about my appearance for so long before they grew tired of me? Is it because everybody you know asks about that pretty *Latin* or *Indian* girl you stay with? Is it because your boyfriend said the words *"Your roommate is smokin' hot. What's her name? Raven? I'm sorry Babe, the guys say she's the hottest thing on this campus…"* Did your face go red with humiliation and rage when you went to the bathroom in his frat house to look in the mirror? Is that why for these last three weeks you've been treating me like a dog?

"Josie, what have I ever done to you? Why do you treat me like this?"

"Like what?"

"Like some stray fleabag you found in an alley somewhere."

"Well, if the shoe fits. Dyke."

"What?"

"You heard me. You think I haven't noticed the way you stare at Chandra's ass like you want to take a bite out of it—I told her and she almost vomited."

I can only stand there with my mouth almost wide open.

"Where is this coming from, Josie? I thought you were my friend."

"I thought you were my friend," she says, Tori Spelling-like mouth twisted in mocking. *"That's what I'm talking about. You're clingy and needy and weird. Look, I know what you want from me now, Raven. But Honey, I don't swing that way. And I'll tell you something else, too. I'm gonna have your thieving ass brought up on charges."*

"Charges? For what?"

"For stealing, Bitch. What else?"

"Stealing? I never stole—"

"For stealing my five hundred dollars I loaned you."

"I didn't steal that money, you gave it to me."

"Tell it to a judge. I hope your new roommate likes living with a fucking thief. Oh and uh... don't let the door hit you on the way out."

I turn to walk out, to run away with my big black suitcase, to wheel it down the hall to the dorm elevator like an airline slut who was just thrown out of one of her college boyfriend's dorm rooms, when the most pathetic and vulnerable place of who I am rises up and turns me around without my consent and forces me to say with a straight face *"I just wanted to be your friend, Josie. Why would you do this to me?"*

"Because you are so fucking pathetic you make me sick to my stomach, that's why. I'm tired of your funny Indian girl face and your greasy black hair. Sometimes you look cross-eyed and you smell like rotten peaches for some reason. And I'm sick of this fake-assed, goody two shoes act, when I know underneath is a whore so fuckin' slutty that she would blow half the professors in this school for a place to stay. You're too old to be a sophomore anyway, you reek of poverty and failure and bad luck—you're like a human stain that I just want to wash off my skin before I get a fucking disease from you. You're like some... some sickening swamp witch who likes to cast a spell on people and then suck the life out of them. I

can't stand the sight of you anymore. I can't stand the smell of you anymore. I can't stand to have your stinking hair in my nose anymore. You, literally, make me want to vomit, and I never want to see your ugly, Mexican Indian slut looking ass again until it's on the other side of a courtroom. You should curse the day your Indian momma shitted you into this world, because if it's the last thing I ever do I swear I'm going to make you pay. I'm suing your ass for a thousand dollars now, Bitch. Now get the fuck out of here."

For the first time in my young life, hearkened from Cherokee County down to Martin County and Old Mill Road, to the college campus in Greensboro where I am, to my place in the universe in front of this 20 year old girl, I feel the lifetime of bad luck and abuse—the lifetime of broken dreams—form into an energy of otherworldly origin, and I suddenly cannot see clearly as who I was a moment ago, as though I am having a stroke. But in this darkness of being, I feel the boldness of a booming presence, that forms the word I know as *Molock* in my brain, and I turn to lock the dorm room of this late afternoon. When I turn back around, my hand is in a fist, and I swing it into her face like Tom Cruise in *Far and Away*, feeling the softness of her nose crumble. She covers her face and screams into her hands, something about *Indians and dykes*, and when I see her face again it is covered in blood from her nose to her chin while she says *My father's gonna put you in jail for ten years you fucking bitch!* But before the thought can fully register, I take her head in my hands, holding it there while she pushes at me, then I punch her again in the nose, making her back away like a she-lion hit with pepper spray, her hands now bloody with the red river from her nose. Then, as if I've done it before, I get behind her and put my arm around her neck while she kicks and struggles, squeezing first her neck and jaw, then repositioning with such skill that I am amazed—then I feel the bone in her wind pipe against my forearm as I listen to her choke and struggle to breathe. She seems as weak as a kitten in my arms as I hold on for at least five turns of the clock, until her body is so limp that I realize I can't hold her upright anymore, and I let her fall lifeless to the floor. With her blood on my arm and all over her pink polo pullover, I look into her eyes and listen at her mouth, and it seems to me that whatever she was has departed the earthly plane forever.

In a place far beyond where fear resides, I stand up calmly. Too numb to be nervous, too far gone to be afraid, I locate two trash bags from the kitchen space, enjoying the silky smooth disconnect they have from the others. Before too long, everything I own—clothes, underwear, hairdryer, makeup, shoes, all dead souvenirs of my time, I empty the suitcase of it into the large trash bags. Then I strip the pink blouse and pretty white shorts and pink thong and pink bikini bra off of her spindly white body, throwing them into the bags with the rest of the trash. It is not much effort to fold her 110 lbs on its skinny side into my suitcase, and zip her body (already grown cold) up tight.

What gives me the right, to the pleasure of discovery! Who do I think I am, knowing, understanding that I am a fish that was choked in muddy waters, which was gathered and thrown by the hand of God into the depths of clarity, where there is only clean and clear water to breathe! These are the waters of contempt—hatred for mothers and their beautiful daughters. I swim these waters of discontent at home, down the hallway of the dorm room in late afternoon, the halls and elevators so blessedly empty, as I push the suitcase and two black garbage bags of my life and death through the lobby of this fine building, hardly raising an eye of curiosity among what few students there are left on a Saturday afternoon, going through the doors with no help at all, pushing my heavy load to the nearby dumpster, where I toss the two black trash bags inside. Now, in the breeze of late afternoon, out for all to see, I pull my suitcase behind me like that slutted stewardess outcast, toward the piece of junk that masquerades as my car nearby.

The blood might run, I hear. *Put it in the trunk*—so I open the trunk in the Carolina afternoon, a sight all too familiar on a college campus—a hopeless young woman sliding a heavy suitcase into the trunk of her seventeen hundred dollar used car.

*T*he closing of the trunk lid closes my vision. I see Simone over the grave of Josephine Joyner, the pretty white girl who disappeared seven years ago, who nobody claims to have seen. I expected posters and news stories of her floating and chattering on every news broadcast, bulletin board and telephone pole—for her rich parents to start a national campaign called *Find the Bitch*, but it never happened. Not a single person at the school mentioned her roommate, because the ones who had remembered me had never thought me important enough to mention, believing I had been long gone before I actually was. I wonder if Simone can feel the spirit of Josephine Joyner the way I can, as she pulls the weeds from her grave. Does she remember the sound she made that early evening here in this yard, when I unzipped the suitcase in front of her? Can she remember the fear in her heart, the pain that it flowed to the rest of her body, when I told her that I had to do it because she deserved to die? Can Simone remember the discorporation of her own spirit from her flesh, as she watched me dig the first grave under cloak of night?

I stroll over to where she is, watching her tend the garden like a house momma. Wondering if she can feel the spirits of the dead.

"Can you remember her name?"

"Josephine," she says. "And I'm sorry baby, but for some reason… I'm glad she's dead." A pause, to hear what message tells this mountain breeze around us.

"Me too. I think maybe I'm bothered because I *don't* feel anything. That maybe I should feel guilty, even though I really don't."

Simone weeds and turns the soil over Josephine, then she moves on to Diane Vaughn, and the pink roses grown from her space. "How can you feel guilty for something you were called to do?" she says. "The same way that a soldier in battle pulls the trigger without remorse—that's the way you pulled the trigger on these sinful lives. These women were judged, Raven. They received their comeuppance that was overdue."

"But what did they do really? I mean, what did they do to deserve what they got from me?"

"From you? What the Sam Hill have you got to do with anything?"

"Huh?"

"What did Abraham Lincoln have to do with the path he walked? From that log cabin to a term in Congress? What did Martin Luther King have to do with the path he walked? From being the son of a poor black Georgia preacher, to the leader of the greatest victory against segregation in U.S. history at that time in Montgomery, Alabama? Huh? What did you have to do with the path you walked, Raven Moon? From the mountains of Cherokee County North Carolina, to a college campus east, and the killing of a woman in cold blood? And you have the nerve to believe that what these women got... they got from you, me, or Chelsea?"

I look at Chelsea over by the sixth and seventh graves, still planting the white rose seedlings in the ground. When she is done, she begins to weed Barbara Raynor's grave.

"No matter what you think they've done to quote, '*deserve*' what came to them, we've all dropped a vase on the hard kitchen floor. None of us are perfect—there're pieces of our so-called morality shattered from the crib to the grave—and so many of these pretty flower vases we tossed into the air like dummies, or we just hauled back and threw 'em on the floor like fools. God is no respecter of persons, Rae, it rains on the just and the unjust. Whatever is going to happen to you in the future was going to happen anyway. You couldn't have stopped this if you tried. And as for these women, how easy has it been for us to abduct, torture, rape and murder them?"

"I don't know... easy, I guess."

"No. It's been too easy. Every time I felt the life slip out of one of 'em, they carried some of my pain to Hell with 'em."

"And that's what you say, huh? To Hell with them?"

"From your lips to God's ears," she says. "Fucking bitches. I hope they all rot and burn in the stinking pits of Hell." Simone spits on grave number one, returning to her duties at number two. Both spaces are joined by two rather large and dense white and pink rose bushes, already in full and lovely bloom for the summer. "You know what I forgot to do? I forgot to take a good, long piss on Number Seven's grave this morning."

As I scan the line of roses from pink to white to pink again, laid and stretched over the joined wooden crosses they hide, I imagine what tulips might add to their little scene, and I find it thoroughly impossible to associate this rose garden with what lies beneath the soil.

Suddenly, we are captured by a most unfamiliar sound. The noise of a *car* slows down from our isolated road and drifts into our yard, apart from where we can see. Together, we gather what courage there is left between us and wander to the front of the house. There, we see a beautiful blonde teenager, reminiscent of Chelsea but at least 10 years younger, driving the same white SUV I saw on this road just two days ago, and that Chelsea and me abandoned out past the other side of Black Mountain this morning. But as my instincts decree, there is no hint of amazement in my breathing, nor the slightest tint of shock on my expression.

The girl gets out of the car in a shape that references her mother's to the point of thickness at the hips and breasts under her gray Boone Senior High School Sweatshirt. "Hi", she says, accent so southern, face so pretty and friendly. Ass so bubbled in her jeans. Teen tits so fat inside her bra. Every part of me wants to jump her and bite and suck and fuck her with blood dripping down my chin. Where do these desires come from? Where on earth are they going to? In me, they originate in my groin, to rise up through my stomach into every muscle that moves me, until sometimes I want to tear my clothes off and howl at the moon in false lycanthropy.

"That's some body you got there, sweetheart."

"No way. You're the one that's gorgeous. I eat like a pig and you can see it."

"We can see it looks cute."

"Thank you. I'm sorry to bother you with this, but my Mom's been missing since Friday."

"Really?"

"We used to drive this road sometimes when she came down here to see grandma. They don't call it Mountain View for nothing do they? We found Mom's car abandoned near the woods on the highway."

"Out on 40, near us?" Chelsea says demurely, wiping the hair away from her mouth in humble cuteness and cute humility.

"No, it was a good 25 miles down east. The area was so deserted. We had to jump her car to get it started. We think she hitched a ride somewhere and just hasn't showed up yet. Mom was like that. She was so friendly, always willing to go too far helping somebody. But she could have at least called."

"Maybe she'll call by the end of the day."

"I hope so. I'm stopping at all the houses around here to see if anybody saw her car go by."

"Does your family live near here?" Simone says, the concern on her face a touching sight.

"We live all the way up in Boone. My Mom's mother lives here. One of those kinda uppity neighborhoods with the old brick houses that look like banks. She lives on Carmen Elizabeth Lane. Pretentious enough, Grandma? I like your house better. It feels like paradise out here."

"We can't compete with Carmen Elizabeth, though can we?" Simone says.

"Grandma's always looking down her nose because when somebody's not going to Harvard like Dad and Grand Dad. Funny thing is, she doesn't even like him. She says *look, if you're father can be successful, anybody can.* He's at a convention all the way in Raleigh for a whole week. I don't even think he cares that Mom's missing. I came down here with a friend, and we couldn't believe our eyes when we saw Mom's truck out there on I-40, on the other side of the highway."

"Where's your friend?"

"She waited with me for an hour until Triple A came. I made her late for work. I think she was pissed off but I don't give a crap. It's like Hey, you... my MOM VANISHED INTO THE DAMNED TWILIGHT ZONE and all she cares about is her pissy little job at Abercrombie's. Maybe I should have got my brother to bring me, but he acts like he doesn't care either."

"Well, have you called the police?"

"I called yesterday, and they were like..." She makes a fake yawning sound.

"Well, I don't know what *we* can do, but, if we see or hear anything... can you leave us your address and phone number?"

"Let me get something to write with—I'll give you my cell number."

The three of us watch her tired, hopeless fumbling for a slip of paper, and the futility with which she writes her cell number for us to never even look at.

"I'm sorry to hear she's missing," I say, rubbing the small of her back and her waist while we walk back to the white SUV, having to resist giving her an inappropriate kiss on her cheek.

"Good luck finding your Mom," Chelsea says.

"It's been nice meeting you anyway," says Simone. "Godspeed, honey."

We wave at her with such sweet and melancholy friendliness as she backs away. She seems sorry that she bothered us with her troubles.

"Should I?"

"You should," Chelsea says.

"You will," says Simone, the three of us strolling towards the back of the house.

The Sunday afternoon sun burns my fervent desire, to feel the body of Amanda Hall's daughter against mine, then to see her in full HD, fully Humped and Dumped. As to whether or not my desire burns to her death and demise—I do not know. All I do know is that there must be reconciliation between my body's craving and fulfillment, until what must be done is done. So even in the midst of a whirlwind of righteous song and dance coming from the TV Chelsea is mesmerized by, the charismatic church and the voice of faith and finance, I gather my phone to make a call I have been resisting for an hour. Whether or not Alison Hall will be fucked here or there is neither, of course—but whether it happens *at all* is what matters, and whether it is today, tomorrow, next week or next year. But in my spirit—the turning of this wheel is set in motion, and the completion of it is set in stone.

"It doesn't matter who you are," the preacher says. *"It doesn't matter what you've done. All that matters... is the Cross. All that matters, is the blood he shed for you. All that matters, is his resurrection from the tomb. All that matters is that he forgave you for everything you've ever done, and everything you're ever going to do, for every sin, for every shortcoming, for every moment, every day, every month, every year of inadequacy— every decade of sin and shortcoming, for an accumulated lifetime of immorality and abomination, there is the blood of Jesus Christ, and the sacrifice He made on the Cross at Calvary, and the life he laid down for you. He laid that life down for you because he loved you, because he wanted you to have the gift of Salvation, the gift of righteousness, the gift of eternal life—the gift of prosperity on this side of the grave—prosperity in your finances, prosperity in your relationships, and prosperity in your walk with him...*

"Some of you have erred from the faith. Some of you are like lost sheep that have gone astray. But there's a reason that Jesus told the parable of the certain man who had two sons. One of the sons began to get too big for his father's house—too full of himself to accept his father's rule. So one day—this son called for his inheritance, so that he could strike out on his own. So, his father, being a loving, kind and understanding father—gave him all that he had coming to him. And the son left. This son went out into the world, to a far away country. Having the time of his life—living it up— spending money like it was water—no longer having to obey his father's rule. But one day, the money ran out. And the young man fell on hard times. It got so bad that he had to take a job feeding the pigs for a farmer,

and he was so hungry that even the slop he gave the pigs began to look good to him. And he began to remember. In his father's house, he enjoyed the finest food. The finest clothes. There were servants to tend to his every want and need. He lived the life of leisure and luxury, and love from his father. So, the boy came to his senses. And he went home to his father's house. And when the father saw his son a great distance away, coming toward the house—he ran out as fast as he could toward his son, and he embraced him in complete and total joy...

"Now, the older brother—the one who didn't leave—was jealous and angry. He got mad at his father because he welcomed his brother back with open arms. Because the father prepared a feast and celebration for his youngest son's return. But the father said to the oldest son—you are always with me. All that I have is yours. But your brother... son, your brother was dead... and is alive again."

My lust for Amanda Hall's daughter hearkens Adina Moses, and the planting of the third rose in our garden. None of the rose garden bushes are red, as this connotates love and devotion, but only the elegance and purity of pink and white, to honor the like manner of His calling.

Adina walks in from the mall to the storefront in long, curly black hair and big droopy eyes and a tanned face very pretty and goofy just the same. When

The Mountaineers

I watch her look through the rack of T-shirts, I see the sad look in her big, dark eyes—and the somber spirit for me to absorb. I condescend to her, telling her how pretty she is in fake tone, so she'll believe I'm just being nice. *I'll be getting off at seven—meet me here and we'll go get something to eat... Adina, right? That's beautiful.*

Before long, Adina and me are drinking milkshakes at Sonic because the food court was just too damned crowded.

I have to be honest with you, she says. *The only reason I came back is because you're so beautiful...*

Thank you. And can I be honest? The only reason I asked you back is because I'm so attracted to you.

Really? Aw...that's sweet.

Its more salty than sweet, Baby. Believe me.

This eighteen year old girl laughs with such good natured confidence that I lose my compassion for her, saying *Let's get out of these lights, huh?*

Fine by me.

How late can you stay out?

My Mom calls me at 10 'oclock every night.

Oh.

I guess I'm gonna miss her call tonight.

And the desire I have for this girl is suddenly mixed with cold judgment and warm resentment—the coming together of these two winds—to begin the turning and swirling downward from the clouds of lore—the growing storm of gore that is my life and time.

I'm not just a dyke. I'm an Indian dyke.

Or Native American lesbian, if you prefer.

Down the street, just a little ways from the bright Sonic lights, to where the nighttime trees stand in darkest waiting. An empty lot. A health care facility, I believe it is… near the hospital.

I hardly even know my Dad, she says. *It seems like he was home about every other weekend.*

What does your Dad do?

He works for Wells Fargo. Travels all the time. I think he's still trying to impress my Mom or something. They were gonna get a divorce but it never happened.

Any brothers and sisters?

I've got one little sister in the ninth grade. She's actually the pretty version of me.

You're the pretty version of you, Baby.

Thanks, but you wouldn't say that if you saw my sister. Her name's Athena. See, she's even got the better name—"

Suddenly, I see the shock on her face appear, in a shower of white milkshake splattered, as her eyes widen and her voice is choked by the thin white rope being held and pulled around her neck from behind.

I thought she'd never shut the fuck up, Chelsea says. *Fake assed shyness. If you were shy you wouldn't fuckin' be here.*

Please let—

Her voice is killed in the choking, as the rope is pulled just tight enough to make her breathing rough and labored.

Aww… what did you think was gonna happen? You thought you were going to share a sweet finger fuck with a pretty girl you met at JC Penney? Something to hold secret—to give you power in your little life—in your resentful little heart? Something to hold over your boyfriend's head?

Over your boyfriend's cock?

Laughter.

Awww… don't cry, Baby. I promise its gon' feel good to you.

Mmmph…

Hmm?

"mmmbrrrmm…

Loosen it a bit, Chelsea.

My Chelsea loosens the rope just enough to allow speech only, but no pretense of escape. None.

I need to be home at 10:00… so I can take… take my mother's call—

You're gonna be talkin' to your Momma in Hell, Bitch, Chelsea says. And the rope tightens again, so she can feel the flames of Hell licking at her feet.

I get out of the car, top light conveniently disabled in my old forest green Camry. There is no Moon. The stars are plentiful. When I open the trunk, there is a light. A beacon of dark hope for one.

Young Professor Cory stiffens in her used model Cadillac paid for. Disbelieving. Unbelieving. Unable to accept what has been. What must be.

Young Professor Cory. A brunette beauty with the world on a string. About to pick up those proverbial shears—and cut her future away. She sees the Indian girl she knows at the trunk. Shining the light intentionally. Unintentionally. Taking a bag out of the trunk. The professor shakes her head—unable to comprehend the blonde in the back seat of the Camry, who must by now be choking a young girl she has never met to death.

The Professor tucks her lips and gets out of the car. In awe of the small city darkness. The isolation. Daring not to pray to the God she believes in. Professor Cory hurries across the dark parking lot, so afraid she's going to be seen. But still unyielding to the eyes of the Lord, beholding the evil and the good. She arrives at the Camry, which looks black in the country city dark, opening the door and getting inside, in fear unlike anything she's ever known.

Oh, yeah—it's on now Baby, says the blonde. Pulling the rope so tight that the girl makes a sickening, straining, groaning sound, her hands instinctively at the thin white rope pulled so tight. Simone looks at the glee, the calm delight on Chelsea's face, then she looks in the front seat at me taking off my clothes like I'm going to shit on the front seat, watching me slide and jiggle out of my pants and underwear as casually as if I'm changing into a bikini at the beach. Then she watches me hurry into my dildo panties—the black leather bikini bottoms with the fake cock already attached good and tight. After I slide it on, I am a naked chick with a dick, and a beautiful Indian face and long hair as black as the dark side of the Moon.

As we approach Armageddon, the end of human history, there is no longer a need to turn a blind eye—to turn a deaf ear to the sights and sounds of innocence lost. Rather, look! Behold the judgment of mankind's darkest hour! Behold the sins which bring judgment, upon the souls of men. Behold, the Indian Woman of Straw, who straddles the girl, with the girl's shirt raised up and black nippled breasts out, and asks her questions about her family and her schooling; tormenting her with an occasional slap or hard bite to her lip or hard twist to her inch long exposed nipples! *Look at the meatballs on them titties*, the blonde says in vitriol, acid burning lust, watching me agree so alike in kind! Rubbing my own nipples to hers, lit up by the lovely novelty of such large nipples, then finally telling the girl to suck my nipple into her mouth, watching the tears and the wetness dampen my breasts from her face. Behold! The Indian Woman of Straw! As she now unstraddles the poor girl and takes the girl's pants and underwear off, taking the knife from Chelsea and cutting, tearing, ripping her t-shirt from her body! The girl trembles now, be it fear or the nighttime air. Behold, the Indian Woman of Straw, who opens up the 18 year old virgin's creamy white legs, nearly darkened to a golden yellow by an ethnic heritage from a grandfather she never knew. Yes, the black blood burns in your white body girl, does it not? Does it give you the jiggly hips I saw in your jeans this very evening, when you thought that I was your friend? Does this black blood give your eyes their dark beauty, is it the soul you project in white woman's glory? Have you been ashamed of the blackness hidden in your family tree, white girl? Is it the strength of hidden blackness which girds you up, at this moment when you are about to die? Behold, the exotic virgin, neck held by rope, with her legs reluctantly open, if only in pleading for her life! Behold, the exotic woman of straw, her rope loosened just enough that we may hear the scream inside the car, when the member slides so deep and gracefully in! What Momma is this that you call for— she can have no solace for thee! *Simone, take your clothes off baby, every stitch.* Behold, the Amazon Woman of Straw! The young college professor, who teaches religion and women to wayward minds! Behold, as she takes off her clothes in as much of a hurry as she can, her face so sullen with worry! Behold the body of a goddess—breasts too big for her form, played upon the highest key, a glimmering glistening storm! In awe, see the woman remove every stitch of cloth, for this abomination to perform!

Chelsea, switch with her... take the rope Simone... hold it good and tight... the Amazon is on her knees in the back seat, the rope held so strong in her fists. Lost, afraid, but feeling her past rise up like a ghost from the mist. In this renewed energy comes frustration, powered into anger, a lust burning deep in the midst. In the paradise of pain and agony, the Amazon woman now exists. The sight of her body, so impossibly curved, lights such a fire in me that cannot be named, but only described by what colors they aspire. Behold, the Blonde Woman of Straw, as she takes off her clothes, burning in blue and black fire! With inherent instinct, with Divine knowledge of fore thought—I am amazed when my Chelsea starts to tend to my Simone, with one hand down below from behind her— causing Simone's face to wash over with intense, melancholy shock, looking Chelsea in the eye—with Chelsea's other hand free to massage those great hanging breasts in squeezing and agony—*pull it Simone,* I say, *kill this bitch so I can cum...*

Behold, the Indian Woman of Straw! As she pumps and grinds like a machine into the dying virgin, her nerves fed by the sound of her choking, and the feel of her twitching, dying form! Behold, the Blonde Woman of Straw! Who is on her knees beside the other, tending to the groin with one hand and breasts with the other hand, while she whispers in her ear *kill her baby, kill her, pull it tight baby, pull it tight...* behold, the Amazon Woman of Straw! The brunette who hath taken a part of perversion, as she pulls the rope so tight around the virgin's neck as to defy reason, until the girl's eyes blow big in her head. Her tongue is blue, and I must descend, before her bruised body is dead! Behold, as I climb this mountain, concentrating, driving, pounding myself in until the member is a part of me, and I am capable of the Witch's Intercourse. Behold the blonde woman's shock, when the brunette woman convulses suddenly, with a gush of warmth in the palm of her hand down below, and the blonde knows it is that rarest of female chasms, where there is water of mystery pushed out as a sign! As the brunette grabs the rope for dear life—to survive the rush through her body, I am the phallic form of my feminine self, and I can see nothing but a purple haze, and hear the voice of an Indian woman's scream in the dark.

In the aftermath of trauma, my vision returns to me, and I see a blonde holding a trembling, shaking brunette as naked as she, and I feel myself on top of a woman in the front seat, whose body is as cold as a cherry tree in winter.

The houses in Amanda Hall's neighborhood are too close together, as greed over beauty decides, giving the impression of neighborhood construction economics on display, and the corporate benefits of urban sprawl. The Sunday afternoon neighborhood is filled to bursting with cars and kids driving and playing and rolling and walking the asphalt to nowhere. The perverted orderliness of working middle class suburbia is deliberate; every house ranging from beige to gray, from the class two cottages with windows marking the roof rooms up to the class three McMansions, and their true second floors proudly and properly boxed in, and a pseudo third floor with those self same roof rooms apparent. I notice that there is practically no space between the houses, big or small, with lawns hardly big enough to give the moms a good sweat who mow them.

Every little landscaped plot of flowers is being weeded or watered, every shrub or bush seems to be trimmed, every other driveway has a group of adults standing with their hands on their hips or their arms folded, all talking about one thing and thinking another, or how they would like to swap husbands and wives for just one night, and then live to tell the tale. The driveways and streets are lined with cars so similar to my own; so reminiscent of the Pride of Life, and the satisfaction of achievement through thrift and labor. And they all walk and visit and smile in the joy of accomplishment, the victory of Sunday afternoon leisure, and the right to see and be seen. The curbs seem to be running with soap and water, from the lengthy and sudsy washings of the new cars and trucks in the driveways.

I am amazed at the number of women in form fitting T-shirts and modern skintight mini shorts in every color. T shirts and mini shorts seem to be the uniform of the day for the daughters and wives who help their daddys and husbands wash the cars, or who stand with the water hoses alone at the bushes and summer wildflowers near the front of the house. The neighborhood is a teeming mass of suburban life; people scurrying about as if preparing for the last days. All this activity reduces me to a sudden shyness, until I remember that they cannot see who I am behind the windows of this new Camry, my sunglasses, and a face exotic enough for them to die for. A force unknown, unfamiliar even to myself rolls me along, until I see the big, white SUV in the driveway of the two story house on Riley Forest Lane. The SUV sits in the driveway beside a charcoal gray Tundra truck, too magnificent to interest most women, though I think if country Chelsea could see it she would have something to say.

A deep breath and another glance around the manmade paradise, to make me queasy to my stomach. May God send an angel with a flaming sword through this ridiculous place and burn the life right out of it and send their deserving souls to Hell for thinking that they have it made, that they have done something worthwhile with their lives! That they live in a place even remotely associated with beauty, as if a fountain somewhere in Europe can be called beautiful with Old Faithful, or the nighttime city lights can be called beautiful with the stars of Heaven. Sunglasses off, thoroughly sickened to my Indian stomach, I step out of the Camry and into the neighborhood street—suddenly struck by the lines of violence running from each home and into the ground, somewhere along a hidden energy line beneath my feet. Sometimes I scare myself, when I imagine that people's motivations—their actions, even the consequences of those actions, are all controlled and destined by God. But I know it was God's only error in judgment that expelled mankind from Paradise—this was our Free Will—our freedom to choose right from wrong, as it was Eve who sinned by choice, and then her husband Adam, who plunged every generation—from the Garden of Antiquity, to the Garden of Gethsemane, to that by the river of blood, the Garden of Armageddon—every generation hath their motivations, their actions of free will under a Divine Curse, so that they sit in hospital wards and jail cells, and the edge of their children's graves, knowing that they could not have chosen a different path in a thousand years of wandering trial and error.

Oh, yes, my dear Simone—what do I have to do with this dark path that I have taken? Where does the Will of Man end, and the Will of God begin?

"Are you Raven Moon? Come on in. Damn, my sister said you were hot. You look like that girl in Rush Hour 2. Even *better*, I think."

All I can do is smile, wondering why the 21 year old boy's enthusiasm is so disarming.

"Is your father home?"

"Naw. That's his truck out there, though. I took 'im to work this morning so I could... take care of a little business."

I wish it were possible to not give in to the woman in me, and become a mousy little girl, so grateful for the hassling attention of some young dog fool in heat. But his attention works its own magic, raising my self esteem to a level higher than where it was when I came in.

"You came here to see Alison, right?"

"Yes, is she home?"

"She's upstairs—let me go—you know what, why don't I take you up there? She's probably on the dadgum phone. Come on."

Come *own* is the sound he makes, pure southern small town accent, impossible to hide.

"My name's Aiden, by the way." He extends a timid, white hand, and I feel the athletic strength in his muscles, born from natural ability and two years as a backup quarterback in high school.

Aidan Hall. A name his coaches surely must have begged God to bless when they laid their little heads down to sleep, grieving to see the boy blossom into a star, which he never did. Was there a black boy on the team, traveling between fourth wide receiver, backup safety and third string QB, named Bellamy Smartnick, that had a long distance sling shot for an arm and legs like a gazelle in tights? Did Bellamy quit football to run track in his senior year, because for some reason, he never seemed to get any playing time on offense, and was awkward and slight as a safety? What if Aidan Hall (the boy who's bony ass is in my face right now up these stairs), what if his name had been Bellamy Smartnick? Would his white mediocrity have ever seen the inside of a helmet? What if Bellamy's name had been Aidan Hall? What NCAA Division I team would he have lead to the National Championship?

Aidan Hall! Lead me to thy sister's fervent, fertile Bosom!

"Aaay," he says, knocking impolitely on her door. "Cain't you get off the phone for five minutes girl? You got company."

I hear the phantom creaking of floorboards under her second story beige carpet. When the door opens, I see the younger version of the woman I buried.

Sunday drifts along the current of time, until evening has crossed over into night. The two of us have enjoyed each other's company through the remainder of the day, such as it is, one looking for something, or someone to fill the empty space left behind by a mother's sudden disappearance; the other—to ease the two fold guilt and frustration. First—of having reached out from Abomination to deprive this poor girl of her mother. And second, that Chelsea Baxter and Simone Cory deprived me of the opportunity to fuck her before she died.

In the parking lot of dreams, we sit in the silver gray Camry, watching the souls drift from their cars to the lights that beckon the cinema where we were, neither of us thinking of the movie we have just seen.

"Look at all those fuckin' losers," she says. "They don't know how good they've got it. That any minute all the crap they love so much could be taken away. Or somebody they love could just disappear and all this stuff won't even matter. Cars and clothes and boyfriends. I don't even see the point anymore."

"Where ever your Mom is, Honey, she wouldn't want you to worry about her, right? Do we really know that she's missing anyway? Maybe she just doesn't want to be found yet. I doubt that anything happened to her. She's probably taking care of something big, something sudden and important. She might even show up tomorrow with the biggest surprise you can imagine. Try not to think the worst."

"I wish I could. But I feel something in the pit of my stomach, Raven. Since you first came this afternoon."

"What is it?"

"It feels so strange. Like maybe you were sent here."

"That feeling—if it could be put it into words—honestly, what would it say?"

I watch her glance off to the side—as though she might possibly hear the spirit gouging her insides, and whatever message it has to tell.

"My mother is dead."

"Alison—"

"No, it's true, Raven. This ball of fear in my stomach is just turning and sending it to my whole body. I'm so scared that my mother's dead and I can't help it. I've been trying not to think this for two days now and I can't stop it anymore. That's why you were sent here. Somebody for me to talk to about it. Where's my Mom, Raven?"

Her look is so devastated, so burdened under fear as to be disturbing. In and around me, I suddenly perceive the spirit of dread, as it applies to both our immediate pasts and tonight in this car, under this parking lot tree, and near into our bleak and uncertain future.

I motion for her to slide over to where I am, and she finally collapses into my arms (like I've been waiting for all day), weeping and sobbing *I want my Mom, Raven* into me. The sound of her crying, the feel of her vulnerability lights my soul afire, until the world I'm in burns with a blue and black flame.

"Sometimes we have to reach out from despair, and just grab hold of the nearest thing and pull ourselves up. I want you to grab a hold of me, Alison." I feel the strength in her young, shapely body as she hugs me tight. "I can make you feel better," I say, kissing her forehead. "We can make each other feel better." I press her head to my bosom, such as it is, making sure she is pressed directly on to them.

"Momma's here, Baby. You just relax now."

From the heart and soul of the Mother Line, through the curse that is bestowed on me, the theater of my mind flashes to the kitchen of Malina Moon, and to the spirits of ghostly depression that haunt and swerve the Walls of Memory, the face of the Indian Woman of Straw—the first time it seemed that she would implode from a despair unknown and unheard of, as she calls me to the kitchen at age nine and tells me to sit in the chair—this, during a violent and vitriolic storm, as the trees outside threaten to sway and snap from their foundations and come crashing into the house. Behind these Walls of Memory, I am nine years old, when she calls me to the kitchen and tells me to raise her shirt up, to roll her shirt up and expose her gigantic breasts that hang down to her waists—pendulous and bulbous for me to see and remember in the storm. She puts her hands on her hips, no smiles or pretense to be had, and she says *help your Momma feel good—* and I know to take them into my little hands and wobble them back and forth. I am a little nine year old Carmen, so pretty and doe eyed in the 3rd grade, newly plucked and carried from the mountains of Cherokee County. Clap 'em together, she says, and I do so per her instructions, watching the two big, black areolas and nipples staring at me like two eyes as I hold them together, still per her instructions, both so floppy and heavy in my hands. Of this kind of private diversion, of what this entails I know is not unique to me, but who can speak of what images they provide! As the lightning flashes the sky outside, I know her spirit is as bleak as the Voice of Doom, when she says *kiss the nipple*, which I do over and over again until the big, smooth areola has shrunken like a raisin and pushed the nipple out, and she says *suck on it*, which I do per her instructions, and I remember twenty years later the shudder in my mother's body—the way her body shook, and the way the house shook from the crack of thunder that split the sky in two—

This, amidst the welcome shower in the night, that washes the people away from where Alison and me sit, and hides our brief solace from the world. Both our shirts are rolled up now, her young, spongy breasts in the same D minor key as mine—only shaped perfectly, with full support all around. "Suck it like you mean it Honey," I say, as she fumbles and flops mine, starting to feel the need in her body for the phantom milk, to drink nourishment into her feminine soul. And before long, I have to return this favor, relishing the veil of rain around us glowing from the street lamps, grunting once when her spongy breast is in my mouth, and the other is squeezed in my hand. Of this, I intend to make her understand—back and forth from breast to breast, watching her pink nipples harden— thinking of the way her own mother had writhed and screamed when Chelsea and me laid on top of her in the yard on Friday night.

"Lay your seat back, and take your pants off," I say, watching her oblige, looking as though she has changed inside a moving car at least once in her young life.

"Yes," I hear her respond to my question "Are you a virgin?" as the innocence washes over her expression and washes my soul free of mercy. I get on top of her and undo my pants, sliding them down and telling her "Close your eyes, Baby—" ushering her legs as wide open as they can be inside a car.

Amidst the low, rumbling thunder, and the noise from the driving rainfall, I slide the thick, eight inch member I have had strapped and tucked between my legs since this afternoon, all the way to her Chastity Gate and beyond it, absorbing her clawing, begging fall from grace as she digs her nails in my back as I stare at her hopeless face. I push hard and deep, so I can hear her cry out in pain, which makes my arms move on their own to pin hers to her side like a human clamp, and pull her tongue as far into my mouth as it will go. So many moons have passed since my body was fed to completion, having been denied my ultimate fare; I take this pound of cure unprevented, unprecedented in the mountain rain, driving into her with quick, hard, deep irregular thrusting—a thrust and pause—a thrust and pause, two thrusts and pause— hardly hearing myself say *put your tongue in my mouth*, remembering those words Malina spoke to me at sixteen in that self same kitchen, remembering the violence of her completion, remembering the last of my innocence fall away like the white leaves of the Autumn Woods, and the sound of her fervent cry in my ears, one she had held in check and repression; pressed down the first 16 years of my life—where it manifested into the scars and bruises I know. Tonight, I let my body thrust as it wishes, sans interference from my will, suddenly remembering the naked, busty hippiness—the hippy, naked bustiness of this girl's mother, which seems to send my hips into a grinding, gyrating motion I cannot control, and I feel a whine twinge my spine like wine, causing my eyes to roll back and my voice to go into a high pitched chime—and then a closed mouth bellowing onto her tongue.

The rain falls in weeping. In mourning over the nighttime mountain chain, and the souls of the Appalachian Wood.

*F*amilies walk the mud of tragedy. On the edge of a dawn of discord. Days removed from the rise and fall of Chaos. The sign of the coming eschatology. Mountains of mud covered debris, some two stories high. Unwashed clean. In the Oklahoma mist, they squint through the haze of revelation in the morning dark, the daytime dark, to find a clearer view. To find the bodies of Clearview in the rain. Inside the path of destruction, in the wake of Armageddon, there are the remains of farm equipment sprawled and twisted in the muddy debris. Equipment from farms 20 miles away. There are puddles the size of small, shallow ponds, where the foundations of houses used to be. In the backdrop of a landscape come and gone. In the morning stillness, in the fading mist of rain, there is the occasional tree left behind inexplicably. To explain without words the beginning of sorrows. In grieving to display the sheets of metal wrapped around themselves, metal from 18 wheel trucks, branches stripped like death in the winter. A mud soaked landscape of vile stench and wetness, strewn across a so-called damage path three quarters of a mile wide, through the wooded remains of where trees and houses used to be. Houses of a new wealth. Streets of old privilege. Every resident of this tiny Oklahoma town—killed in the rumbling that tore through. When the Saturday skies were darkened.

Days and miles, years removed from Clearview, the families that had left are drawn to devastation. Driving in on what roads were not torn up and taken. Knowing death at first sight. At the first smell of what *The Great Clearview Tornado* has left behind. Behind the clouds of grieving, the sun rises on the sons and daughters of tragedy. Of cataclysm. Gazing northeast now, in the growing light. Daring not imagine where the bodies of their mothers and fathers, their aunts and uncles, their sisters and brothers were taken. Staring at the brief Oklahoma woods, and the path that is cut between them.

Walk this path of revelation, in the loss of Clearview in the rain. See the remains of the brief forest, the stumps and sticks of where there were spruce and pine. Look to either side of you and walk, loved ones, at the stripped branches along the borders of this half mile wide phenomenon, betraying the signs of the strongest twister on record. Walk the giant mud path a half mile wide through the forest, where spirit saws and phantom bulldozers scraped the ground. See the border trees stripped of their bark and leaves, splashed with mud from Armageddon. Walk the edges of disbelief, at this brief sign of His coming. Now, turn away from the small woods of the plain. Go back to where the houses remain. In tiny pieces unknown. Pieces of lives shattered. Twisted. Broken. Buried in the mud.

Woman, close your eyes. Take comfort of thy husband! Feel the mist of rain dissipate in the breeze. Woman, remember thy mother! Of the calls you used to make. Of whatever promises were made to be broken. Understand, dear woman, that there is not a single promise that He hath made to be broken. Know that his promises never grieve to be broken. This, the promise of annihilation. The promise of the end of this age. The promise of Judgment. Wander the debris, dear Lady! Dry your tears in the morning breeze. Look upon the sign of his coming. Walk the Streets of Eschatology. Listen to what each lonely tree must prophecy, of what was born in the Garden of Antiquity. The Garden of Gethsemane. See the end of the Age of Grace. Talk to the reporters of your mother, Dear Lady. Of where it is that she could have gone. Speak to the reporter woman, Dear Lady, of the cloude that took your mother. Eyewitnesses, she says, say that it sounded like an earthquake—like a thousand tanks rumbling from the distance. Now, react to the video she carries. React to the technology of this age. The rumbling, black cloud as wide as Creation. See the cloud on the little screen, Dear Lady. The cloud that took your mother away.

*C*helsea Baxter counts the money. This, from the window of earthly progression. Another day spent in wondering over what lives, what situations, what circumstances these bills will pass through. What corruptions, what atrocities, what abominations must be; what immoralities, what sins and shortcomings, what negative energies, spirits and Divine Rights of Vengeance saith the Lord must be. What forests of wickedness, what trees of dibble and dabble in sin must be. What skies of passing clouds of melancholy endurance— what protracted years of family perversions there must be. What tears there must be to stain and taint these dollar bills of want and need, what chills of haunted greed. What ills, what sicknesses of the soul, what dandelions of diseases fly from one field of dreams to the other, to plant and grow disruption. What hands of unearthly progression— of inhuman Capabilities, of such Divine negativities wrought—what cruelties perpetuated are these?

Chelsea Baxter counts the money. Of the businessman who lays off his workers to increase his profit margin—these are signs of the times. The minister who burdens the guilt of tithes upon his congregation, then paddles his young children's buttocks to blood, like a flood of thunder and pain. The white lady judge who sentenced an eighteen year old black boy to six years behind bars for drug possession—be they crack rocks or what ever—watching the black poverty mother sit quietly and shake under the agony of this sobbing, that her young son is going to prison instead of college, this lady judge watches this with no compassion, while her own son sits in his bedroom at a pastoral rehab resort in another state for a $1,000 dollar a week cocaine habit—these are signs of the times.

The cheerleader who starts a rumor that another girl is pregnant. The football player who cheats on as many quizzes and tests that he can, the teacher who rides him in the back of her minivan—these are signs of the times we are in. The teacher slides, she hides, straddles and rides, with no such remorse as to not do it again. The girl who invites her best friend over to her house to spend the night, then jumps her with two other girls, beating her off and on for an hour, the three girls holding her down under a sheet on the bed while the girl pleads, the girl who cuts herself until she bleeds—the mother who tossed her new born baby in the weeds, these are signs of the times we are in. The mother who drowns her children for spite. The father who goes to his daughter's room at night—the mother who antagonizes her daughter to fight—this is the end of the age we are in. The mother whose daughter lost a beauty pageant show, and was beaten until there was blood—the flood of immorality and sin—these are the signs of the times we are in.

All day long, Chelsea has counted the money. From the window of non-judgmental confession, she has taken their money stained with their lives, and given new money to be stained by them. Her last transaction of the day, a note from Abraham Lincoln from the bottom of a working woman's account, so that two gallons of gas might last until she is paid again. Chelsea delivers this bill in satisfaction to the young Hispanic mother, to the beautiful brown Mother of Straw, long black hair shiny in the afternoon, aching to get her two daughters, eight and five, home to the belt whipping that awaits them. Two licks apiece, she will say, not being satisfied by any of the licks, will call the girls back to the living room to perform the two hits again, this time with all her strength, but being unsatisfied because both girls have learned from the numerous beatings how not to cry at first, believing that tears only makes the pain worse. And so the frustration will get to this Hispanic Woman of Straw, and she will break her promise of two licks apiece—breaking down into a flurry of belt lashes the girls have rarely felt upon their skin, until their screams penetrate the empty walls of the apartment next door, and the young Hispanic mother's satisfaction knows no bounds, as neither did her lack of compassion—the smell of the new bill still fresh in her nostrils, and the memory of Lincoln's face in her brain.

"Chelsea, can you come in here please, before you go?"

My young blonde switches into the office of Connie Green, bank manager, who has laid smiles and inference at Chelsea's feet the entire five years she has been working patiently as a teller, with silent and suggestive promises of a bright and corporate future. *As long as you're here Chelsea I'll take good care of you. You do well as a teller, with your education and professionalism there's no telling how far you can go in this company.*

"Chelsea, I don't have to tell you how bad the economy's been, and our industry is taking hits like you wouldn't believe. It's become necessary for us to have to make some changes in individual branches across the country. And as you know, since they bought us out they've been doing some major restructuring, and that usually means that some of our best workers will have to take a hit."

Connie Green's dowdy, matronly face washes over with guilty corporate compassion—the kind that extends as far as the door of her office, and lasts until five o'clock in the day. Connie Green watches the blonde beauty suddenly grow fidgety, and her eyes begin to widen with sadness and fear.

"Honey, I wouldn't worry about this job if I were you. You can do so much better. There's no telling how far you're gonna go in life."

Though the blonde tries so hard, something will not allow her to turn the other cheek. It is the rising of seven ghosts. To touch her with fire and regret.

"When we drove down to Charlotte last year Connie, what did you say?"

The question cuts through their new corporate sensibility, turning on a deep breath from Connie Green, burning through dowdy, plain eyes and a violently loud exhale filled with *I never liked your blonde bimbo in a business suit act anyway, Kelsey or whatever your name is.*

"Look, Chelsea. I fought for you as hard as I could (*a yawning, disinterested call to corporate suggesting severance pay over a two weeks notice*). They considered making you work two more weeks and then giving you no severance. But I at least got them to give you two weeks outright, without having to work for it."

Chelsea does not know that her head is tilted to the side, eyes anguished in puzzlement and frustration, staring at the face of a corporate betrayal—one that goes as deep as a canyon in the Himalayas.

"You said to me *I'll see to it that they never lay you off. Chelsea, I swear as long as I've got a job here, you've got a job here…*"

"That was last summer. Things change over time, Honey. I really thought I could keep them from getting to you. I tried but I couldn't stop it…"

"People do what they want to do, Connie. If you wanted to you could keep this from happening. There's probably five tellers you hired since last summer."

Connie takes another deep, high rise wishing, bureaucratic breath, suddenly complacent in the machine as a moving part—the part equipped with a sword, to cut would be threats to their future position off at the knees.

"All part timers," Chelsea says. "You don't have to pay them benefits do you? How much money does a company save, hiring part time employees? Firing the full time ones?"

"Well, I don't know what that's supposed to mean. That's not it at all."

A pause. One where truth and lies try to coexist, but like warm and cold air, being unable.

"Five years. I just didn't think that... never mind. Well, do I get my pay?

"You'll get it in the mail. Seven to ten business days."

"I've had an account here for five years. Can't you just deposit it?"

"We have to mail it to your home. Technically, you're no longer an employee, so..."

Fuming, Chelsea stands up to walk out, but stops and returns to her chair.

"*You'll get it in the mail? Seven to ten...* what the fuck kind of talk is that Connie?"

"Excuse me?"

"There *is* no excuse. I'm standing here looking at you and it's like I don't even know you. You just fired me after five years and it's like you don't even care."

"Well, if we're being honest Chelsea, you don't really know me."

"What?"

"I mean, yes we went for one weekend down to Charlotte last summer, but that didn't mean we were close friends. I'm sorry If I gave you the wrong impression."

"The wrong impression? What impression did you get from that little trip, Connie?"

"I wouldn't necessarily call it friendship."

"Oh, so now that I just got fired I'm not your friend anymore."

"We were never friends, Miss Baxter."

"Miss Baxter? Was I Miss Baxter when I let you feel me up and put your dry, cracked lips in my face?"

"I won't sit here and be slandered by a disgruntled ex-employee."

"The only thing disgruntled in here Connie is your ugly face. I whored myself out to you and your nasty assed hands. I should have never let you do that."

"Good day, Miss Baxter. Or do I have to call security in here?"

Connie Green stands with the desk phone in hand, angry and fully immersed in the bureaucratic mentality.

"I could tell 'em what you did."

"And I swear I'll sue you for slander so fast it'll make your head spin."

A pause, to consider the flood of angry tears on the blonde's beautiful face.

"Now why don't you get out of here before you really get hurt."

Chelsea gathers herself at the end of this corporate journey, suddenly feeling about as worthless as the ink they used in signing her psychology degree. She stands up, refusing to look the woman in the eye again. Whirling a slow turn from the small but highly decorated office with a door slam such as was never before heard behind these walls. In false dignity and humiliation, she wipes her eyes and strolls in her long skirt past every remaining lookie loo of the day, across the entire bank in front of all the eyes that stare, and finally out the heavy tinted, bullet proof glass front door.

Chelsea strolls across the breezy parking lot, adrift on a current of freedom. At her blue Saturn, she turns to take one last look at the money cathedral, breathing a sigh of relief that her days there are over. Watching some of the employees exit their livelihood for the day, trying not to see the tall, stylish pretty girl at her Saturn on the day she was laid off. *A lay off is as good as a firing*, they all think, as the rumor starts that Chelsea Baxter got fired after an argument with the bank manager.

Staring at the Money House, a sudden vulnerability accompanies her relief, to begin to devour it, leaving the vulnerability alone. And as she remembers the souls inside, and their dependence on the flow of wealth, their worship of every dollar coming in and going out—their hopeless waiting for every feeble payday—Chelsea's own vulnerability morphs into apprehension, realizing now that she is suddenly unemployed with a new car to pay for. And then she remembers that Simone's idea five years ago had been brilliant—that we only live on her meager professor's salary and whatever I could scrape up besides, paying all bills with her paychecks, with whatever extra money we needed coming from me. Inside this very institution lay the remains of a five year dream realized, of what happens when *every penny* of a salary is saved five times per annum.

And so, relief floods back into her system, as she remembers the day the three of us sat in the Money Cathedral together, making sure all of our names were on this special account, and that the three of us had equal access. To withdraw this money and use it any time, which we have not. And though the plan was for all three of us to pour money in—cars and clothes soon took their rightful places over discipline, until only Chelsea's paychecks were going in. But still, a six figure savings has a power all its own, and she is struck with a sense of overwhelming relief again, where the tension of worry cannot prosper, like when a widow stands at her husband's grave at the burial ceremony and wonders why the tears won't come.

I look up suddenly from the rack of skirts that were mulled over by a pack of teenagers—a pack of skinny pretty white girls with more time and money on their hands than is possible for most grown women. Straightening out the mess they made, I look up to see a tall, beautiful, smiling blonde in a long, flowing blue and black skirt and high heel black boots, walking towards me like a ghost in the afternoon. "Chelsea," I sing, shocked to see my beautiful doll here today. She drifts all the way up to where I am—a mysterious, giddy look on her face with a sprightly twinkle in her eye.

"Guess what?"

"What?"

"You'll never guess."

"What is it?" I'm on the edge of laughter myself now. "Come on now, what is it?"

"I got fired."

In a place we've never known, where The Joker himself must surely hearken from, we both lock eyes... and burst out laughing like somebody died.

"So, now what?"

"I don't know. Another bank maybe. Another job closer to home. But with the way I talked to that bitch on the way out…"

"You can still use her as reference. If anybody calls her she'll give you a good report."

"No she won't. She'll say...*well, she can be a bit temperamental at times, like she's above criticism or being told what to do...*I think my ship has sailed, Honey. I'm tired anyway. I'm wore out. All the driving and working. The digging and planting. I feel like I just want to go home and go to sleep forever."

"We had one helluva long weekend, didn't we?"

From our food court table, Chelsea seems distracted by a sophisticated, older version of herself—walking so un-casually into a clothing store nearby, blonde hair slicked and pinned back into a loose ponytail over an ivory crème blouse and gray skirt down just below the knee.

Chelsea's expression is somber again.

"People would be shocked if they knew how their mothers really were inside. If they knew who their grandmothers had been when they were young. Our mothers. The ones we're supposed to trust the most. The ones who are supposed to keep us safe. To teach us right from wrong. Who are supposed to dry our tears, and not cause them."

My mind is suddenly adrift, to the familiar house on Old Mill Road.

"My bank manager... Connie Green. Last year when we drove up to Charlotte, to the judge's house, she put her hands on my knee while we were driving. And she ran her hands all the way up my thigh, and she said *Honey you have inspired me to think things I didn't even know were inside me. Please tell me you understand.*"

"My God. You never even told us."

"For some reason I couldn't talk about it. She said, *The next deserted spot we come to, lets pull over so we can discuss your future.*"

I suddenly forget the milkshake I'm drinking, able to see the woman's sky blue minivan in my vision.

"Is Connie Green married?"

"Happily. With four grown children. Two sons. Two daughters. She just didn't seem like the type Raven, I don't know. She's kinda Helen Mirren-ish, you know. I always thought she was sort of good looking but I didn't even imagine she was the type."

"Deep down, they're all the type, Chelsea. Especially that bitch. Dyke was written all over her face."

"You think so?"

"I know so."

"A loan officer at a bank. A bank manager now. I thought she was somebody I could trust."

"How old is she?"

"About 50, but kinda shapeless, a little dowdy."

"Dowdy? Ms. Cuntie Green? You must have really liked her to think that. She was too Mrs. Tingle to be dowdy."

"She kept her hand on my leg for a long time—rubbing it up and down while she drove. The whole time she talked about what a bright future I had, and how *it's not what you know in life that matters as much a who you know*. She was so filled with it, Raven. It was burning her up so bad she had to take an exit into some town along the way."

"Exit 31. Oh, My God, we thought you guys had stopped to get something to eat. Simone said *'that's Chelsea's appetite.'* You guys turned right on that country road. We thought she had family somewhere, so we decided to get back on the interstate. We waited until we saw you. We saw that sky blue minivan pass right by us. We couldn't believe it—we thought it was over. We had even talked about going back home."

"When we turned right down that road, we parked the van by a grove of trees. There was nothing but trees and an old cropfield that probably hadn't been used in years. There was this, like, hundred year old looking barn thing close by, and I remember that no cars would come, Raven. No cars would come to make her stop. She put the car in park and turned off the engine and said *You don't mind this at all do you.* And I couldn't say anything else but *No, I don't mind.* I mean, I'm not a virgin or anything, right? *I want us to get in the back where we'll be more comfortable,* she said… and I got in the back seat first. But she got out and walked around, and she opened the sliding door and got in. I remember being so scared when she was walking around the van towards me. I think I jumped when she opened the door. And I knew this was something I had to do. She got in and said *Slide up beside me,* and she kissed me full on the mouth. Her lips trembled, and she exhaled and moaned like it was the best thing she'd ever felt in her life. I don't think she'd ever kissed another woman before."

Any and all who walk by our mall table who might glance at our faces, are curious as to why this beautiful blonde has such a distant, somber look while she talks, and why the exotic brunette has such a bewildered, anguished expression.

"What did you do?"

"What could I do? I wanted to keep my job. I decided to give her what she wanted. I moaned and I gave her what she needed. What she liked most was sucking on my tongue. Sucking it up and down while she had her hands on my panties. She said *I have put myself to sleep at night a thousand times like this. I have dreamed this all my life and it's still so much better than anything I could have imagined. Your lips are soft,* she said. *Your tongue tastes sweet.* I was thinking, like, Of course it does bitch, I just drunk a Mountain Dew, what'd you expect? She said *I want to put our pussies together. Do you want that to?"*

"She actually used that word?"

"Yep."

My look is suddenly a disapproving frown, shaking my head. Distaste. Disdain. I despise the word 'P'-'U'- 'S'- 'S'- 'Y'. *Cats* despise the word 'P'-'U' -'S'- 'S'- 'Y'.

"Boy, she had it bad."

"She undid my shirt and squeezed my breasts over my bra. She kept saying *Oh, yessss. Oh, yesss*, like she really meant it. A deep, sultry voice. I remember thinking how the Hell did her husband get to fuck this dyke four times?"

"What?"

"She's got four grown kids, remember?"

"Oh. Did she… did she get to you?"

"I don't know. Kind of, I guess. I never thought about her that way before. Her acting sexy was just too weird. She kept squeezing on my breasts until she pulled one out, and she put her mouth on it and sucked it like she was trying to get milk out of it, and she made this long groaning sound like an animal, kinda shaking her head real fast. And she was sticking her fingers in my crotch."

"How did it feel?"

"Terrible. I wanted to stop. I felt like I was being raped. But I guess I deserve it, don't I?"

I can only sigh and look away, understanding that whatever wrongdoing should befall either of us is the reaping of seeds sown.

"After a few minutes she laid me down and spread my legs open, then she said *I'm going to push our pussies together Baby. Just relax.* She raised her skirt all the way up and got on her knees, and slid herself right onto me. To me it seemed like she was taking a dump. She must have been horny as Hell, I could feel how swollen she was. She started moving and grunting like a sow pig scratching against a wooden fence. *I've never felt it*, she said. *Oh God. I've never felt anything this good in my life,* she said. She shook her head back and forth real hard. She pushed and ground herself into me until she found it, and then she kind of leaned forward, holding on to the seat with one hand and my breast with the other. Meantime I'm laying there wondering how the Hell it is that my bank manager can be doing this. I still can't believe it, Raven. I kept thinking I was gonna wake up from a dream. Then she leaned down and sucked my breast like she had a gift or something. I remember it was an absolutely perfect suck. Hard and soft at the same time. She let it go and just stared at it and breathed on my nipple. I'll admit I started to feel something. I couldn't help it. While she was bent over she started moving her hips really fast and hard and I knew it was coming, so to speak. She closed her eyes— her mouth was open, she looked like something had control of her body, the way she was moving. The way she was humping. Then she said *Oh, Lord have mercy*, and she started to make a sound like crying. Like that noise Simone makes. And that sound just kept getting louder until it rung my ears. Then she shook like a jack hammer and screamed like she couldn't have stopped it if she tried. I almost felt sorry for her that she had to do that to me. That she had held that in for so many years. Maybe that's where that masculine ambition comes from in some women. When we sit on that pornographic lust and press it down and pretend it's not there. What she did… it reminded me of going to the bathroom. How no matter how long you try not to, eventually you're gonna have to go. That's what it seemed like with her. Like if she hadn't got it out of her system it would have made her sick. She was actually crying when it was over. She just sniffed and wiped her eyes and laughed a little like she couldn't believe it happened. I think for 20, maybe 30 years it had burned in her like a sun, and I guess when she met me, she just couldn't hold it in anymore. She seemed relieved. Almost happy. For the rest of the trip, it was like a weight had been lifted, and she talked to me like she had known me her whole life."

"So that's Connie Green."

"Yep. The one her church group doesn't know about."

"Is she really a church woman?"

"She's a member of First Assembly of God. She goes every Sunday. I went with her a couple times, remember?"

"Oh yeah. That *was* her you were going to church for that time, wasn't it?"

"Yep."

"I asked you why you were driving all the way down here just to go to church. Wow. That was this winter, around Christmastime. So that means she had already done that to you last summer."

"Yeah."

"God, wait 'til Simone hears this."

"No."

"What?"

The look on her face, the epic fear and shame, ripples the calm of Spirit Lake, to send a shudder through my soul.

"It's too pathetic, Raven. I don't want her to know this about me."

"Why not?"

"Simone is too smart. Too strong. Too beautiful. She's got a PhD. She owns her own house. Where would I be if it wasn't for her? I feel like she saved my life. I just don't want her to know I'm that pathetic."

She takes a deep breath and closes her eyes, and here in this ridiculous place, this Palace of Corporate Greed, I watch tears flow from two closed eyes of beauty.

"Oh, God I wish I'd never been born. What kind of a person am I who would do the things I've done, and who somebody as normal as Connie Green could think they could just piss and shit on and get away with it? What kind of a person?"

The pain burns her insides like an iron over sin, and I know it's everything she can do to keep from sobbing. The suffering of her marketable looks is so tragically appropriate in these surroundings, as though she is now a living work of art, called to express the inner pain of those poor souls around her, those that float through life in smiles and laughter, who wear them as a cloak and a mask of joy.

"I gotta go," she says.

"Let me go with you, Honey."

"No, you go on back to work. I just want to go home."

We stand together, two women, hugging each other in the busy mall as if it were the lobby of an airport.

"I love you," she says.

I only nod, refusing to speak it, telling her with my eyes how I feel. I watch her turn and walk away, down the Corridor of Lost Souls. She waves at me one last time, and I return our farewell wave, watching her turn the corner and stroll out of sight.

*C*helsea Baxter counts the miles. Along the highways of manmade progression. Rolling casually along, she feels the calling from near and far, from high above where the sun rolls towards the Western Gate of Eve, that chariot driven by the God of the Sun, hearkened from a journey began many eons ago, many hours ago, when Aurora tolls the Eastern Gate of Morning. Chelsea rolls the miles North and East, bidding a fond farewell to the Amazon Beauty in her heart, rolling smoothly toward forgiveness and absolution on the Streets of Chesapeake, and the asphalt roads of Camille Harbour. Knowing in her heart that somewhere North, in a region so far away from here, her earthly Redemption draweth nigh. As the sun fades to the golden amber of sleep, where men can look upon it with longing, Chelsea counts the miles towards the place that calls and awaits her arrival in the turning of the evening day.

What tears along this road do you cry, Dear Chelsea? What solace have you known? Does this trip to the Virginia border hearken days of leisure bygone, and the sophisticated brunette you met that day who was not yet old enough to be your mother? Ms. Patty Southern, Ms. Patricia Southern, divorced with two teenage daughters at the great park in Williamsburg? A 40 year old woman of straw, with a sixteen and a seventeen year old daughter at the park, who when the three of us spotted, you said—*you guys go to the car and wait, it might take me two hours but I swear to God I'll bring her*—watching us both nod our heads and touch and agree. Could you catch your breath, Dear Chelsea, as we phased from consciousness and your heart began to beat faster as you walked toward this woman who seemed alone when her daughter's left, wearing her ivory pearl pants, with matching ivory tank top underneath the open sky blue button down collar shirt. How easy is it to talk to her, knowing that even her mature, refined good looks are no match for your own?

What an impressive figure you are! A lonely blonde in the prettiest purple and plumb flowered white dress under the sun—a queen among minions and servants in this park. You are lucky, dear Chelsea, that the woman looks twice at you when you wander up beside her, taken aback by your appearance, that in real life there is such a woman as thee. *Excuse me*, she says, *are you an actress? Or a model maybe?*

I eat too much to be a model, you say—*and I couldn't act good enough to play a tree in the woods*. The creamy skinned brunette laughs her pretty, black eyed laugh, confident already that the two of you are going to have lunch more pleasant than what she has known in a long time. How many rides, Dear Chelsea, does it take to get her drunk? To stagger her on new wine, this fantasy of friendship she has, spilling every detail of her suburban tragedy as you wait in the lines to the rides—even the big roller coasters, that now she is not afraid to go on now that she has you. *I don't want to sound weird or anything*, she says, *but you have a quiet strength. I know it sounds creepy, but I'm a psychiatrist—I read people for a living. And there is just something so comforting about you* Chelsea—*you seem so mature for your age. You're not walking around in skin tight clothes and listening to the Black Eyed Peas and trying to compete with these little young girls—even though you could if you wanted to—*

When you sit on the seat on the big coaster, what does she say to you, Dear Chelsea? *I really felt like I needed to take a big stop and do something crazy*, she says. *Well, this is it,* you say, with a facetious, mischievous glee that makes both of you laugh, knowing that whatever strains toward bonding there were are about to be loosened, where there is only a running towards one another in unabashed enthusiasm and a hug strong enough to take your breaths away. What does she say, Dear Chelsea, as the coaster climbs the Tower of Fear? Do you feel the same tickling of Death's bony fingers along your spine as they do? Or do you gaze as casually as a hawk, plaintively across the park as if you were perched by choice alone? *I can't believe this is happening*, she says, her forty year old face twisted in silliness now, dragging up more inner contempt from you than you already have. *Oh, My God this is it Chelsea* she says, beginning the loud, hollering scream just below high pitched, a loud long woman's scream that you hear with your eyes closed. *It's a good scream*, you say to yourself—*I need to hear it again. I'm going to torture you when we get home, so I can hear you scream again—*

During this wild ride, as you fly through the air on the back of the Great Yellow Dragon of Loch Ness, you long for the feel of her breasts pressed against yours, and the sound of her screaming as you try to break her fingers while holding her hands behind her back underneath her. Where does this come from, Dear Chelsea, this sadism from beyond the sea? Toward the wide and sounding sea you drive, to the house in Camille Harbour, where your forgiveness and Redemption draweth nigh.

Walk me to my car, you say, in the Heart of Memory. *You being from New York and everything. I don't know when I'll know see you again.*

Honey I'll be glad to, she says. *It's too bad you have to leave, though. I'm trapped here probably for another three hours, my girls will be here until dark before they'll let me leave. Then we've got to drive all the way back to New York.*

There are too many souls in the parking lot are they not? This will have to be done by a sinful plot, to blot out her life and time. A crime, Dear Chelsea, as she listens by way of her profession as you tell this woman of how much your mother despised you, and how it is such a good thing you had a chance to tell her about it, and how you didn't really want to come today but something inside said you have to push forward and go to Busch Gardens, and breathe some fresh air. *Ooh, that's a pretty car*, she says. *I was going to get a Camry.*

Wanna sit with me a minute before I go?

Well... oh why not, I'll be here 'til 9 o'clock anyway You've got more you want to talk about, don't you?

Yeah. I do.

You are so strong and beautiful to her, Dear Chelsea. She is mesmerized by your presence in the world—the purple and white dress and the beautiful blonde hair is almost too much for her—and though every instinct tells her to flee from your golden spider clutches, she is helpless to oblige—ignoring her instincts because you are so *White And So* Pretty, and she slides into the back seat with you against her own better judgment, wishing already to be away from you and back with her girls. *Just relax with me for a few minutes*, you say. I *know you want to get back in the park with your daughters...*

Dear Chelsea, do you remember the thrill you got that day, when the Indian Woman opened the door on the Southern side? Do you remember the shock on her face, when the beautiful Amazonian brunette opened the door the rest of the way so quickly and slid in the back seat, pushing Patricia Southern toward the middle of the seat? Did Simone Cory seem like a super heroine to you that day, such big curves around the small waist; such long, silken black hair framing the ivory skin? Do you remember me, Chelsea, as I parked my Indian ass in the driver's seat and cranked the car without a word, my evil eyes staring in the rear view mirror?

Who are these women, Chelsea? Where are we going—I have to get out of here, she says, as she tries to violently push past you to get to the door. But a lovely hand so firmly, so gently around her throat calms her like a chicken on a chopping block, and you hear the Cory voice say, *No, Baby. It's my time now. It's our time. You're going to sit calmly, and tell us all about yourself—*

She's got two teenage daughters, you say to Simone, Dear Chelsea, while I say *Oh, yeah Baby, Oh God yeah* from the feeling and sudden pressure in my groin. Then you watch while Simone puts her hand to the Southern breast, you holding Patty's arms back as she struggles against a perverted hand and a good, angry cry. *I'm going to hear all about your daughters*, Simone says, *starting with their names…*

Are you in awe, Dear Chelsea, as Simone interviews the lovely psychiatrist, as she discovers the incestuous attraction she has to both her daughters? What happens inside your body, Dear Chelsea, when Simone exposes the Southern Breast, and fellatios the nipple with such power as to make Patty Southern have to close her yes and breathe a prayer to God? Does Simone get lost in what she is doing, moaning and sucking the breast as though it feeds her body while you hold on to Ms. Patricia so tightly? What pain does this relieve in your body? What fires does this relieve—to see this mature, capable, confident woman broken down to nothing?

I know you're all gonna rape me… I can feel it, she says, wiping her eyes on the high pitched, cracking last syllable. *Chelsea… Chelsea I just want you to remember what… what a powerful connection we have. We know one another. We understand one another. Our Mommas did things to us that we're never gonna forget. My Momma used to send us to bed without any supper if she was just in a bad mood so I understand. Chelsea I just want you to remember how much my daughters need me…*

And the car rings with a sudden scream, as Patty exclaims the pain of her nipple being twisted by Simone. *Okay, okay,* she sobs. *Chelsea. Chelsea please. Please find it somewhere in your heart to have mercy on me. Chelsea Honey, look at me. Look at me, please.*

You just wanna go home, don't you?

Yes, with your permission. With y'all three's permission.

Y'all three? Simone says.

I live in White Plains, but—I mean, I was raised in Alabama.

Patty Southern from Alabama. Well ain't that the sweetest little ol' thing you ever heard?

In the rearview mirror, I catch her attempt at a tearful smile. Looking back and forth between Simone and Chelsea with such goodnatured pleading as to be heartbreaking.

What else did your Momma do to you, Patty Southern? And I want the truth.

Chelsea Baxter counts the miles. The time and distant roadway, stretching on forever as we go. Listening to the begging forty year old mother—finally conceding to taste of the dish she hath prepared. *You want to live, don't you,* Chelsea says.

Yes, please.

You want to go home to your daughters? How bad do you want to live? Hmm? I want to feel how bad you want to live.

With her single breast still partially exposed—the woman slides over and smartly presses her wet face full on Chelsea's cheek for a hard, smacking kiss. Then she cuddles herself onto Chelsea's bosom, sniffling tears loudly. Biting her thumbnail.

The Mountaineers

Chelsea Baxter counts the miles. Those that govern the years come and gone, from those of today and yesterday, to the tiding of Number Four, and her tragic introduction to Mountain View Road. Chelsea, as your day dies on the North Road—do you remember? Do you remember the strange compassion you felt for Patty Southern, that you allowed yourself to be a comfort to her while we rolled the wilderness west, toward the line of mountain blue? Do you remember the somber fire that began to eat you alive, when you thought of the betrayal you had to deliver? Do you remember when her sobs, hopeless longing for a reprieve fed your spirit like pain medicine? The more she begged, as we walked the lawn to our brick cottage in the mountains, our brick cottage by the sea—this, the sea of loneliness and regret—do you remember the way I stopped us all at the front door? The way I whirled around in a quiet, simmering disgust that had been building for three hours, saying *Look, bitch—your fucking grave has already been dug—*

I still see the look on her face, Dear Chelsea. Can you see it too? The way her expression waxed cold in fear—the way her eyes widened and her mouth opened as I said—*so you might as well shut the fuck up, before I kick you in the stomach hard enough to make you vomit.* What seeds of past agony did this relieve in you, Dear Chelsea? What pleasure did it send to the ghostly phallus that you feel? As the earth turns toward the evening, Dear Chelsea, can you remember the wailing in her voice when you told her to take off her clothes? Can you remember the begging and the pleading for her two daughters, Dear Chelsea?

You walk over to her and you slap her hard enough to make her bellow like a gelded bull on her way to the floor, so weak from the stress of her calling. *Get the fuck up*, I say, pulling her up hard by the hair, at the very end of all patience and compassion, as the Devil will be on the Day of

219

Judgment, for those who are cast in the Lake of Fire. After you are naked, and your member hangs down from your groin, strapped so firmly into place, you keep the promise you made to us, to open the camera's eye for the first time, and record the evil that we do—placing it on the low table in the living room—pointing it at what we do. The camera records a pretty brunette with dark eyes and ivory skin so mildly tinted cream, a short, wavy suburban hair cut and pretty gold rope chain around her neck, with perfectly rounded breasts in D minor above a slim waist, and hips as slim as my own tend to be. We stand around her, the three of us with our cocks a part of us now—watching her—unaware of the camera's probing eye, waiting for the Spirit to tell us what to do. *Do you want to live?* I ask her... *get on your knees then, bitch... Simone, this bitch wants to live. I want you to test that with your cock. I want to see how badly she wants stay alive...*

Do you remember, Chelsea, when Simone trembled at the merest touch of this woman's tongue to the tip of her cock? *You wanna live, don't you baby*, Simone says, *then let me feel it...* How did you feel, Chelsea, as you watched her choke and spit on the rubber dick, sliding it in her mouth and swallowing it down her throat like a 4th generation lady sword swallower, holding it there, looking up at Simone with tears pouring from her eyes from the gagging alone? How did you feel, Chelsea, when Simone pulled her cock out from Patty Southern's mouth and the spit fell in beauty to her thigh as she gagged? Did you like it, Dear Chelsea, when she was forced to take ours into her mouth as well, and do the same to all three of us back and forth, round about, until she was so exhausted it wasn't possible anymore? Do you remember the one we called Cock Robin, because we walked round robin as she was down on her hands and knees, waiting for us to eat her alive? I remember the look on your face, Chelsea, the nearly epic sorrow and bitterness, as you knelt down in back of her and said *I want you to get off, Bitch, your life depends on it...*

As the woman nods, she puts Simone back into her mouth briefly, taking hold of mine with one hand, and I admonish *you better relax and concentrate bitch, if you don't cum you're fucking dead.* And I watch the Spirit of Perversion overtake her, as she begins to say *fuck me Chelsea—I want you to fuck me*, and I can hear how clearly she means it. What does it do to your body, Dear Chelsea, as you slide your cock all the way in without mercy, as she lowers her head and screams like a virgin? Simone and I watch you, Dear Chelsea, as your face is anguished over—in where a Witch's Crown is the reward, when there is the Intercourse of the Tribade, when the member is yours in your mind, an extension of body and spirit. Do you feel every inch of it as your flesh Chelsea, as you slam it into the back of her with a slow, determined rhythm? So much slower than my rabbit rhythm, or the slow fumbling tiger's rhythm of our Simone, but yours is as a she dog turned human—keeping every push separate and in perfect check from the other, rattling a ripple through this bitch's body with each thrust. What I see is perfection, as the Spirit is so inclined, giving you the gift of this abomination. I even hear the lower pitch in your voice when you say *tell me when you're gonna cum,* and I watch the woman put both hands on the floor and stare at Simone's big cock, saying almost at once *I'm cumming*, and I watch you put your head back and say *I want you to get off... I want you to .. get OFF!*

And when you scream, the spirits that govern such perversity runs through Patty's body, and she jerks forward one gigantic time, screaming loudly just once, and your own rhythm is suddenly faster, Chelsea, until you deliver two high pitch yelps through the walls of our house, and into the summer mountain night.

Now, watch me rabbit fuck her Chelsea. A quick, fast as lightning orgasm for myself. Now, watch Simone have to rest inside her forever, hardly moving at all, then suddenly exploding that siren from her Witch's Crown, which leaves her spent and clinging to me for comfort while she shakes like Angelina Jolie's lips in winter. How does it feel, Dear Chelsea, as you hold Patty Southern still for me, as I choke her to death with my bare hands? How does it feel, Dear Chelsea, as Patty Southern screams for God and Christ, from the curling iron Simone brands her with in her back? How does it feel, Dear Chelsea, as the woman you befriended struggles for air and then breathes her last, choking breath in your arms? Do you remember the smell of her burning flesh? Do you remember?

Chelsea Baxter counts the miles. Along the highways of earthly progression. From the mountains in the west, where the sun rests golden amber in the day, to the places where friends in beauty work and play. Chelsea Lynn Baxter rolls the miles upwards, cruising along the Wealthen Stream, but this only an abundance of love for two friends she has known, and an abundance of Golden Beauty besides. Beneath these clear skies of obsession, in the gloaming of the day, she is drawn from where the light of hope did reside—away from the Land of the Setting Sun, towards another place, a calling farther east among the houses of Camille Harbour Estates, and the mansion on Harbour Wood Road.

After this final sun hath come and gone. When the sky has phased to another light—to where only an echo sings what remains of the day. Echoes of another journey through the Land of Shattered Dreams—where hope hath faded to hopeless pain and despair. On the edge of this new life, Chelsea cruises the Wealthen Stream, grieving for the land of plenty. Along this stream of beauty she rides—this, the beauty of manmade obsession—perfectly landscaped trees and lawns and bushes and flower gardens, all placed around each house and mansion of earthen clay, burned into the bricks of hardened determination; decisions forged, fired and finished in stone, the will and ways of man's pursuit of happiness, as it pertains to house, home and community.

Chelsea climbs this new hill, this new mountain of expectation and desire, burning with the fires of renewed splendor, the final rendering of want and need. On her blue path among the stars, she rolls the Saturn into the driveway of a finer dwelling, a finer resting place, under the early evening sky. Remembering the faces of two who loved her without precedence, two who loved her unconditionally, who loved her without judgment for who she was, nor any of the things she had done. In Beauty, she steps out of her Chariot of Harvest, into the Lawn of Reckoning— where she steps in divine delusion in the evening day, toward the fine mansion of manmade hope and dreams. She takes one step in front of the other, perceiving the turning of the day, the moving of the Great World toward the shadow of night. Beyond where she can see, every star beckons her imagination, every burning light near and far, from the few that she can see twinkling in the early night, to all of those that burn from the edge of earth's feeble vision, on the line of pearl and infinity, whirled throughout the second heaven.

Suddenly, through the falling of a tear unknown, from a place she never knew, from where she had felt but had yet never dared to know, she declares her love for her Lord and Savior, believing that he died for her, that even if she believeth on the Cross, that she too might be saved. She steps in the middle of this fine lawn and property, staring beyond the twilight sky, seeing the mercy of one true and living God, from earth and upward through the cosmos, and the infinity which is the second heaven.

From these tears of renewal, from this place of knowing she reawakens, resurrected to a new life in an instant, transformed by the renewing of her mind, to where she is no longer a prisoner of this life, but has been set fee and born again.

Down the avenue of awakening, Chelsea walks the path to the door of veiled eternal damnation—the doorway of failed expectation—toward the front door of the house on Harbour Wood Road. To the beauty who bore her in blood, whose talking voice has already been heard in the calling, knowing that her daughter hath come for redemption, to receive whatever reward of forgiveness that is due. And in concession, she hath agreed to see her lovely daughter, on the edge of this new life and time, to make right the years of bitterness and venom—to hold her in righteousness, to speak words between them that have never been spoken, to at last put to rest those haunting ghosts of a past lived in poverty, and the time when they were a mother and daughter of sin. These were the Women of Straw, both born under a curse, who now seek resolution, restitution from the years of pain and suffering.

This beautiful daughter rings the doorbell. Eyes still a mist of those tears where Redemption was made bye and bye. And when the door slides open, in her mother's beautiful, lioness eyes is the power of Heaven and Earth, the key to Life and Death, as she raises her arm out to her daughter. In the haze of slow motion, Chelsea reaches out to her mother's hand, having not understood that what she sees is a *gun*, hearing a loud noise echo like a firecracker around her, feeling a hard and painful thump into the middle of her chest that lifts her off her feet and carries her backward and away from her mother so slowly, reaching out for her mother to save her from falling down, downward to the ground. With a gun in her hand, Donna Turner, Gretchen Turner, Gretchen Baxter pulls the trigger of automatic death, causing the woman she knows as her daughter to fly backwards to the ground.

In the cool of the evening. In the haze of this slow motion dream. The daughter perceiving a lifting up, amidst an overwhelming peace and purity. Hearing another popping sound in the air, and the disembodiment of a lost soul, and separation from it for an eternity.

Part Two

In the Heart of Memory, I see you still, Dear Chelsea. I am the unblinking eye that sees all—the eye of the camera you wield with natural skill, to record the Tiding of Number 5, the planting of our Grandest Rose. It is Victoria's deepest and darkest secret, a lust that boils hotter than the sun.

The fast and loose laugh of the beautiful wife of Simone's colleague. The spindly, nerdy, four eyed fop of a geek named Joseph Drinkwine, professor Joseph, Professor Joe—Dr. Drinkwine, I presume. Lucky enough to have met his beauty at a brief stint at Boston University, by way of a Master's degree at Princeton, and a Ph. D not yet acquired until after she will die. *I think Vicky would want you to go get that Ph D, Joe—it's the best thing you can do to remember her.* Missing for almost two years— since a Christmas Banquet in Raleigh. A gathering of religious professors and their wives from every school in the State University system, a pointless exercise in holiday futility, a glorified Christmas party at a mansion, to raise awareness and money for the ever shrinking raisin of Religious Studies— now a refuge for the bitter, the traumatized and the dispossessed, as they look for answers from Fate, Destiny and God. Why, Oh Lord, did you let my wife die of Cancer? Why, Oh Lord, did you kill my son by a drunk driver? Why, Oh Lord, did you knock the towers down on Nine Eleven? Why, Oh Lord, does my skin bear the burn marks of my Momma's depression—why, Oh Lord, is my beautiful wife missing?

I noticed you staring at me... I just had to come talk to you. You work with my husband don't you? A handshake as big and phony as Marilyn and Jane's, a hearty laugh from both of you, that two such beautiful and big breasted brunettes have bounced into one another. *You wanna get outta here*—Simone says, with an Amazonian wink and a smile—not letting this beautiful and bodacious woman out of her sight—taking her by the arm and dragging her to the coat room and then outside in the cold. *Oh, no. its freezing*, she says.

I've got to go anyway. Walk me to my Cadillac so we can talk for a minute...

Mrs. Victoria Drinkwine. Former acquisitions editor at a publishing house. Wife of murder suspect Joseph Drinkwine. Curves now unrepressed in the chair, by the roving, unblinking eye. The eyes of the Lord are in every place, beholding the evil and the good—the eyes of the Lord are in this place, Victoria. Watching you die.

I stand beneath the Seven Sisters. Gazing into sparkling light. I watch the earth stars blaze a trail—across a fervent winter's night. On this clear, icy winter's night—I take a breather in the mountain cold—wearing the long winter coat over my nakedness, taking a break from the camera's eye, and the screaming of a dead woman. *You stupid bitch*, I say to myself— thinking how easy it was to chloroform your dumb ass by Simone's Cadillac and drag you to my brand new Camry. You are the Camry's first victim, my sexy Dear, and when you woke up screaming in the back of my car thirty minutes from home, Chelsea and me looked at one another in shock, and I must admit that it is the closest I have ever come to pissing on myself from fear.

We let you out of the trunk on the black road home, I remember, so many miles from any light but the cold stars in heaven. Outside under the blackness of space, still too far away from home—we introduce you to the spirit of a man's lust in a woman's body, when Chelsea drags you over into the grass we see, by the edge of a grove of trees, and we hold you down fully clothed, and listen to you scream yourself exhausted in the cold, covering your mouth when we hear a passing car. I remember Chelsea's trembling as she ran her hands up and down every inch of you, Mrs. Drinkwine, so lucky to have found such an ambitious little man with such an appropriately poetic little name. Your breath is still hot from the liquor at the party, my dear, and your lips are bitter from the sour taste of it. Is this a nightmare for you to wake up from—this foreplay, this Rape of the Sabine Women? Do you recognize the stars in this December sky you see?

Yes, my Dear Lady. My dearest Woman of Straw, these are the seven stars that form the tiny question mark—a question posed through the eons, but heard by few, and answered by fewer still. What must you do to be saved, dear woman, on the night where you will begin to die? This is the end of the Advent, and you will suffer in our home for three days before you die.

Your mouth duct taped so tight now, as are your hands and your feet, you lay fully clothed on the first night, waiting for Simone to come home from the party. Simone walks in the house on the winds of the Christmas season, a week from the Spirit of the Nativity, and Chelsea takes her coat and her purse from her, so that she can look upon what she has done. *One of the signs that you have answered a calling*, Simone says to you, *is the rising of Divine Luck and protection—to see you along your journey. Nobody saw you leave the house with me. They thought nothing of you being gone. Because you're a busybody, your husband Joseph said—like mother, like daughter he said. I didn't know that Joseph had a 15 year old daughter, one that his mother hardly ever sees—he says, because you're so in love with your damned jobs and going on vacations. Vice president of an insurance company now, is it?* If it weren't for the holidays I'd never see her—he often said. But now he can see and feel you every day, in the heart of his fervent memory.

I see your extreme curves in blood soaked bra and panties dear lady, your hands bound helplessly to the dining chair and your feet bound tightly together. Your curves having grown the phantom cock between my legs, Baby Doll. Thirty seven years of pin up perfection like I have hardly seen in my life, your nearly black areolas shining clear in the wet white bra, your gigantic cleavage still apt to tremble when you sob, when you are broken down from the New York sense of self and purpose, from the big city sensibility you were raised in. *How do I get home*, your spirit may ask in your sleep? Make a big city wish, or two , or three!

Your tits wiggle mightily from the Chelsea slap, when she puts the camera down and rushes to where you are, slapping the Holy Hell and taste from your pretty mouth. Your straight, short cut brunette hair is beautiful in the slap. Chelsea opens her knife and says *who the fuck do you think you are bitch? The next time Simone asks you a question you will answer it, or I will cut your fucking face off like Hannibal Lector in Silence of the fucking Lambs.* Your scream is too much for me, Mrs. Drinkwine, as Chelsea puts the tip of the sharp little knife in your face under your lovely jawline. Through tears and shock, your crying eyes are blue. The blood running down your lovely neck is red against your white skin.

When you spank your daughter, do you use your bare hands?

I use a pa...

A what?

A wooden paddle... I make her stand up near the wall and put her hands behind her head.

Every time?

Yes.

Have you ever beaten her with anything other than a paddle?

With a belt.

Ever used a hair brush?

No.

Why not?

I just never thought about it.

What?

Chelsea steps forward—

Because the paddle turns me on! she screams. *Because I get a tingle in my crotch when I paddle her ass with the wooden paddle... God, I can't help it....*

Even to your captors, there descends a silence we cannot break, at the admission of such deep, unspoken depravity.

Did you ever fantasize about paddling your daughter?

Yes. God help me, yes! I wait for her to slip up, to say the wrong thing, to fucking just think the wrong thing so I can knock on wood.

That's what you call it?

Yes, I tell her if you bring home a C on your report card we're gonna knock on wood until you're black and blue.

You've spanked bruises onto her?

Oh, God yes. I live for it. God forgive me, I live for it!

Have you ever molested your daughter?

No.

Did you ever want to?

I...

Answer her!

I don't know, she says.

Did you ever want to fuck your daughter?

No. I swear to God no.

What did you want to do?

I... I can't say it out loud. Please..

A glance over at Chelsea loosens her tongue.

I wanted to ssm my dottit

What? Chelsea says.

I wanted to suck my daughter's tits as a punishment.

Why?

She met a boy at the mall and missed curfew… she makes me so fucking mad I can't think straight. I wanted to hold her down and suck her tits until she was crying from the pain.

Why didn't you?

I just couldn't. Something wouldn't let me.

Oh, so you were going to go through with it.

I was going to try. But I couldn't do it. It's one of the worst paddlings she ever got that night. I made her pull her pants down and take her shirt off and raise her bra, just enough to expose her little tits so I could watch 'em shake when I hit her. I beat her so bad that night. She was crying and begging me to stop and I wouldn't. The next day her legs were bruised all the way down to the back of her knees.

Because she missed curfew?

But she missed it by an hour. Her defiance was deliberate. She was at the mall with her giggling, silly little friends. All those little bitches, I hate every one of 'em. Those sassy little cunts… they all think they're so smart and they don't know a goddamned thing about life. They don't know shit.

You wish you could teach 'em, don't you?

Yes. I wanna spank the blood out of ALL their little asses!

You do, huh?

Yes! Let me go. Just me go and I swear I'll dedicate my life to it. I'll plant the seed in all their mother's heads that we need to beat the fuck out of their little asses until they learn to close their legs and go home.

And learn to be chaste, good little girls.

Yes.

The Mountaineers

Girls who sit quietly at home and mind their Momma's and Daddy's. And one day they'll learn to be a good wife and mother. Like you.

At the end of your third day, you are exhausted, having only drank water, having only slices of apple for strength. Our Simone has your ropes cut by me, and we watch you remove your own blood stained bra and underwear. Had I enjoyed pulling your nipples forward while Chelsea held you from behind, pushing the safety pins into your areolas to watch you shake and scream to God and Christ? Did the blood run from your breasts and down your body until it seemed you would bleed to death? Did the sheer size and sexiness of your breasts get to me at long last, until I admonished you to relax—with my hands shoved between your legs until you shook with another kind of scream? Did I watch your bleeding breasts latched by pins, and your wiggling wide hips jiggle as you shook to endure the aftermath of trauma, which was the rubbing of your clit after your orgasm, to the deepest torture you have known this side of pain? *Let me hear it through your voice*—Simone had said—and you obliged with such an undignified grunting, bellowing and convulsing as I have never seen.

Stand now, Northern Woman of Straw. Stand now, New York Lady of Leisure! Upon you is the stench of death, covered in the most delightful perfume. But doth thy perfume smell the tiniest bit as sweet, as the roses above your body in bloom? The pink roses that will shine in the sun at noon, that will glow in the light of the Summer Mountain Moon? You act this final role in blood, Dear Lady, as though you don't know that you're going to die! Stand there, with your big, jiggly ass out, white and ready to feel the pounding of the paddling wood. *Not one fake sound from you bitch*, Chelsea says in brilliance, to heighten the tension. Simone hands me the paddle, and I strike the first blow of your demise, square across both of your fat, shapely buttocks, watching the paddle sink in and out of the Jello wiggle, leaving a red mark as big as the paddle across your whole backside.

We stand there. Watching it get redder, listening to you sniff and whimper quietly, afraid to make a sound. The second whack is as hard as the first, across the same spot, raising a quick grunt which you suppress, leaving a deep, dark red spot where the end of the paddle dug in. The three of us know that this is your threshold, thought it is only the beginning, and when the third whack is brought down, a siren comes out of your voice that grows the cock in all three of us, and I quickly give you the fourth whack with the paddle, which breaks you down and your hands slip from behind your head to the white living room wall.

This is still the Tiding of Number Five, before my Chelsea hath flown. The Tiding of Number Five, under the winter Mountain Moon. Drink the wine of your comeuppance, Lady Victoria, as you near three hundred swipes upon the board! The skin of your backside is unrecognizable as normal, only a mottled, red and blue mess of dark bruises and broken skin, whereby the paddle itself is stained with blood. You stand leaning against the wall now, bellowing long like an animal and slobbering. And now comes the surprise, Mrs. Drinkwine, as Simone takes the thin boards she put together and brings them down hard over your back. The boards break into pieces all over the floor, and Simone grabs your weak, stumbling body and beats you in your face, making your lip bleed in the flood. The flurry of abusive blows, ending with her walking around you in her big bra and underwear, picking the boards up from the floor and stacking them loosely in her hand, and she wildly slams them into your bruised, bloody back again.

Stumble to the floor again, Dear Lady. Lay there crying, sobbing because you feel like a rib is broken, and your buttocks and the backs of your thighs feel like they have been burned in fire. Lay there on the blood stained carpet. Spitting, breathing. Suffering inside. Wishing for a home you will never see again.

Now look up. Watch three demons in women's bodies. See The demons power the bodies forward to action, to especially the voice of the Amazon who says *bring Moby Dick* and you wonder—what does a novel have to do with thee! And you understand what it is that she means when I bring out the biggest dick you have ever seen, which slopes down all of 12 inches like the big banana dick that it is. I help Simone strap this monster around her waist, and you say *please* with your last living breath, and the last ounce of sanity there is. And then, Chelsea and I join her, our members inferior to the Cory libido tonight.

The rags of our brief modesty lay scattered with the bleeding wood, and we are on our knees beside you (with Chelsea's knife to your throat) while you lay on your raw back, with Simone pushing the whale in to split you in two. Now scream, dear woman, wail to the God you never prayed to before, as the woman whose breasts are even more magnificent than yours kills you with the gigantic spear, which you feel further up inside your womb than you thought possible. Surely, you must know that on the other side of this leap is no solid ground, that there is only a plunge far and away downward, where you hear professor Simone Cory's screams mingled with your own. It is the gift that Simone and I share, likewise as the angel blonde—that our strapped on penises become real after just a short time, and too much thrusting sends us into orgasms we can hardly endure.

Careful, my dear Lady. Don't move against the Chelsea blade! Lie still against the siren in your ears, as the brunette you once trusted cries out to God, then lays down and trembles every inch of her body on top of you. I wait for her to rest, and then I take my part of you, until I have climbed this selfsame mountain and fallen from it again, even tasting the blood from your nipple on my tongue, holding your big, blood stained tit in my mouth so I can cum. And then at the last, at the long last, I am again the roving, unblinking eye, and I am as the eyes of the Lord, watching the blonde rack her own body with this buildup and release of energy, and I hear her evoke the name of Jesus when she shakes, even as you begin to choke your last breath past Simone's hands clamped around your throat.

In the Heart of Memory, I see my Chelsea Doll on her knees at the foot of the Cross, planting the fifth rose in the garden by the Appalachian Woods.

On the edge of Mountain View Road—underneath the fall of night—
I wait for the Chelsea Doll to round the rings of Saturn, having no idea where
it is in the universe she could have gone. And although I have felt uneasy
since this afternoon, it is only because I know how unsettling it must be for
her to have lost a job, rather than the despair brought on by her boss'

apocalyptic betrayal. *She'll be fine* is the medicine I keep taking, whenever a feeling rises in the pit of my stomach that something might be wrong.

Nighttime summer skies are so much clearer in the mountains, giving us the clarity after dark not seen down in the Piedmont, where the stars are dimmed by the haze of city lights and pollution. But the mountain air is clean and pure—and when there are no clouds in and about, it can be seen why the astronomers build their little round houses on higher ground. From Kitt Peak to Pine Mountain—these night skies are clearest to behold.

High above me, I see the Northern Cross, and the haze of light that arcs across the celestial sphere from one side to the other, the tiniest echo of God's glory. This is the haze by which we understand the cosmos, and the infinity of his mind and will, a sight that glows with truth too far away to see, and beauty too far and wide to understand. Beneath the arm of the Milky Way Galaxy, in my spirit there is a truth that glows the light of a revelation too far away for me to see.

Where's Chelsea is the sound squeezed from the storm door hinges somewhere behind me. I hardly look back at all, turning my hand just enough to be sure Simone is coming towards me. Her steps get louder and louder in the mountain night.

"Here. Sit."

I open the folding lawn chair and sit down, breathing a sigh of profound gratitude. Looking back up into the field of stars, I notice a bright spark falling in a long, fiery arc towards the horizon.

"Please tell me you saw it."

"That falling star," she says. "I saw it."

"I know it means something. But what?"

"Make a wish just in case. It could be a Divine symbol of hope. It could be an angel. It could foretell some future event, a major change coming. We'll just have to wait and see. When it happens, we'll know."

"It's the biggest, brightest one I've ever seen."

"It could mean that it's over," she says. "That our garden is full."

"I think maybe she *was* the last one."

"Maybe?"

"Well, you never know."

"Raven, it had to end sometime. I felt a sense of completion with this one. A finality. Don't tell me you didn't feel it too."

I don't answer.

"It's the strangest thing, Simone. I know God didn't approve of what we've done, but at the same time, He knows that we couldn't have done anything about it. We couldn't have stopped it if we tried. There was a spirit driving me. Pressing down on me. I felt it enter me when that girl— no, no it wasn't then. I think it entered me when I was a child. When I was about nine years old."

"That was when Malina called you to the kitchen the first time."

"Yeah. After that I started having dreams about women. Grown women. The first one I remember was two women with their butts pressed together over the toilet taking a dump."

"How'd they accomplish that?"

"I don't know. Two beautiful, long legged women. They got it done somehow. Since I was a little girl, I remember every night, going to bed with lesbian fantasies in my head. It's like they were waiting for me. In my heart. My mind."

"Mine too."

"Really?"

"Since I was about 13. I used to imagine two of my female teachers with no clothes on wrestling in an empty classroom. They were always standing up, trying really hard to flip the other one down but not being able. I even dreamt that once. It was so real. Very intense."

"Weren't you 13 when Jennifer called you to the bedroom?" I barely see her nod her head in the dark. "So what are we saying?"

"Only God knows."

A pause, to consider what Wisdom wanders among the stars, and what is still unread in the manuscripts of God.

"There was a show that used to come on. Malina used to watch it—it was called Alice. Remember that show?"

"Vaguely."

"It starred Linda Lavin as this middle aged Mom who worked at this diner, with two other waitresses named Flo and Vera. One of the first fantasies I had was about Alice and her skinny, goofy brunette friend Vera. I would see Alice on all fours with Vera behind her banging her real hard. This was before I even knew what a dildo was. I don't even think they used one, I can't remember. But Alice would always close her eyes and start yelling *oh, no*…like she couldn't take what was coming, so to speak. Then she would just explode with this big orgasm at the same time Vera broke down with hers. And Vera would grab Alice's tits and pull her up and they'd both be kissing and moaning like it was the end of the world. It was a recurring fantasy I couldn't stop having. I couldn't keep it out of my head. But I never thought about being with other girls myself. I just thought it was normal to have private fantasies about women being together."

"Did you ever have a boyfriend in your life?" she asks.

"No."

"You are a raging dyke, honey. And you didn't even understand. If you did, you might have been happy."

"What about you? When did you know?"

"I was the same as you. Thought my sexual attractions to other women was normal for everybody. But still, I knew it was something you couldn't discuss. But I turned down at least one guy a week my whole life it seems."

"With those tits, I can imagine. Didn't you get hit on by women, too?"

"When I was a senior at Wake, about to go to graduate school—one of the professors in the Dept. of Religion—"

"No."

"Yes. I swear to God, yes."

"How come you never told me?"

"I don't know. I think it's too embarrassing. It was a female professor. Older woman in her late 40's. She said *Simone, I just have to tell you, your bosom is magnificent*. I got to tell you, I was shocked."

"Did it lead to anything?"

A pause…

"Let's just say that… she was hungry."

"Come on now, you've got to tell me something. I told you about my stupid Alice fantasy."

"Well, it's pretty humiliating but…"

"What?"

"I became her assistant for the next four years. Through her 50th birthday. All the way through graduate school. And I never had any trouble getting published. She admitted to me that she had wanted to do it for a long time. Since her husband showed her this German softcore, she said. The desire used to burn in her so hot that she almost approached her own daughter."

"You must be joking."

"You know I don't joke about this subject, Babe. There is secret mother-daughter heat everywhere you go. And believe me it is a secret. One of the deep, dark secrets of mankind."

"Well, tell me about you and her."

"She used to sit at her desk in her office chair, my shirt would be off. And I'd have a white t-shirt on. She said she loved the way my breasts looked in a T-shirt with no bra. She would fold my t-shirt up and she would be nursin' on 'em like she was trying to get milk. The first time she did it, I came. Just like the whoring slut I am. My professor just held on to me. Kinda loving, actually. She said *I always knew things like this were possible in real life. I always knew it. Simone do you know how lucky we are? How privileged we are in the history of the world to have experienced that?*"

The scene carries me back to the afternoon, and what Chelsea had told me about her bank manager. About Connie Green.

"This afternoon, Chelsea said that people would be shocked if they knew how their mothers really were. How they really thought. The things they did in secret."

"Speaking of Chelsea—where is she anyway?" Simone asks. "Is she gonna spend the night in Winston? If she does, I don't blame her, I've done it before in Greensboro. But she could have called us at least."

"Yeah. That's it isn't it? She's gonna spend the night in a hotel. She said she was really tired. Probably had to go clear her head. I'm sure she's got a lot on her mind. Sometimes I'm tired too. I wish we didn't have this long commute every day. After seven years I think it's getting to all of us."

"Well, she could have at least called."

"Have you tried to call her?"

"I already left three messages. But she won't answer."

"I don't blame her. She just got fired from her job, for God's sake. She's probably embarrassed as Hell."

"She doesn't need to be embarrassed with us about anything," Simone says. "I hope she knows that."

"She knows."

"You know, I wonder how unique we really are. Among the population as a whole, I mean."

"As murderers?"

"No. As daughters," she says. "We both had our mothers shove their naked tits in our faces when we were growing up. Both our mothers actually sucked on our breasts for their own sick, sadistic sexual needs."

"You and Chelsea were both raped by your mothers."

"You were raped too, honey," Simone says. "Penetration's got nothing to do with it. The law would call what she did to you "indecent liberties with a minor." Rape is the tool of the powerless. Used to gain the power and control they don't have in their everyday lives. Dicks in pussies don't have a damned thing to do with it. But we're so focused on that, that we don't realize if a man had any brains he could rape a woman by dry humping her while holding her down. And even though that is every bit of a rape, he couldn't be charged with it. Dicks and pussies. Dicks and pussies."

"Simone, that word."

"Sorry. But it pisses me off. I'm strong enough to hold a skinny, weak teenage boy down under me. And the three of us together can hold down a grown man. I guarantee you if the norm was for women to jack men that way, the whole concept of rape would be redefined. If a man as much as stares at my ass too long, it should be some form of rape crime. Rape by Penetration? Hah! Rape by penetration should carry a fucking life sentence."

"I don't give a fuck about men. I mean it. If a man ever raped me, I swear to God and Jesus he would be *dead*. I would wait outside the courtroom like a sweet little Indian mouse. And I would blow his fucking head off. If that Bobbit bastard ever in his life raped a woman, then God bless Lorena. And as for my mother, she used to go up and down on my tits like she was blowing a cock. She grunted and groaned and licked and sucked like it was her greatest pleasure. Our mothers, Simone. Our mothers did these things. How unique are we?"

"I think there's a lot of us out there, but like I said, it's a dirty little secret. And it's going to stay just that. The Mother Daughter Dynamic, Raven, is the single most compelling sexual dynamic there is. Of all pairings, it is number one. The most perverted simplicity there is, because it encompasses the dual lust of two women together, and the forbidden lust of incest, but made even more powerful by the age difference, unlike sisters or cousins. Not even Aunts and nieces because aunts don't give birth to their nieces. The aunt niece relationship is not sacred like mothers and daughters. And because we all worship female sexuality, there's a part of us that is forced to accept it. Especially if the mother and daughter are sexy or beautiful enough. In other words, the Age of the Hot Mom. The cougar. The mother lover. And when you mix the Mother Daughter

Dynamic into all of that, all of those longings—its explosive. Two older women together? Whatever. Two younger women together? Whatever. But an older woman and a younger woman together? Its twisted. It begs the mother daughter question, which haunts us all down to the core of who we are. And yet it is just too perverted and sick to admit it's something we have all thought about. Nobody is going to admit how hot it is to imagine that Chelsea Clinton might strap it on every now and then and give Momma the screaming anal sex she might need behind closed doors once or twice a year. Or how about when Martha Stewart got out of prison, huh? Did her daughter fuck her up the ass as some kind of a spiritual release or right of passage? If they did, we're never gonna know about it I promise you, but it's hard not to imagine it. I do know that there are plenty, and I mean *plenty* of older women who want to have sex with a younger girl so bad they have to get off on the fantasy to make it stop. And this is running through all of us at some level. This forbidden fantasy, the beauty of mother daughter sex. This modern sexualization of the mother daughter dynamic is pervasive, Raven. Getting worse all the time. And nobody is going to listen to us complain because Mommie put her bit titties in our mouth. How can they listen to us complain about it Honey? They get off on it."

"I get off on it. I always have."

"And it's not just because you're Lesbian babe. It's because you're human."

"But are we Lesbian… because we were molested by our mothers?"

Professor Cory takes a breath of mountain air, gazing up into the second heaven.

"It may have activated what was already in us when we were born," she says. "Our mothers may have sensed it subconsciously and were drawn to it. Does homosexuality run in families? I don't know. I have never been attracted to men. Never even imagined being with one."

"You *know* I haven't. And Malina never had a boyfriend after my father left."

"So, we're probably Lesbian from birth. Whatever it is we are, I know that somehow, it was written in these stars… before the beginning of time."

$\mathcal{I}$wake up beyond the call of midnight, feeling a profound sense of relief, having just dreamed that Chelsea came home in the best mood I have seen in a long time. Her hair was blonder, her skin smoother, her eyes bluer than the waters in the Sea of Galilee. Of what earthly joy this is I feel, I do not know. I know only that I'm able to go back to sleep now, and rest for the remainder of the night.

On our blue path among the stars, we circle an infinity. Pulled along by the Global Stream—speeding towards our Destiny. Lords and Kingpins, users and pushers. Families are torn apart, by the sea of thunder rising. By the greed of tears asunder. Drawn into Hordes of Legion. Entertained by the violent color. Waiting to kill…waiting to die.

Somewhere in the midst of chaos, the seed of doubt remains. Corrupting goodness into bile. Causing idle hands to lust for power. We must return to the darkened room, to reverse our path to dark eternity. A path leading to worlds unknown. Breaking into bands of animosity.

We are told by the elite that our path through the storm is done and complete. She will take no particular offence, when told the sign of the earthquake is wrong.

On our blue path among the stars, we circle an infinity.

Again and again, all roads lead to the barren plain. Around and around, beneath the skies of eternity and grief. Rising into Chelsea's Place. Having no energy for the present. But the Idyllic Path is stopped. Buried underneath brimstone and fire.

Human life goes to Heaven. Transformed by a miracle.

$\mathscr{D}$awn is the morning twilight, nearby the edge of night. Shadows recall fair birth of light, beyond their feeble sight. From where the new sky rises in the east, burning blue and black fire—past where Professor Cory rides to another day on campus, the new day rolls toward the Appalachian Range, until the stars are faded in the light. I awake again at about seven in the morning, when dawn is killed by the light. This is truly a new day for me, after a night of strange and wonderful dreaming—from the top of a snow capped mountain peak somewhere, to shores past Elizabeth City, and the roaring waves of the Crystal Coast and Cape Hatteras. It is a renewed sense of freedom, I believe—that the suffering of our lives has ended, and we are past our earthly calling, to deliver judgment to the deserving souls of women.

The Tiding of Number Seven is but four days old, from Friday afternoon until today, and perhaps in these waters there rests a cleansing spirit that has washed us clean, that has ebbed our sickness away and out to sea. Somewhere in my heart, I know he has forgiven me, and I am glad to be alive, and I look forward to a time to live, and then a time to be happy.

What image is it that I deliver in my jet black hair, black sports bra and tight black Hanes to match? When I turn the TV on, and when I see myself in the mirror in the hall, I am truly amazed at the unnatural prettiness of the woman I see. But how is it that a part of her is so filled with self hatred, and the inability to feel pretty at all? In the bathroom mirror, I gaze at the Indian girl I see, the thirty one year old failure thus far, on the edge of believing in her potential. "They're going to ask you to be manager," I say. Then you'll finish school and get your MBA, and then you'll go as corporate as when the Devil wore Prada in the city. *Say hello to my newest executive assistant, Raven Moon… she started out on the sales floor in a mall so she knows the business from the ground up…*

I'm suddenly pulled from my morning daydream at the mirror by a woman's deep, sultry voice on the morning infotainment—the colossal, corporate clowning and concocted candor—foreordained fawning and phony, false faced sincerity—*"Police investigators were called to a wealthy suburb in Chesapeake, Virginia this morning to investigate a murder-suicide that occurred there after sundown yesterday, where it appears a woman shot and killed her estranged daughter on her front lawn, and then turned the gun on herself. Police have not yet released either of the women's names, but is believed that the thirty year old daughter was a bank teller from Black Mountain, North Carolina...*

...Relatives are still grieving the loss of nearly 100 lives this weekend when one of the strongest F-5 tornados on record devastated the tiny town of Clearview, Oklahoma on Saturday, killing nearly all of the 104 residents who lived there. With nothing left of the tiny town but what one reporter called "wet sticks and mud," the Governor has publically referred to the incident as quote, 'an act of God, that has taken Clearview off the map forever'..."

Somewhere in the whirlwind, in the funnel cloud of words drifting, there appears parts of phrases that I cannot fully discern or comprehend, having something to do with Chesapeake, Virginia. And when I see the word *teller* come around again, this time it is attached to the same devastated sentence as the words *Black Mountain*, and like the fool on the highway of certain death, I see now that what I see whirling at me is that tanker truck filled with gasoline, and it is already too late to run.

I have no sympathy for whatever Hell bound souls were blown out of existence in the deserving Oklahoma town. All I can do is rinse the toothpaste out of my mouth and throw myself into these blue jeans and black shirt, with my hair flying, gold hoop earrings in place, and red lipstick where it ought to be. *Chesapeake... bank teller... Black Mountain...* For whatever reason, I know I may as well not waste time with questions; pointless phone calls that won't be answered. There are so many miles to cover. Such a long, long way to go.

Driving. Speeding. Flying down the highway east. Why am I blaming myself, for whatever I imagine has ensued? How foolish am I being anyway—a profession and the name of two towns does not a dead girl make, does it? Surely, it is the tragedy of another mother that has befallen the community of, what is it, Camille Harbour? Why am I thinking of Camille Harbour, anyway—I don't remember them mentioning it. There's probably a whole network of those places in Chesapeake, right? Why am I blaming myself for what probably hasn't even happened? Why does my mind flash over and over again to something Chelsea said yesterday, about being tired, and just wanting to go home? Surely, there wasn't anything to read in the Hug of Grand Departure, and the look she gave me when she turned the corner, and the wave like a passenger on a boat, slowly drifting from a loved one at the edge of the wooden dock.

I was supposed to think nothing of it, right? I was supposed to back off, and give her space to breathe in. Time to recover from the humiliation of being fired from a job she liked just fine, by a woman who violated her in ways that no one would believe or understand. She needed the hours to herself, to contemplate the end of the age, and the abominations which are the sign of his coming. Should I have held her hand the rest of the day, like she were a weakling child without the strength of character to persevere? To stand up like a woman once and for all, on this side of morality, and take up her Cross and follow Him? But what is this I feel, my Dear

Chelsea, when there is a gulf fixed between you and I, and I cannot know where it is that my beloved could have gone?

The Triangle of Miles is all I can fathom now, beneath the Triangle of Tears that bore it. Three points of light in the cosmos, darkened by their point of origin, dimmed forever by accidents of birth, where there were not sufficient forces to ignite them properly, where sorrow and disillusionment are often burned away. This Triangle of Years, from where phases these roads I must travel from Black Mountain to Greensboro, to Chesapeake, Virginia.

Let thine eyes see clearly, thou Indian Woman of Straw. Monitor thy accursed condition, lest you be distracted by your grief. If you look down, Dear Lady, you will know why the flashing lights have appeared behind you on the highway east, admonishing you that the cardinals do not sing the trees and fences of your new path, and the owls lurk silently in the dark.

Jonathan Lovejoy

"I can't make it—on my own—
No one likes to be alone
She drives me crazy, like no one else—
She drives me crazy, and I can't help myself"

The Mountaineers

The town is normally copasetic when I drive through, as I am apt to have occasion to go to work every day in a woman's paradise, and play with fine casual for a living. *They're going to ask me to be manager* keeps playing in my head like a stuck disc as I get closer to the mall. But today, there is no giddy anticipation—no satisfaction of fun park sensibility as I drive into town to the nearest gas station for a breather and a drink—still hardly able to believe what has begun to ring in my spirit, unable to accept that what I feel is true. Sipping a Tahitian Treat in the summer breeze, I fill the Camry to bursting with oil from Vesta's Reserve, gazing mindlessly once at the trunk, remembering Amanda Hall without pity.

As I return the nozzle to its place, I hear the call of an angry blackbird nearby, which seeks to unnerve me as a purveyor of doom. But what is that to me, having carried their dark energy for 31 years on this earth? What image do I project, returning the gas nozzle to its place, walking back to my driver's seat in the rising summer wind, hair flowing past my earrings and my shoulders in the Carolina breeze? As I start the car and roll away from the Amaranthine Station, a wave of satisfaction floods me that even though I alone was enough to put awe in their suburban minds, those shapely and misshapen, fat tittied and fat bellied, pretty faced and ugly faced suburban bitches I just ignored would have had a heart attack if they had seen Simone Cory, unable to accept what they saw without anger or gossip or laughter, and unable to get the image of Goddess beauty out of their minds.

Back on the Highway of Lost Souls, my mind is drawn to the Cory sensibility, and the anticipation of thunder. The lightning bolt of my sudden appearance, splitting the air in two, and the sudden crashing of it back together again. I cruise this hop, skip and a jump from Winston to Greensboro. Newly settled into the delusion that what I heard this morning was coincidental at best. How silly I was, crying when the trooper asked to see my license. *Oh, come on now, it ain't that bad is it darlin'? We cain't let you go 70 can we?*

No, I had said, *it's not that. My friend's been missing since yesterday. I'm just really worried about her.*

Was I trying to gain sympathy from the bureaucratic mentality? Was I trying to get blood from a stone?

I tell you what, he says, *I don't usually do this Maam, but I ran your license, and I see you've got a perfect driving record. So I'm gon' accept that you might have been genuinely distracted by your friend being missing. You keep it down to under 60, cause I guarantee you if you get stopped again you gon' get a ticket...*"

But what mercy of God was this, as the blood did trickle down the rocks of Calvary, nearby the foot of the Cross? Without the shedding of blood, there is no remission of sins, and with God, all things are possible. *Have a good day, I hope you friend turns up soon*, the trooper had sang in departure, with the requisite tip of his drill sergeant hat, knowing he had about as much power to give me a ticket as he would have Michelle

Obama. The spirits that have called me to do what I do, they are in the divine order of things, protecting me from all municipal eyes that stare. What flames that burn here do so unabated, until they have consumed what they may, according to his will and purpose under the sun.

Get back in your car and drive away, asshole! Flash the light in somebody else's mirror!

In this selfsame mirror, I check my makeup at every stop, as I roll slowly down the university streets. I find a space in the summer parking lot, remarkably full it seems to me for summer school. What misery this must be, trapped in these dusty old classrooms on such a day, when the sky is as blue as the Caribbean Sea, and there is not a cloud in sight? Parking pass in its place on the mirror, I step into the rarified university air, which smells of failure and lofty aspirations, shattered hopes and broken dreams intellectualized away. It is the stench of secular humanism, which carries the life of graveyards in its wake, and the rotten, putrid smell of the grave. The place—the people, the purpose of it all makes me sick to my stomach as I walk—a place where intellectual innocence goes to die—a place designed to weed out those who would cross over, but are unable. As I walk past the girls and women, I do so as a stuck up dyke bitch and I love it, made confident by the fact that if the spirit had so moved, one of these twits would have been assured of two things—that they would disappear off the face of the earth, and two, they would fucking die screaming.

Screams of days and years gone by. The howling, wailing voices of souls trapped forever swirl all around me as I climb the concrete steps to Gilbert Hall, where the Department of Religion hides and resides. Waist in, titties out far, I find the nearest open door in the echo of my black boots down the hallway, peaking inside with no pretense to phoniness nor friendship, but being pleasant just the same.

"She's in class right now", the black woman says, "but I think it's over at eleven, and she always comes back here and works in her office 'til about three."

I thank the pitiful, underpaid woman who calls herself a secretary, turning to leave, but suddenly deciding to ask what building Simone is in.

"Go outside the front door and walk to your right. Then turn right again on this little street out here and deep walking about a mile till you see Brown Hall, you can't miss it. She'll be on the second floor in Room 207."

A brief smile and a nod from me, and a pleasant wave, turning on restraint and mild contempt for her dressed up mediocrity, trying not to wish I could run in and just slap the shit out of her for no good reason and scream unspeakable, racist truths in her cute, brown Momma face for her own good, to see her get the Hell out of this place and just go home. But truthfully, who am I to judge? A bitter, despondent criminal, a scourge—a blight on the fabric of society? Should this woman be proud of herself, that she runs with the big dogs here in Academic Heaven, if only as their second rate servant and companion? Why am I jealous of her, because she is a University Department secretary? I think it is the rising of my true self again, which is devoid of self esteem and the ability to believe that I am worth a damn.

The Mountaineers

I walk past two lady professors talking in the hall, one in a long, kaki skirt with her back to me and her hands in her pockets—skirt stretched across an ass unlike anything I have ever seen outside of a fantasy. *God...DAMN*, I say in my mind, while the twinge of light pricks my groin. The sheer width of her backside, her hips, is burned into my mind now, something she must be aware of at least in part. *Honey get to the nearest full length mirror and turn around with your hands in your pockets. I'll bet you won't wear that skirt again. Our Lady of the Hips*, is the chorus I sing as I open the big front door, realizing that along with the worry in the pit of my stomach is now the agony of my accursed lust, and the despair spoken into my life by Malina Moon. *"You might as well quit school and go to work,"* she said when I started the eleventh grade, with her hands around my throat in the kitchen *"'cause you ain't never gon' mount to nothin' no way. You ain't nothin' but a Indian bitch. Good for a farm or a factory. You think you gon' school your way out of what you are? A straw dog? If you lucky you'll find a man that won't beat your ass every day. And that little eye roll you just did? Its gon' cost you. I swear to Almighty God and his son Jesus it's gon' cost you some lashes after supper, Miss Baby Doll. You think you look like a baby doll? Huh? You think you got baby doll eyes?"*

What few smiles I have left are gone now, as I stroll the Campus of Dreams, down the Avenue of Aspiration, unable to despise the meadow and forest life of green, equally unable to tolerate the walking and talking life of black and white. I am overwhelmed with apprehension (which I am practiced at hiding), having to remind myself that what they see when I walk is just too damned hot for them to ridicule in their hearts. Beauty is my saving grace, my protection from the outside world, but inside I am a monster, corrupt and fearful, and full of hatred for the mothers and daughters of mankind. What love I have in me is for the souls of those accursed, out of respect for my Lord and Savior, though their flesh I care nothing for, as neither a loving flame can care for the condemned witch it embraces in the night. *They all deserved to die* is what keeps burning inside, to help reduce my fear and worry down to nothing.

Brown Hall is another brief stroll from the Avenue (after I realized I had almost walked past it), across the street and down a long, concrete walkway to the high brick steps, which I take in renewed energy of expectation. *Simone is in here? Really?* The boys and men making an effort to see and be seen by me hold no interest, but I myself must often work to not turn my head to stare at a pair of young breasts or a face too pretty to ignore. The girls all look at me at least once, as though I were somebody to be looked at in my long hair and tight jeans. But the one who catches my attention is a woman with short, blonde hair ten years older than me at least, as pretty as a dancer, reeking of a suburban sensibility I have known. I lock eyes with this woman on my way up the stairs to the second floor, putting my hand to my hair like a teenage girl at the front door on Friday night, smiling this *M*other *I*'d *L*ike to *F*uck up and down, wanting to follow her to wherever it is she is going. At the top of the stairs, I turn and watch her go out the door, catching her look as she goes out, knowing that she is lucky there was already the Tiding of Number Seven, and the planting of the seventh rose in the garden.

Amidst the quiet of my slow, determined footsteps, I see that the door of room 207 is open, and I hear a voice so sultry and familiar, so filled with passion about her subject, teaching the summer graduate class Women in the New Testament, saying something about the woman at the well, and the metaphor of living water...

"... And Jesus was particularly sympathetic to women. He knew us. He understood us. And this woman was taken aback that Jesus was talking to her in the first place, because she was a Samaritan, and she knew that Jews didn't have anything to do with Samaritans. Yet here is this man—this Jewish Rabbi, asking her for something to drink. And even though it was his job as a Rabbi to always avoid even the appearance of so-called evil, he had enough integrity to not worry about what anybody else would think, if they saw him talking to this woman. And the kicker was that not only was she a foreigner he was forbidden to associate with, but he knew she'd been married five times. And the man she was living with now was *not* her husband. And did he judge her? Did he condemn her? Did he use it as an opportunity to make her feel bad about herself—about her life? No. He used it as an opportunity to put the focus on God. Telling her that God is a spirit, and he should be worshipped in spirit and in truth. And something about the way Jesus spoke made her think about what she'd heard in a prophecy, that supposedly a 'messiah' was coming, somebody who would 'tell us all things,' she said. And then Jesus said something to her he hadn't even said to the religious leaders of the day yet. He said, *I am the Messiah.* He spoke this to the woman at the well, and she was so excited, she left her pot of water right where it was, and she went into town and said, *I have seen the Christ.* The most important element of his mission as a prophet— and he reveals it to a woman who had five husbands and was working on number six. *Whosoever drinketh of the water that I shall give shall never thirst*, he said..."

At that moment, this Woman of Power looks at me, a tallish woman in glasses and a long, tight charcoal gray skirt, her navy blouse in grieving to hide a disproportionately large bosom. I hardly recognize this intelligent, confident person, having never seen her immersed in her gift, to stand in front of people every day and give impromptu speeches—prepared or unprepared—a lecturer *par excellence*, I think, though I know she has chosen to soon retire from lecturing to research and write. This beautiful Woman of Knowledge looks at me, looks into me—with a sudden shock to her system, having not ever imagined to see me haunt the Halls of this Campus ever again. I turn away from her and stroll to the side, listening to her dismiss her class ten minutes early, telling her to read the book of John chapter 4 again before class tomorrow and to think about this 'living water' that Jesus was talking about.

I wander over to the side—a little down the hall towards the corner by the stairwell. The students all file past me down the stairs, their stares being neither here nor there for me. The stench of their youth, their false confidence and drowning naiveté grates my last nerve, and I have no smiles left, nor eye contact unfleeting. When the last hopeless one of them is gone, their beautiful teacher brings up the rear, wandering over nearby to where I am.

"Gee *whiz*," I say, referring to what sings the key of G major under that navy blouse.

"What?" she says, in full Diana Prince regalia. Hair pinned, glasses tight.

"Let's get out of this hallway."

She follows me, bewildered, back to the classroom. I take a seat in the nearest chair by the door, watching her gather her books together and put them in her leather carrying bag. Truthfully, I can only nibble at my red nails while I watch her swim the ocean of her calling.

"Am I supposed to guess?" she says. Stepping back out from her desk over to me, pointing stick in hand as if she intends to use it. As I lower my head, I feel the stick at my chin, gently raising my head up to where she can see into me.

"Speak."

My mouth trembles, but to speak—I cannot. She puts her stick on her desk and walks in seriousness back to where I am, sitting down in a desk beside me, bosoms nearly making it impossible not to notice.

"I heard Ann Curry on the Today Show this morning."

"Oooo. *Mama San*. Did she call the house? Cause if she did— "

"She said that an F5 tornado wiped out a whole town in Oklahoma. Clearview, I think."

"Is that what you came all the way up here to tell me?"

"Before that, I heard her say something about Chesapeake, Virginia."

Melancholy revelation. It is what splashes the beautiful professor in her face, and washes the comic bewilderment from her expression.

he earth flows the River of Time, from one to the next evening day thereafter. Simone and I have hearkened to every voice of reason, under the stars near Chesapeake Bay, with me trying to convince myself that our journey here had been in vain. *It's a nice trip but I don't know why we came here,* I say, even while we drive from our hotel to the Police Department downtown, to try and get more sympathy from them in person. Not one detail beyond what I heard on the news would they give Simone over the phone. But when the two of us walk in their office after sunset, the three officers on duty are powerless against these fervent spirits, telling us rather quickly that the woman who was murdered was named Chelsea Lynn Baxter, which implodes my soul into a thousand pieces. In a pain I have never known before, with the ache of cold steel through the pit of my stomach, I turn and hurry out of the police station in the evening, and look helplessly to the dim stars trying to appear. When these stars begin to whirl about, as the coming of the night before Armageddon, I feel strong arms lift me from an impending fall, and walk me to the silver gray thing I hardly recognize as my car.

What tears there are to cry are bound up inside under a pressure too great; what screams, what convulsions there be are under lock and chain. My protector, my strength escorts me to the other side of the car and helps me get inside. Soon, she is in the driver's seat, a place I am normally accustomed to. But as she turns the key and rolls us away from the police station, I know it is as it should be, because even now, in the aftermath of trauma, I wonder what I would do if I were behind the wheel. I see the whirling of broken glass—I see the twisting of metal, and the explosion of airbags in our faces, to keep us from seeing how it is that we died.

As we cruise these unfamiliar miles, I cannot look around or speak, nor can I acknowledge Simone's kind hand on my knee and my leg. *You can identify the body*, they said. *They'll do an autopsy tomorrow, but it's pretty clear how she died. There was so much blood we think the bullet must have—*

"We'll get through this, Raven. We have to be strong. Being strong is what we do, Honey. It's who we are. And that's exactly how she would want it. We're gonna wait until they do whatever it is they need to do, and then we're gonna take her home."

"Where? To Black Mountain?"

"Maybe not in our... I mean... someplace nice. A real place where she can rest."

"A place where she can rest." I shake my head, afraid the speak the question of whether or not she would have died if it were not for me. Did her meeting with me bring the same curse I had into her life—the curse of fire and blood? Had I not spoken to her that day seven summers ago, would she have given place to evil, and helped me take a life? Would she have gone to graduate school, and medicated her pain with knowledge and brain pills and educated wisdom from the psychiatry books? She might have become Dr. Baxter, a woman with a deeper understanding of her patients' pain than they realize, knowing how and what to say to them for a healing. And even as we near the place where she lays, the morgue at Northampton Medical Center, I hear the ghosts of Mountain View Road calling us home, and they sing a ghostly, somber refrain in the summer evening, this Chorus of the Leaves, that tells me my Chelsea Doll is come and gone.

What is this place, this strange, unfamiliar place we are in—these trees I have never heard, these cars I have never seen, these dead and uncaring souls I have never known? I don't know if this is a frown I feel on my Indian face, as the nurse takes Simone and me down below—I only know I need to chloroform her and take her to these Virginia woods for a beating—for trying to tell me that my friend is lying still and cold somewhere down and far away below. Down, down blink the lights of our earthly obsession—these elevator lights that blink on and off but just once, where the door slides open for us beneath the earth—and we take the fool's step with the skeleton faced nurse into this darkness, this unknown place that stinks of cold and death.

She opens the square metal door with no compassion, as though she were pulling a sandwich from a silver refrigerator, sliding a body in a white sheet out to where Simone and I can see. My head is already shaking no, because I know that there is no way under the sun that this is where my beloved could have gone. Then the nurse touches the sheet of the maiden that lieth underneath, whoever she may be, this lying form they say belongs to us, and she turns the sheet respectfully down from the face of Truth and Beauty. I yip like the kicked straw dog I am and turn away, grabbing Simone by her blouse and pushing my face to her shoulder. And then I look again—and my voice begins to wail a sound wave, textured by the rising word *please,* and the rhythm of *look what her Momma did to her*, and then a long and painful shriek tears its way out of my body as I hold on to Simone for the last ounce of life and hope I have left. Holding me tight, a paragon of strength and power, she comforts me by rubbing my hair and my back, while she stares at the pale, lifeless face of the blonde woman we once knew.

*U*nder the drowning mist of rain, the yellow police tape is removed from the property in Camille Harbour Estates, and the world has forgotten this place again. Having spent one day with the loving, understanding family of Gretchen Baxter (Donna Turner, they all knew), we know all along as to what things must be—such as when and where Chelsea should be laid to rest. One week after the Seventh Rose, the funeral service is on this gray, rainy Saturday, packed with well wishers and lookie loos, and other fair weather followers of misery. There are 500 people in attendance, not including ourselves, who have neither the guts nor the patience to battle crowds at a prestige funeral. Neither do we attend the dreary, drowning burial with at least a hundred nosy stragglers left, to watch the rich suburban man bury the mother they heard about on the national news, who shot her own daughter in cold blood, then turned the gun on herself and pulled the trigger. We wait through the rainy afternoon of this encounter with nature itself, physically mourning the Death of Beauty, and of a woman who fulfilled a divine calling of hatred for her daughter.

When the very last body has left from the tent, we get out of our car and stroll casually through the mist, which is now a driving rainfall fed by the waters of Chesapeake Bay itself. The rain is noisy on the tent above our heads. We look down at what has been lowered beneath the ground, a mother and her daughter, absorbing the loss of a loved one, and the symbolism of what we see. It is the Death of Civility between mothers and daughters, the burial of old ways of thinking. I see the flooding of the Great Dismal Swamp, the overflow of eschatology along the banks of the river. Gone are the days when mothers were the caring and nurturing towers of strength and virtue, when daughters were naïve and trusting innocence and purity, looking to their mothers for guidance and protection from harm. This is a time to remember, yet one that will indeed last forever. From here until the end of the age, there is enmity set between a mother and her daughter, because the mothers hath corrupted themselves. Having lost their divine place in the order of things; having fallen from grace, choosing to carry the sensuality of their youth deep into middle age—feeding upon it, placing it on display until even the world at large must acknowledge it in vulgarities like M.I.L.F. and Cougar, inciting younger men to a lust they can neither resist nor understand, and a bitter rivalry with the young women half their age, the Daughters of Zion, the fallen young girls and women of straw, who now look to their mothers as examples of inspired lust and impropriety. It is the Death of Moral Civility, where immorality awaits with impudence, to permanently corrupt the mother-daughter dynamic, and spiral this corruption outward into the modern age. In these last days, He will uncover all behind closed doors sin, to show the world the fallen nature of man, and the seed of corruption passed down through the mother line.

As these Atlantic rains fall down in weeping, in mourning for two souls departed, even I can feel the power in the lives I see and remember, and I feel the fervent energy of what they have left behind. The end of these two lives is the beginning, I think, a divine acknowledgement of what is coming upon the earth. Chelsea, though we have no rose to give to thee— lay thy head to rest in Abraham's Bosom. From there, across the gulf affixed thereof, you can have no pity for the woman you see, who is tormented in this flame for eternity.

The rain falls in weeping. In lamentation for those upon the earth. Simone stands at the balcony window of our hotel, hardly able to process the turning of events. Though much of my own grief has already come out through my voice and the slow, steady flow of tears, Simone has not seen fit to cry once, believing that Chelsea would have wanted it that way. But like the raging floodwaters of a hurricane come ashore, the rising tide of grief cannot be denied, until it spills over into a life, and washes away every pretense of strength in hiding.

Simone looks out the second floor window of her resistance, seeing the waters of the Atlantic coursing the streets of this town, the place called False Dignity where she resides. "The rain is a sign of her forgiveness," she says at the window. "God always mourns the loss of one of his children, but at the same time, he rejoices."

"How come?"

"To be absent from the body is to be present with the Lord. And I believe that's where she is right now. I can feel it deep down."

"Me too. And for some reason I actually feel pretty good. Almost like a weight is lifted. It's not really joy as much as it is inner peace. Part of me is really glad she's gone, Simone. That she doesn't have to stay here and live this life anymore. That she can rest now, from the pain of what her mother did. From what all our mothers did to us."

But what I say, my feeling of relief has a strange, opposite effect on Simone, which she is in grieving effort to conceal. At long last, she turns away from the gray view at the glass door, walking over to the foot of the bed where I am and sits beside me.

"Are you okay?" she says pitifully, a veiled acknowledgement of her own soul's impending doom. "I think I'll make it," she says. "I just keep thinking about how, how it seems like when she died, the best part of what I had left died too, Raven. Even underneath the rage, there was a spark she had, a sweetness and a humility I hardly ever saw in seven years of teaching on that campus. Somewhere underneath it all, Raven, she was a good person. She was just angry. She couldn't help the things she did. And now she's gone. Chelsea's gone, Raven."

The wind blows hard against the walls of our brief shelter, driving the rain hard against the window. Although I'm able to stay calm, to stand fast in this storm, I know that the madness of grief has threatened to bury my Simone, to take her precious control from her, to make her endure the loss of dignity. I watch her hug her stomach with both her arms, sitting on the edge of the hotel bed, and she opens her mouth to no sound, and she squeezes herself as if to endure agony in her bowels. "Oh, God," she says. "Don't make me feel it, please..." I try to touch her, but she recoils as politely as she possibly can, shaking her head, refusing to be comforted.

I stand up and walk to the glass door, with her hardly aware that I have moved at all. Truthfully, I have no choice—as the waters of a creek rising in the rain give no place to the carpet of dead leaves that wish to remain. I am carried along toward this driving rainfall by a silent scream, one that I know she will hold in check for as long as she can, and let it go in waves small enough for her to endure. She refuses to sob; the stubbornness is epic. But when the long, loud and bellowing noise comes out of her, I know that this is private and not my place, and I gather my new umbrella and raincoat, long and black, and I step out onto the balcony in the wind and drowning rain. Before too long, I have contempt for this warm, weak Atlantic weeping, and my umbrella is closed and plopped horizontal on the wet balcony at my feet, soon joined by even the raincoat I have no use for just yet. A straw dog in the rain, eyes closed to the thunder and the lightning—aware that there are moments when every life connects again to where it began, and I open my eyes to the electrical sparks in the clouds with due respect, and take my full circle moment like the woman that I am.

*P*reordination spins the axis of events. Along the calendar of the Moon, and the time clock of the rising and setting sun. Somewhere behind these clouds of grieving, the time keepers spin around the earth, marking every second of every predestined hour, recording the past, present and future. The gray skies of Chesapeake have followed us south, even to the end of our journey. While the wind whips the waves into the beaches of Hatteras Island with renewed intensity, we press onward in the summer storm, to answer the call of the outer banks, and a view of the lighthouse above the Diamond Shoals. This is the Graveyard of the Atlantic, but not only for the ships that were captured in the shifting sand, but for where those that understand that they are at a crossroads must come, to complete their walk towards the end of this life.

We park the silver gray Camry on the side of Old Lighthouse Road, hearing the crashing of the waves as we step onto the sandy shore. This is no leisure walk we must undertake—to see the light on the outer banks— the light that shines a day's walk through the wilderness. In the wind and the rain, as I look 200 feet above me, the black and white pattern spirals in beauty against the gray, and I realize that God loves simplicity.

"It's beautiful. But what are we doing here?"

Simone looks away, towards the roaring waves—the wide and sounding sea. *And there shall be signs in the sun, and in the moon, and in the stars; and upon the earth distress of nations, with perplexity; the sea and the waves roaring; men's hearts failing them for fear, and for looking after those things which are coming on the earth: for the powers of heaven shall be shaken.* As she turns her back to me, to look away from my question, from my dim begging of why this must be, I know that answers are as vast as the ocean we see, and as elusive as the ocean air we breathe.

"I love you."

"I know. I love you too Simone. I always—"

"No."

She shakes her head no, wet hair blowing in the storm and mist.

"I think it happened the moment I saw you. I felt a spark. My heart literally, as they say, skipped a beat. The whole time I was driving you home that night I wrestled with it. I tried to deny it. But when you took my hand… it was over for me. Any dreams I might have had of being straight, of being normal—they died for me that night. I didn't tell you because, well, at first it was because I didn't want to scare you away. And I didn't want us falling in bed like two disgusting alley cats. I loved you so much that I was more than satisfied with just being there for you. And the other reason I didn't tell you, and this really hurts but… because I knew that you were in love with Chelsea."

"Simone, I didn't—"

"Shut… up. Shut your mouth. Don't you stand there and insult my intelligence and make a bigger fool out of me than you already have."

"Why didn't you just tell me?"

She turns like the big, white tiger she is and grabs my little head with both her strong hands. The strength of pressure she gives is masculine.

"I *told* you why," she says, shaking my head on the *told*, making me think of being drug up to the shore with my hands tied and held underneath the water and beaten with a stick, par Malina Moon herself, and a bathtub run full when I was 13. "Because I know you would have ran like a scalded dog if I had opened up to you like that. And because when you showed me that girl's body in our back yard I nearly shitted in my pants from pure fear, and yet I still loved you so much I helped you bury her and I chose not to call the police. I let you live in my house and use my lights and eat my fucking food like a goddamn stray cat… I even did dishes and vacuumed the floor topless so you could get off on it you nasty bitch…"

And on the choked word *bitch,* she throws me to the side like a wet scarecrow, causing me to lose my balance and fall.

"And after I let you into my life, after I let you suck on me like a leech on Rambo's fucking neck, you bring that fucking blonde *BITCH* into my house and act like I don't fucking exist anymore. And then you turn me into a fucking killer. A goddamn sex predator. I did all of this shit for you, Raven. And you were in love with Chelsea and you didn't give a damn about how I felt. Oh, you think I didn't know about you two? That you were fucking behind my back?"

"Simone—"

"Don't you deny it!" she yells at me, rushing at me and grabbing my hair while I'm still on the ground. "Don't you deny it or I swear I'll kill you with my bare hands and leave you here for the fucking *birds*. I knew it. I knew it since that trip we took to Hawaii four goddamned years ago after we killed that college bitch in the parking lot. When I was on the beach and you and her took a whole hour to come down from the hotel. Did you think I was stupid? And you didn't respect me enough to tell me? You didn't give a *damn* about me. All you cared about was your fucking self. You selfish—"

When she pushes my head and begins to walk away, I climb fully ashamed to my feet and hurry after her, but when I touch her she turns and attacks me with such strength as I didn't know she had. But my job is to hold on, to fight my way through the demonic attack until I am at her bosom, embracing her as if she could get me a seat on the Ark before the Flood. I hold on while she pries and scratches and claws and beats at my head and face. But I will not let you go, my Simone. I will not let you go until you bless me.

We both stand still in the misty rain, with her holding me tight again, amidst the sound of the pounding, crashing waves, and the voice of a woman saying over and over again, I love you.

𝒯he weeks pass into oblivion. From our wedding in the rain, under the lighthouse at Cape Hatteras, to our journey west again, disturbed by detours of days—and twenty five miles down east. In the Heart of Memory, we cross the miles from Elizabeth City, where we gather a long and lasting look at the house that bore her into this world as Maria Coronado. In so many lives, there is a House on Sycamore Avenue, where the spirit of unloving parenthood reaches in the heart of a child, and kills every part of joy and hope for the future. A house on Sycamore Avenue, white washed from the pale green remembered as a child. Behind these walls are the ghosts that roam, the spirits of childhood anguish and agony, where the rapes and the beatings first began. *Curling irons and wooden paddles,* Simone had said, neither of us bothering to even get out of the car. It seems that the clouds that mourn have followed us, keeping hope and happiness at bay, drowning us in a solemn mist of rain.

We cruise the miles from Elizabeth City, crossing the Roanoke River into Williamston, where Simone's family struggles on, her five brothers and four sisters all younger than she, and a mother that was widowed in the Dead of Winter. As we sit and stare at her mother's brick home, I hold the hand of my Roanoke River bride, and try to comfort her on a rainy day.

"Do you want to come in?"

"I can't."

"I know. I'll try not to be more than a few minutes, okay? I just need to see her. Maybe talk about some things. Just to get things started, you know. The universe wasn't built in a day, I know it'll take some time. I probably shouldn't be here, but—"

"Just go, Honey. I'll be here."

After a kiss of profound support and grieving, I watch Professor Cory step out into the cold summer rain, her long coat as gray as the oppressive clouds in the sky. Are they even *home*, I say to myself, as she takes the last brick step up to the porch and rings the doorbell. I am as shocked as I've ever been as a fifteen year old beauty opens the door in all smiles and capris delight, and lets Simone into the house. I close my eyes, lifting from the car as a spirit into the rain—where I am pulled screaming back to earth, through the roof and into the brick Cory house, long enough to see the friendly 15 year old Angela Adriana Coronado in her mother's bedroom, telling her mother that her 33 year old daughter has come out of the past like something out of a cemetery on a rainy Halloween, asking to see her. I see the fifty something woman put her hand to her mouth then shake her head in a determined, direct no—against her young daughter's wishes, until she has to grab young Adriana by the shoulders and shake her with an anguished, growling *no* that carries through the house and down the hall to where the beautiful thirty three year old woman closes her eyes against the pain. She listens to the footsteps of her sister in the hall, each compounding fear and devastation on the other, until Adriana steps into the Cory sight, slamming her with the third part of the Truth in ice and destruction.

She hugs her little sister, a stranger she has never seen before, and I am suddenly back in my body in the car. My eyes open from the daydream of Eve, in time to see Simone wave to young, exotic Adriana as she walks down the concrete driveway into the street, then into the car with me.

"I heard her in the bedroom," she says. "Little Adriana, she's tough. I don't think she's got a problem handling my mother. I just knew she'd be able to talk her into seeing me. But I heard her voice. It was the most profoundly intense refusal of anything I'd ever heard. I don't think I've been that frightened since before I left home."

"What about your grandmother?"

"It'd have to be at Woodland Hills."

"Well, let's go. Maybe you can talk her into—"

"It's a cemetery."

We roll the rainy streets of Williamston, then the highways of Martin County to Jamesville. My hometown is little more than a collection of houses decorating the woods— and the roads that run between them.

We spend our lives running from the past. And though we learn to live in the present, and strive to move forward to the future, our bond with the past can never really be broken. Oh, they weaken and they fade from chain to rope, and then from rope to string, from string to a single silken thread, harmless as a butterfly in the spring. But even the occasional butterfly is as black as the years between the stars, to remind us that the Beauty of Creation is tainted by the fall of man. On our blue path among the stars, there is the future and the present, bound inextricably to the far and distant past, when Eve walked the banks of the Crystal Stream, in the Garden of Antiquity.

In every life, there is the echo of the past that calls to those who choose to live there, and to those under the delusion that these ghostly ribbons have been cut, and that the bonds have been severed and broken. There is no mountain, the song says, that climbs to such great heights toward heaven, nor corporate high rise, nor foreign village, nor exotic desert nor wilderness exploration far enough, wide enough, nor deep enough to hide from the Spirits of the Past, and the fear, sorrow and regret they must bring. Those that haunt Old Mill Road are activated by my passing— joining with those that followed me through my tragic life, bending the trees we pass in warning to flee, to run far away from the streets of this town, and the abandoned House of Straw and Wood.

Simone rolls the Camry in front of my old house. Slowly turning into the dirt space that passes for a driveway. The dirt space extends from beneath our car to the road—back across the patch of ground that never really tried to be a front yard. As a blessing from above, the rains have ceased for the moment, that I may step out of the passenger seat into the half wet mud that is my life and times. The heels of my black boots do not sink down into the hard, wet dirt as I step through it alone, climbing the ridiculous smooth, concrete steps onto the faded, falling apart excuse of a wooden porch. The sign up ahead of me says 'condemned,' inside the screen door, attached permanently to the door window. Mercy sees fit to have the door unlocked for me, and I do the ghosts that grieve an eternal favor, opening the door they have mourned to see opened for over a dozen years. In my long, black coat, I step a black boot into the daytime darkness, not so far removed from the memory of this living room where I was beaten every day, then every week of my childhood until I left home at eighteen.

The paint on the old, paddle boarded walls is still blue, no more faded now than it was when I was ten. Twenty years from that little girl in the black Indian braid, that little elementary school straw dog, who lived breathed and walked in fear every day, afraid to go to the bus stop, afraid to go to school, afraid to come home. Afraid to go to sleep at night, because Malina might wake me up in the dark with a wooden spoon on my head or hand or somewhere else on my body, and drag me outside into the back yard and leave me there all night. And though I can see you, Malina Moon, Cherokee Woman of Straw, standing faithfully at the stove to cook chicken and rice for you and me, I can feel not the smallest longing, nor the tiniest affection for thee. They say you died 12 years ago when I was 19. Dropped dead in this kitchen from a massive stroke—they found the gas stove burned out, with a pot of your famous chicken and rice burned black from several days before, with the violent and poisonous smell of burning and death in this home. Yes, Malina—these walls are darkened with soot, from the blue and black flame of our age, and the raging heat of your own lust and sin. As I step through the Kitchen of the Dead, opening the back door, I see the black dirt of your misdeeds, the upgrown grasses of your neglect, and the fervent trees of your skill at causing pain, in the woodlands of our discontent. Yes, Malina—on this old, broken down nothing of a back porch, attached to this anachronism of a relic and ruin, I do see the ghost of a little girl named Raven Moon, who cried unholy terror to the evening skies at night, that God might send the stars down as angels to ease the fire burning on my skin. In these grasses, there lurks a spirit made of white, who appears at the onset of every rain, who lurks at the edge of these forgotten woods—still wondering, after your body is interred so long, still wondering where it is that her beloved mother could have gone.

I am pulled back—away from the edge of these atramental woods, forward through time to the present day, where I am still adrift in power Penny Casual, taking again each stylish, steadfast step back though the blue living room of pain to the front door, back through this whirling gray portal to today and tomorrow, hardly able to fathom the strange, beautiful woman in the driver's seat, who is mesmerized to tears at the dirt and the tall grasses around the condemned house I was in.

We roll the road west. To the only place we know. Leaving the rains of our loved one's departure behind. Knowing that though we tried as hard as we could not to think it, neither of us had wanted to go back to Black Mountain, and we know that along the way, there is one more stop that we have to make. One more necessary thing we have to do.

The Mountaineers

When we arrive at the bank in Winston Salem, we are fevered by instinct. A white tiger, and her sister panther in the forest. This, a forest of callousness—avarice, greed and parsimonious, rapacious depravity. We step out of our silver chariot. Two beauties in style. Looking, smelling every inch of the money temple we seek.

After four in the afternoon, we walk so casually in. Both in our skirts of beauty, me in my black collar shirt, my black and beige kilt pattern skirt, down to my black boots. Simone in snow white blouse and big, white bra vaguely detectable, long black hair, tight black skirt and short black heels. We are prepared for the beauty of the middle class dance, the sophisticated and middle class romance we once knew. We walk strongly, purses in hand to the door of a woman every bit of 50 years old, sitting at her desk pretending to be hard at work at something or another. An attractive, almost pretty older woman with sandy colored hair down to her neck and piercing blue eyes like a lioness, B majors bound up so tightly in her off white summer tee, married to her tight beige skirt and thin brown belt, in high spirits to stand up and reveal only a lightly thick, slightly matronly middle. A sexy older woman? Maybe so, even through her obvious love of white cake squares and classic white icing.

"Excuse me, Connie Green?"

We hardly wait for the answer, stepping oddly, rudely into her big as a suburban bedroom corner office—both of us smelling of Estee Lauder and Freshen Up spearmint gum, speaking so candidly, so kindly and humbly about having a very deep and private problem to discuss and "can we close the door?"

With a smile and a nasty walk that switches her wide hips back and forth for no good reason, she obliges, even walking past us and closing the door and the blinds, which is our last and greatest cue that this necessity is preordained. While she returns to the desk, I lock the door, and Simone grabs her so tight around her mouth as to be air tight, as I rush back over to them, and hold a tiny knife to her throat.

"Shut the *fuck* up, bitch. Shut... the... fuck ... up."

Beside her desk, the three of us stand pressed so close together.

Breathing.

"She told Raven what you did," Simone says, "and after Chelsea died, Raven told me."

And upon that syllable, I punch her in the stomach with inspired precision, making her emit a stifled yelp into Simone's hand, with my knife still at her throat to prevent sound. Then one more quick punch and another, more pitiful grunt, sounding as though somewhere inside her bowels are ruptured. She coughs once into Simon's hand while I put the tiny knife in my pocket and press hard up against her.

"You fucking pervert," Simone says. "You think you know what lust is? If she hits you one more time I'm gonna cum. Do you hear me? Chelsea as much as killed herself because of you, bitch. You raped her on the side of the goddamned road and then you fired her because she was nothing to you. You humped and dumped her. You humped and dumped my Chelsea?"

The woman opens her eyes wide as shock itself and stifles a gruff yell, at the feel of my hand beneath her skirt, clamped over her underwear and vagina.

"Be still," Simone says. "That's it. Just be still before you make me blow a load in my panties. I feel like I'm gonna piss myself. I'd bet you'd like that though, wouldn't you?"

The tears flow freely, as the woman turns to stare Simone in the eye.

"I like your tears on my hand. I can feel your tears on my hand. You like crying for me. Hmm?"

The pressure clamping between her legs makes her nod her head again in the bank office, amongst the tears that fall.

"She's gettin' turned on, Simone."

"Of course she is, Babe. Fear is the best aphrodisiac in the world. The only reason I'm not biting you and breaking your fingers one by one is 'cause of where we are. Oh, God how I wish I could hear you scream."

She clamps her beautiful, lovely white teeth onto the older woman's ear—who by now has calmed to a state of unwelcomed arousal.

"Listen," she says, unbiting the woman's ear. "If I hear a cop over this. If I see a cop. If I smell a cop, when I get out of jail we're comin' back. And we're gonna take you up into the mountains—"

"And fuck you with Chelsea's cock."

"Oh yeah... Oh, God yes. If either of us gets in one minute's trouble— I'm gonna tell 'em all what you did to Chelsea. And then I swear to God and Jesus we're gonna bury you alive and listen to you die."

One, final pinch to her private makes her jerk with hardly a sound, then a defeated, quiet cough and a sob. I remove my hand from her skirt and Simone slowly, quietly takes her hand away from her mouth. Her cheek is red from the pressure.

"You scream," I say, "we'll kill you before they get in. We'll decorate this fucking wall with the blood from your neck. I want to do it. I want to soak Simone's white bra in your blood."

My Simone pulls tissues from the box, admonishing Connie Green to wipe her tears and fix her smeared makeup, and to sit calmly at the desk for another 2 minutes, hands away from any panic buttons hidden, lest she die from a cut throat. When I peep through the blinds, we are of knowledge that the coast is clear, and it is time for us to leave.

"Any sounds they might have heard," Simone admonishes, "yes, it was crying, because you heard that one of your favorite former employees was killed three weeks ago in Chesapeake, Virginia. Shot to death by her own mother."

And on the final chord, as Connie Green sits devastated to ruin, we open the office door in all smiles and sweetness, and we take the long, leisure strides through the bank as if in slow motion; all flowing hair, fabric and boots. The white tiger—and her sister panther in the woods.

They shall die of grievous deaths;

They shall not be lamented.

Jeremiah 16:4

As it was in the days of Noah, so shall it be in the coming of the Son of Man. From the Tiding of Seven Roses, to the planting of a red rose bush far and away alone. From a burial in the rain by Chesapeake Bay, to ghosts of 25 miles down east, we endeavor to achieve acceptance in lamentation, of the answer we gave to our Divine Calling, and to the forgiveness He gave when they made him march to Golgotha, and nailed him to a cross on Calvary's Hill. Offences must come, saith the Lord, but woe unto him by whom the offence cometh! There is salvation ready for every soul, be they liars or murderers, but as per the curse bestowed from Eden, there are consequences preordained for choices made in this life. These hold true even for the elite, that although Fate controls every action, there is still the freedom of choices made, and the predestined outcome for every path chosen.

We have been at uneasy rest in our mountain paradise these many days, rising east with the Sun and falling west on the Moon. Every star is a great beacon light of hope to us, and we look to even the passing clouds for help in the noonday, to feel the absolution He hath promised, when he set his bow in the clouds, and to know in our hearts that our Redemption draweth nigh, and that despite all the evil we have done, He has still prepared a place for us, and that we are truly not alone. So many of these long summer nights, we have tried to believe that the past is as dead and buried as what lies beneath our rose garden, and the rest of our life is simply there for us to live, and for us to be happy. But there is recompense that is always due—there is always such a vile and bitter comeuppance overdue. And although Simone and I can choose to live our lives in leisure, helping others with our time and pieces of over one million dollars of our angel's money, (a gift from four policies of her death bestowed), there is truly no hope from our earthly view of the stars in heaven, and there is no peace for us under the sun.

Sometimes I watch her without disturbing her. Walking our lawn in the morning or the evening, sometimes sitting on the ground by the road or the weeds, even walking the great field of grass across the road, always looking away to the heavens as though she is waiting, burdened I know, by the same hopeless longing I have felt my entire life. I have listened to her scream in the morning when she wakes up, or in every hour of the night sometimes—always talking about seeing the Cross on fire of Hell, and that there is no forgiveness for her sin. Always with a bible in her hand, refusing to think or talk of Chelsea—sometimes sitting on the porch with her arms clenched about her waist as though she has been stabbed with a two edged sword. Perhaps it is my fault, that I pulled her into something she would have never thought of if it were not for me, and after seven years of living with my curse, her mind and body can no longer endure it. Its killing me, Raven, she'll say, *I know he can't forgive me unless I'm made a sacrifice to Him. Help me to go home, Raven. Please help me to go home.* This is what I have dreaded for so many weeks for myself—the Tiding of Number Eight & Nine—a final call bestowed to us by birth, spoken by the women who gave us life, and as it is written, took it from us so abundantly.

In the morning dawn, I go to the back of our home—to prepare the place of her demise, dragging the Cross of St. Andrew to the lawn and laying it diagonal at our picnic table, where we had never sat again as a family—to eat, drink and be merry, watching the trees whish and whisper in the summer mountain breeze. I return to the house, where my Simone stands in the middle of the floor as a victim fully nude, her hands bound in front by rope. In my Indian Braid, feeling the Mohawk inside that I will never cut to my hair, I take her by the arm without mercy, pulling her out the front door and into the lawn with one hand, holding a birch wood cane and leather nine chorded whip with the other. She is a victim to me now, I am her executioner—and the love I have for her has swirled into a bitterness and anger at Fate, Destiny and God himself for bringing us to such a tragic state.

As we walk past the shadows of death, I feel her sense of peace with what must be done, and I can hear the farewell in her spirit while she looks around her, at the grass and our brick home, at the elegant garden of roses nearby, and the trees of the Appalachian Forest. And then I lay her body nude upon St. Andrews Cross facing down, her gigantic breasts exposed and hanging white, with no cloth wrapped for her dignity. I guide her arms and legs to the X shaped wood where she will lay, strapping both her arms and her legs in black leather on the wood, and I take the birchwood cane, for the blue fire of her abomination, for the flaming Energy of Lust, and I proceed to stripe the skin of her buttocks to open sores bleeding, from her backside down the backs of her thighs to her feet. Then I take the flagellation leather (with its nine leather strands knotted to cause greater pain), that same leather used to curb the demons that once haunted the Royal British Navy—this flagellation leather, for the black fire of her abomination, for the flaming Energy of Violence, and I lay into her back like a Roman Soldier—watching her stiffen and try to relax, but being unable—and then I whip her over and over again in the dawn, savoring every scream in the glowing of the day, until her back is cut in ribbons, and the blood runs in angry streams down her back and over her striped buttocks, dripping to the grass beneath her feet. And then I unlatch her and turn her over, infuriated with sorrow, having greater contempt for her broken condition—her weeping, begging position. She screams of her back when I turn her over, strapping her back to the X cross, back to the bleeding wood. With the knotted whip chord, I whip the front of her body without mercy, savoring the screams all the more, watching the blood pour freely from her gigantic bosoms, watching it run from the torn skin on her stomach and thighs.

When she is striped to blood, I loosen her restraints again, and I escort her stumbling to another cross further away in our back lawn, built for a stage play of The Passion, the cross fashioned as the Cross of Calvary. I help the bleeding, trembling woman to the small platform, strapping her legs firmly to the vertical wood. Raising her arms and strapping them to the horizontal beam, until she is the image of her own absolution in the mountain morning. There, I leave her to suffer in the baking sun until the noon day, when I return as the sun passes behind a cloud, to give her the vial of poison to drink, and I listen to her say with her fading life "Thank you, Raven. I love you." And though she trembles in pain and blood, so much of it crusted over in brief time, I know she is at peace now, to reconcile her belief in form that her soul is forgiven, and that the blood He shed has finally made her whole again.

And what I do now, I must do quickly, as I hurry to the picnic table and its macabre display for the 4 six inch nails and the hammer resembling a small sledge hammer. I place a nail in the palm of her hand, causing hardly a stir, bringing the hammer down onto the nail—and she stiffens and yowls an unholy, unearthly sound with madness in her eyes, with shock and regret on her face, but I nail without mercy, knowing the poison she drank works with a speed that can outrun the devil himself.

I must wait but a moment. Going around to the other hand when her head is down and her body is limp, nailing the other hand in like fashion, which brings no movement at all from the Maiden on the Cross, who hath shed her own blood for her absolution, suffering a strong delusion bestowed by a curse that she may believe a lie, and die as she had lived. And although I pick up another nail and kneel downward, I think better against it, knowing that I cannot bring myself to harm one part of her beautiful feet. Tossing the hammer and nails to the ground, I step back to see that my Simone is upright and nailed to her cross, in the like manner of her Lord and Savior.

What I see is but the flesh of this world, set now to go forth to the dust from whence it came. And now in the remainder of the day, when the mountain sun has passed behind the single cloude, the shadow falls over the life that she was, and the profound death she has become. I see a curse removed from the face of the earth in the mountain bluebird perched in the branches of the greenest tree I see. Then the bluebird flies away, the angel I know He sent to escort her to Paradise, where 1000 years is as a day, and there is love, joy and peace in everlasting life.

I turn away from where the bluebird hath flown—to prepare my own body for burial. Inside our mountain home—I bathe myself in the finest soap we own, shampooing my hair in strawberry just the same. I dry my body and my hair, until I am as naked as the day is long, with black hair about my shoulders and halfway down my back. With what skill I have learned, I fashion my eyes lined Egyptian dark, with even the bluest eye shadow I have always loved but only pretended to despise. There is no need for a concealer or base, but my lips are full now and ruby red, as ripe as a strawberry in June. In the aroma of Estee Lauder, I sit naked before the Lord, reading his word as unto him, believing in my heart as the disciple that he loved, that *in the beginning was the word, the word was with God and the word was God. The same was in the beginning with God. All things were made by him, and without him was not anything made that was made. In him was life; and the life was the light of men.*

As the light of this day begins to fade, I put away my Bible and I go to my closet, retrieving the snow white Indian Leather Dress, trimmed as blue as the mountain sky in summer, or as the feathers of the mountain bluebird. I slide it on as an Indian bride, prepared to meet my end as a bride of Christ, in hopes that my heavenly father will look upon the Lord in my heart, which has washed me white as snow, and count me worthy to hear him say *Well done, thy good and faithful servant. Enter thou into the joy of the Lord.* And so, in the cool of the evening day, I drink the poison as unto my Lord and Savior, and then I sit at the foot of the Cross, and lay my head to rest. Here, I dream the sleep of the dead, where I am no longer an Indian Woman of Straw, but I am a bride of Christ the Lord, and child of the most high God.

In the midst of a mountain paradise, as the evening day fades to night, our bodies lie in sacrifice to Him, underneath the stars of Heaven.

Epilogue

(AP Video: "The Mountaineers")

"They're already being dubbed 'The Mountaineers.' Three beautiful women who lived together in this brick rancher on Mountain View Road in a town called Black Mountain, North Carolina. The world may never quite get over the shock of what an insurance agent stumbled upon on a visit to the women's home back on July 24th:

> *"I knocked on the door and there was no answer—but I noticed two very nice cars in the yard, one was a Camry, the other a Cadillac. And being an insurance man, we're nothing if not persistent, so I went to the back door, and that's when I made the discovery and called 911..."*

The Mountaineers

"When the flood of police and highway patrol cars arrived at 1910 Mountain View Road, they were shocked beyond their wildest imagination to discover a nude woman dead and nailed to an upright wooden cross in the back yard, and another woman dressed in a traditional Native American white leather dress lying dead on the ground at her feet. A search of the house turned up their identities and a disturbing revelation of what had been gruesome happenings on this property.

The woman on the cross was 33 year old Simone Cory, a professor of Religion at the University of North Carolina at Greensboro. Lying dead at her feet was 31 year old Raven Moon, a sales clerk at JC Penney in Four Seasons Mall in Winston Salem. The two women lived with 30 year old Chelsea Lynn Baxter, who had been murdered by her own mother just a month before in Chesapeake, Virginia. A camera recovered in the house shocked investigators further, when they learned that three of their victims were seen on the videos being beaten, humiliated, tortured, then finally raped and murdered. One of the killers was heard on the video saying "you're going to the rose garden," which led investigators to begin digging in a small but elaborate garden in their back yard near the Appalachian Forest. A massive excavation soon uncovered the bodies of seven women, one already identified as Patricia Southern, a 40 year old psychiatrist from White Plains, New York, who was reported missing after a trip to Busch Gardens three years ago. All seven women were apparently abducted and murdered by the three beautiful, seemingly normal women who lived in this modest, attractive home on Mountain View Road. Cora Leeds—the Associated Press."

Jonathan Lovejoy

ℳddendum

Excerpt from *"Mother Daughter Sex: The Modern Sexualization of the Mother Daughter Dynamic"* by Simone Cory, Ph.D (Viking University Press)

"For those of us who are cursed enough to believe in the timeline itself, the ebb and flow of it—whether or not there will be an end to the flow of history, we find the signs inevitable, impossible to ignore—these are signs of the times. Just as there are signs that a road traveler must read to know when he is nearing the end of his journey, a traveler on this road of life, this road of history, must be able to read the signs of the times—to know when we're nearing the end of the age and for those of us who believe, the Second Coming of Christ. But whether you believe in Christ's return or not, one must still remain realistic and objective about human behavior—the evolution of behind closed doors family violence and perversion, much of it perpetuated not just by fathers and sons and brothers—but mothers, daughters and sisters as well. This is the first generation of the sexualized mother—where women who 20 years ago were be-bopping to She Bop and Girls Just Want To Have Fun, have grown up to have husbands, sons and teenage daughters of their own. Women in their 40's and 50's who have decided that they have no desire to age gracefully, and are fighting bleached white tooth and acrylic polished nail against it.

Any detour off the information super highway to a good porn site will reveal what has become the modern dumping ground for our most perverted psychologies—where the term M.I.L.F. originated—Mothers I'd Like to Fuck—a middle aged woman morphed into a mountain lion like something out of a

Michael Jackson Video, or a Cougar she is sometimes called. These women have an advantage over their own daughters in so many cases, one being that their faces and bodies have matured with time, where their beauty becomes more seasoned and exotic, more alluring, and their figures are softer and curvier about the breasts and hips, which are still number one and number two—not piss and shit, mind you, but tits and ass...

And from this pornographic detour, to a trip to a local church, or a local mall, or an amusement park far and away, reveals a difficulty in telling mothers from their daughters—who's the sister? Which one is the mother? And which of these young men is a mother fucker? Which one of these young women is one besides? And these older women develop a synergy with the younger women—feeding off each other like a ying-yang ball, until they learn to wield a new kind of sexual power in the world. It is a modern phenomenon, born of end time perversion—the modern sexualization of the Mother-Daughter Dynamic, and all of our secret desire to watch them perform in every walk of life as a pair, to satisfy the burning, deep rooted, deep seeded lust in the core of who we are... and I know by first hand interview that this pervertedness is spreading, where some have revealed underground suburban Mother Daughter Exchange Clubs (something not confined to pornographic fantasy), and some have even taken to becoming incestuous "friends with benefits," with these mothers thinking nothing of straddling their own adult daughters in a hotel room during their busy mother daughter travels, bouncing and grinding themselves to orgasm... it is one of the last and most subtle, and most powerful signs we have that we are on the edge of Christ's return, and that this is the evening day of man— and the beginning of the end of civilization as we know it..."

Simone Cory, Ph.D

ABOUT THE AUTHOR

Jonathan Lovejoy is a graduate of the University of North Carolina at Greensboro, with a B.A. in Religious Studies, and a graduate of Liberty University with an M.A. in Theological Studies. He currently lives in Winston Salem, North Carolina.

For more info on the author's life and career, visit jonathanlovejoy.com.

The Mountaineers